Praise for *New York Times* bestselling author Brenda Jackson

"[Brenda] Jackson's characters are wonderful, strong, colorful and hot enough to burn the pages."

—*RT Book Reviews* on *Westmoreland's Way*

"Jackson's trademark ability to weave multiple characters and side stories together makes shocking truths all the more exciting."

—*Publishers Weekly*

"Jackson is a master at writing."

—*Publishers Weekly* on *Sensual Confessions*

Praise for *USA TODAY* bestselling author Olivia Gates

"No one does seduction and reparation better than [Olivia] Gates."

—#1 *New York Times* bestselling author Sylvia Day

"Gates is a master at writing emotionally charged, passion-filled stories."

—*RT Book Reviews*

Brenda Jackson is a *New York Times* bestselling author of more than one hundred romance titles. Brenda lives in Jacksonville, Florida, and divides her time between family, writing and traveling.

Email Brenda at authorbrendajackson@gmail.com or visit her on her website at brendajackson.net.

Olivia Gates has always pursued creative passions such as singing and handicrafts. She still does, but only one of her passions grew gratifying enough, consuming enough, to become an ongoing career—writing.

She is most fulfilled when she is creating worlds and conflicts for her characters, then exploring and untangling them bit by bit, sharing her protagonists' every heart-wrenching heartache and hope, their every heart-pounding doubt and trial, until she leads them to an indisputably earned and gloriously satisfying happy ending.

When she's not writing, she is a doctor, a wife to her own alpha male and a mother to one brilliant girl and one demanding Angora cat. Visit Olivia at oliviagates.com.

New York Times **Bestselling Author**

BRENDA JACKSON

ONE NIGHT WITH THE WEALTHY RANCHER

HARLEQUIN® BESTSELLING AUTHOR COLLECTION

ISBN-13: 978-0-373-01021-9

This edition published by arrangement with Harlequin Books S.A.

For questions and comments about the quality of this book, please contact us at CustomerService@Harlequin.com.

HARLEQUIN®
www.Harlequin.com

Printed in U.S.A.

CONTENTS

ONE NIGHT WITH THE WEALTHY RANCHER 7
Brenda Jackson

BILLIONAIRE, M.D. 165
Olivia Gates

Books by Brenda Jackson

Harlequin Desire

The Westmorelands

Texas Wild
One Winter's Night
Zane
Canyon
Stern
The Real Thing
The Secret Affair

Harlequin
Kimani Arabesque

Madaris Family Saga

Secret Love
True Love
Surrender
Sensual Confessions
Inseparable
Courting Justice
A Madaris Bride for Christmas

Harlequin
Kimani Romance

***Steele Family* titles**

Beyond Temptation
Risky Pleasures
Irresistible Forces
Intimate Seduction
Hidden Pleasures
A Steele for Christmas
Private Arrangements

Visit the Author Profile page
at Harlequin.com for more titles.

ONE NIGHT WITH THE WEALTHY RANCHER

Brenda Jackson

To the love of my life, Gerald Jackson, Sr.

To everyone who joined me on the Madaris/Westmoreland Family Reunion 2009 Cruise to Canada. This one is for you!

Provide things honest in the sight of all men.
—*Romans* 12:17

Chapter 1

"What are you doing here, Summer?"

Summer Martindale's eyes froze on the document in front of her at the sound of the husky voice. It was a voice she hadn't heard in almost seven years, yet she distinctively remembered the sensuous timbre and how every audible vibration could stir her senses in a way that even today she could not explain.

In a way she wished she could forget.

She inhaled deeply and after a moment, she lifted her eyes and stared into Darius Franklin's dark and intense gaze. It was a gaze that was emitting a chilling glare.

Summer could just as easily glare back but refused to let him know how disturbing it was to see him again. What had once been between them was over and done with. He had made sure of that in the worst possible way, which she could never forgive him for. His actions had caused her pain—a degree of pain she vowed never to experience again.

"I could ask you the same thing, Darius," she finally responded. Her tone was just as sharp as his had been.

He stood tall, all six foot one inches of him, as he leaned in the doorway with his arms crossed over his chest and his gaze fixed directly on her. She thought at that moment the very same thing she'd thought when she'd first laid eyes on him. Darius Franklin, with his pecan tan complexion, close-cut black hair, charcoal gray eyes and neat pencil-thin mustache, was an extremely handsome man. But there were other noticeable changes. His cheekbones appeared more pronounced and his lips seemed firmer.

His dark stare, as well as the way a muscle seemed to twitch in his jaw, were all the evidence she needed that he wasn't happy to see her and if truth be told, she wasn't happy to see him, either. It would be a lie to claim she hadn't thought about him over the years, because she had. Yet at the same time, the memory of what he'd put her through—the humiliation, heartbreak and pain—made her regret ever lowering her guard and letting him into her life.

He stepped away from the door and she watched his every move, wishing she weren't drawn to how fit his body was, and wishing a tug of desire had not invaded her stomach. Although he wasn't as lean as he used to be, he wore his masculinity well. Well-toned muscles outlined his chest and shoulders—muscles she could easily see through the material of his chambray shirt. And then there were jeans that hugged his firm hips and strong thighs. They were thighs that could keep a tight hold on hers as he thrust deeper and deeper inside of her.

She forced the turbulent memories away. Her gaze moved back up to his eyes and she tried not to flinch at the cold look in them. Something inside her shivered and she wondered how a man she had once fallen in love with so deeply could end up treating her so shabbily.

"I live here in Somerset."

His voice cut through Summer's thoughts. *He lived here in Somerset? Maverick County?* That information immediately filled her with apprehension and dread, as well as curiosity. *When had he left the Houston Police Department and why?*

"I live in Somerset, as well," she heard herself say. "I moved to town last month to work here at Helping Hands as a social worker."

Surprise lit his eyes. "A social worker?"

"Yes."

She understood his surprise. When he'd last seen her seven years ago, he'd been twenty-four years old and a detective with the Houston Police Department. And she'd been a nineteen-year-old trying to escape the clutches of an abusive fiancé by the name of Tyrone Whitman. After she had broken off their engagement, Tyrone had refused to get out of her life, to leave her alone. He had stalked her for months before he'd finally caught her alone in her apartment, and for three hours he had held a gun to her head, threatening to blow her brains out.

While the SWAT team had been trying to talk Tyrone into surrendering, Darius had broken into the apartment by coming through a bathroom window. He'd apprehended Tyrone and saved her. That night, Darius Franklin had become her knight in shining armor.

He was the same man who had stopped by her apartment the next day to repair the window, and the same man who, after learning that a not-too-smart judge had posted bail for Tyrone, made it his business to become her protector until the trial. After that, he was the same man who she began seeing on a daily basis, who would drop by when his shift changed to spend time with her, to show her how special he thought she was.

The same man who during that time, for one night, had been her lover.

"So, you went to college and got your degree?" he asked, and for a split second she could have sworn she detected a degree of admiration in his voice, but the look in his hard gaze told her she'd been wrong.

"Yes, I got my degree," she responded, proud of her accomplishment and quickly remembering he was one of the few people who'd encouraged her to do so, and convinced her that she could. He had made her believe in herself. And a part of her had believed in them, in a future together. He had proven her wrong.

"Congratulations."

"Thank you," she said briskly, putting aside the document she had been reading. "So, why are you here, Darius? Although we've established the fact that we're both living in Somerset, I'm sure this town is big enough for the both of us. What brings you to Helping Hands?"

"I'm here to install the security system as well as the billing account for the shelter," he said, as if that explained everything.

She nodded. "I was told the Texas Cattleman's Club

would be sending someone over to do those things," she said, finding it hard to concentrate.

She had heard a lot about the Texas Cattleman's Club, a group of men who considered themselves the protectors of Texas and whose members consisted of the wealthiest men in Texas, mostly from old money. The TCC was known to help a number of worthy causes in the community and Helping Hands, a newly opened women's shelter located in the small, impoverished section of wealthy Maverick County, was one of them. They provided all the shelter's funding.

Summer had interviewed for the position at the shelter and once she had been offered the job, had decided it would be a good way to have a fresh start. She had made the move from Austin, where she had been living for the past six years.

"How did you get the job?" She couldn't help but ask.

He shrugged. "I own a security company."

She raised a brow, surprised he had gotten out of law enforcement. He'd made a good police detective and she'd figured it would be his career. "How long have you been living in Somerset?" she asked.

"Around six years."

It was the same amount of time she had lived in Austin. He had moved here a year after they had broken up. She quickly recalled that they really hadn't broken up since they had never truly been together…at least not like she'd assumed they had.

"If you're through with your interrogation, I'd like to get to work," he said.

"Fine. I'll get out of your way if you need to work in here for a while," she said, getting up from her desk. Seeing him again after all this time was just a bit too much. Bittersweet memories were trying to invade her brain and she was determined to fight them back.

"If you need anything, just let the shelter's secretary, Marcy Dillard, know. I'll use this time to go to lunch."

She grabbed her purse out of her desk drawer and quickly moved past him toward the door.

"Summer?"

She paused just before reaching the door and turned around. "Yes?"

He still had a hard look in his eyes. "I would say welcome to town, but I wouldn't mean it."

She narrowed her gaze. "Then I guess that means we'll have to learn to tolerate each other, doesn't it?"

Without waiting for him to respond, she turned and continued walking out the door.

Darius leaned back against the desk and watched Summer until she was no longer in sight. It was only then that he made an attempt to begin breathing normally again. But it was hard because although he couldn't see her, he still managed to feel her presence.

Seven years was a long time, yet today when a startled Summer had looked up at him and met his gaze, he'd felt a sensation that was like a swift kick in the gut. Potent memories had flooded his mind, forcing him to recall what she had come to mean to him in such a short period of time, and just how deep her betrayal had cut.

He hit his fist on the desk, angry and frustrated. How could he still find her so desirable after all this time? After all she'd done? Why had seeing her sent sensuous shivers down his spine? She was seven years older, no longer a mere nineteen-year-old who hadn't decided what she wanted out of life other than to be free of an obsessive ex-fiancé. She was just as stunning as he remembered. Even more so.

She had matured beautifully. She was about five-eight, tall and slim with shoulder-length straight brown hair and hazel eyes he could always drown in. Her skin tone, the color of café au lait, had always tempted him to lick her all over.

Darius bowed his head momentarily as even more memories he had tried so hard to forget resurfaced.

After college, he'd gotten a job with the Houston Police Department as a detective with aspirations of moving up the ranks. Authorities had been called to the scene regarding a domestic dispute, and Darius and his partner, Walt Stewart, had been the first to arrive.

A young woman who had obtained a restraining order against her ex-fiancé was in danger. The man, named Tyrone Whitman, had broken into her apartment and was holding a gun to her head, threatening to kill her unless she took him back.

While Walt tried talking him into surrendering, Darius was able to get into the apartment through a rear bathroom window, overtake Whitman and free Summer.

Concern for her safety when Whitman was released on bond allowed Darius to convince himself that it was important to keep checking on her. But then it became obvious it was a lot more than that. Point-blank, he had been attracted to her and thought she was a special woman who'd gotten mixed up with the wrong guy, and was trying to get her life together. Against his better judgment, although he'd been warned by Walt that Summer wasn't really what she seemed, he had fallen for her, and fallen hard.

He'd assumed he had gotten to know her, and thought she felt the same way after a night they had spent together filled with so much sexual chemistry that it could only end one way: they had made love. Deep, passionate love. Shudders passed through him just remembering that night and the effect it had on him. It was a night he could never forget, although over the past seven years he had tried like hell to do so.

And it was a night that apparently had meant more to him than it had to her.

The following day he had left town when he received word of his brother Ethan's near-fatal car accident. He'd had to leave immediately for Charleston and when he couldn't reach Summer, and had been unable to leave her a message because her voice-mail box was full, he'd left word with his partner to let her know what happened. When he had returned to Houston a week later, he discovered that Summer had packed up and left town without leaving word as to where she'd gone. She'd told Walt to tell him that she wanted to build a new life for herself and was leaving town with an older man. A very wealthy one—something Darius was not.

After nearly losing his brother, it had almost destroyed him to find out that he had lost her, that she had turned her back on what could have been between them to take up with a man with money.

A hard smile formed on his lips and he wondered what she would think to discover that he was now a wealthy man, thanks to smart investments and the success of his security firm. She thought he'd been hired as a laborer for the TCC—he could just imagine her reaction when she discovered he was a member of the

Texas Cattleman's Club. The same club that was funding the shelter, including her salary.

Another thought crept into his mind, one that made his skin crawl. What if she knew already? What if the reason she was in Somerset was because she'd heard about his success and assumed after all this time she could ease her way back in his good graces? A woman looking for a wealthy husband would do just about anything. He'd been gullible before and wondered if she thought he would be gullible again. Considering her actions seven years ago, he wouldn't put anything past her.

He leaned against her desk as those thoughts filled his mind. She wasn't wearing a ring on her finger, which was a good indication that she wasn't married. And she *had* acted surprised to see him. But then it could have very well been an act. He had found out the hard way just what a good actress she was. One thing was for certain: he wouldn't be letting his guard down. She had taken advantage of his heart before but she wouldn't be doing so again.

He was about to begin the work he'd come to do when his cell phone went off. Recognizing the special ringtone, he pulled it off his belt and clicked it on. "Yes, Lance?"

"Hey, man, sorry I missed your call earlier."

"No problem. I just wanted you to know that I heard from Fire Chief Ingle. I'm meeting with him tomorrow evening to go over some things. He indicated that he'll have the official report ready in a week and that it contains proof that the fire was deliberately set."

Lance Brody was Darius's best friend from college at the University of Texas, where the two of them, along with another good friend, Kevin Novak, had been roommates. The three had forged a bond that would last a lifetime. There was nothing one wouldn't do for the other and Darius could rightly say that he could give his two friends credit for his financial success.

Lance, along with his younger brother Mitch, had come from old money and together they owned Brody Oil and Gas Company. The two had included Darius in a number of successful investment opportunities. So had Kevin, who'd made his fortune in real estate development.

Lance and Kevin had grown up in Somerset and had tried convincing Darius to move there after college but he had opted for the job in Houston instead. Then, shortly after that incident with Summer, he'd decided he would move to Somerset to start a new career and a new life.

He worked closely with his friends, and Lance had hired him to investigate a fire at the Brody Oil and Gas refinery a few weeks ago. Although there was significant damage, no one had gotten seriously hurt. Darius had no doubt the fire had been the work of an arsonist, and now Chief Ingle had confirmed his suspicions.

"I can't wait until we nail Alex. I intend to make sure that he rots in jail," Lance was saying.

Lance and Mitch were certain they knew the identity of the arsonist. He was the longtime hated rival of the Brodys, a man by the name of Alejandro "Alex" Montoya.

"Calm down, Lance. The man is innocent until proven guilty," Darius said.

"Wait until the report comes out. Mark my word, Alex Montoya is the person behind that fire."

"That may very well be the case," Darius said, knowing just how convinced Lance was of Alex's guilt. "But it has to be proven. How's Kate?" Darius asked, trying to change the subject. Lance and Kate had eloped to Vegas a few weeks ago.

"Kate's fine and I know what you're trying to do, Darius."

Darius couldn't help but chuckle. "If you know, then humor me. I need like hell to laugh about now."

"Sounds like it's been one of those days for you," Lance said.

"You don't know the half of it. Summer is here."

There was a pause. "Summer? *Your* Summer?"

Darius could have really laughed out loud at that one, since Summer had never truly been his. But at one time he'd thought she was, and he had told Lance all about her. "Yes, Summer Martindale."

"What's she doing in Somerset?"

Darius sighed deeply. "She's a social worker at Helping Hands. I showed up to set up security and work on the billing system for the place, and walked right into her office."

"Must have been one hell of a reunion."

"Hey, what can I say?"

Lance chuckled. "You can say you need a drink. Sounds like it, anyway. Meet me at the TCC Café when you're ready to take a break for lunch."

Moments later, Darius hung up the phone thinking Lance was right. He needed a drink.

Summer settled into the booth at the Red Sky Café three blocks from the shelter. It was the first week of August and such a beautiful day that she had enjoyed the walk. It had given her a chance to compose herself after seeing Darius again.

She glanced around the café. The Red Sky was a place she had been frequenting for lunch since working at Helping Hands and she had become friendly with the owners. The Timmons had grown up in this section of Maverick County and had been instrumental in approaching members of the TCC about the need for a shelter in the community.

The shelter was a full-service center that provided a safe place for women who'd experienced all types of violence to heal and plan for their future. Helping Hands had opened their doors a few months ago and she'd been hired as part of its counseling team. Summer couldn't help but appreciate the members of the Texas Cattleman's Club for funding the shelter. She of all people knew how important such a facility was.

She had dated Tyrone for a few months, but it was only after they'd gotten engaged that she'd discovered his mean-spirited, possessive nature that on occasion would become abusive, both mentally and physically. She had sought the help of a shelter in Houston and there had found the strength to break things off with him. The social worker at the shelter had helped her to see that although she couldn't control Tyrone's behavior toward her, she could control how she responded to it and remove herself from the situation.

Her choice to end things was something Tyrone couldn't accept and he had begun stalking her, which was the reason she'd put the restraining order in place. Months had gone by when he'd appeared at her apartment one night, and forced his way inside, threatening her life. Chills went up her spine as she remembered that time.

After her own horrible experience with Tyrone, not to mention her heartbreak with Darius, she didn't trust her instincts where men were concerned so she just left them alone. Over the years she had buried herself in her books, getting her degree. After college she had concentrated on her work as an advocate for battered women.

"What are you going to have today, Miss Martindale?"

Summer smiled as she glanced up into the face of Tina Kay, one of the waitresses. Tina had been one of her first clients at Helping Hands and at seventeen, one of her youngest. A runaway after being shifted from foster home to foster home, Tina had become the victim of physical abuse at the hands of her boyfriend, a guy who had convinced her she deserved the beatings he'd been giving her.

Summer couldn't help but recall her own story. After high school, she had wanted to see the world. Aunt Joanne, who had raised her after her parents had been killed in a car accident when she was thirteen, tried to get her to remain in Birmingham. But she'd left Alabama to work her way to California. Along the way, she ended up in Houston where she found a job as a waitress at a chain restaurant. That's where she'd met Tyrone. The company he worked for frequently made deliveries to the restaurant. Something told her he was bad news, but she had wanted to believe there was some good in him. Boy, had she been wrong.

"Just the usual," Summer finally said, relaxing in her seat, looking forward to her grilled chicken salad.

She took a moment to study Tina, who looked so different than the young woman who'd come to the shelter with a swollen eye, cuts around her mouth and bruises on various parts of her body. "And how have you been doing, Tina?" she asked.

Tina's smile widened. "I've been doing fine. The Timmons are letting me use the apartment above their garage. I've enrolled to take classes at the local community college next month and thought I'd brush up on my math. That's always been my weakest subject. I ordered one of those do-it-yourself math books online."

"And how are those self-defense classes going?" The shelter offered the classes weekly and attendance was always at capacity.

"They've been great. The instructor is just awesome. I've learned a number of techniques to protect myself."

She could hear the excitement in Tina's voice and felt good about it. The man who had roughed Tina up had left town but there was a warrant out for his arrest. Summer's thoughts shifted to Tyrone, who'd gotten a twenty-year sentence. It would have been less if he hadn't told the judge just where he could shove it. She shook her head, wondering how she could have ever thought that she loved the man. She could now admit that at eighteen she had been young and rather foolish.

"I'll be back with your order in a second," Tina said.

When Tina walked off, Summer settled back in her seat, allowing herself to think about the man she'd left at the shelter. The one man she had tried so hard to forget. She'd thought moving to Somerset would be a fresh start. A new town. New people. A new job. She hadn't figured on being confronted with a blast from her past.

One thing she told the women she counseled at the shelter was that they could confront and conquer any challenge they were presented with, and she knew she needed to take that same advice. Fate was playing a cruel trick by putting her and Darius in the same town. But she would handle it. And she would handle him.

An irritated and frustrated Darius walked into the TCC Café and glanced around at his surroundings. What used to be a twenty-six-room mansion had been converted into a place where the TCC members could unwind and relax, which was just what he needed.

In addition to the café, the TCC also included a golf course, a state-of-the-art spa, riding stables and an air-conditioned pool house with a retractable roof as well as numerous meeting rooms, game rooms, a well-stocked library and a formal dining room.

Darius, Lance and Kevin, along with Mitch and another friend of the Brodys named Justin Dupree, spent a lot of time shooting pool in the game room. Last fall they were practically glued to the club's projection television screen during football season.

He saw Lance sitting at a table in the back. The café served both lunch and dinner and it wasn't uncommon for Lance to meet him here for lunch. However, nowadays Lance was quick to rush back to the office since his new wife Kate had decided to remain at Brody Oil and Gas as Lance's administrative assistant.

Darius shook his head. Knowing Lance the way he did, he doubted his best friend let Kate get much work done. Hell, he wouldn't either if he had the woman he loved pretty much underfoot all day.

The woman he loved.

Something twisted in his gut at the thought. Thanks

to Summer, he doubted he would ever be able to love another woman again.

"I need a beer," he said, frowning, sliding into the booth across from Lance.

"I've already ordered you one. I was looking out the window when you drove up," Lance said, studying Darius carefully.

"Thanks. I had hoped to at least get the security analysis completed on most of the computers today so I can decide what software will work best," Darius said, smiling a thanks to the waitress who placed a mug of beer in front of him.

"So, you're going to do it instead of one of your men?"

Darius nodded. "Heath left yesterday for Los Angeles to guard some actress who's been getting death threats, and Milt is still in Dallas," he said of two of the six men who worked for him. "The others have been assigned to various other projects around town. That means I'll have to go back over to the shelter when I leave here."

Lance nodded as he took a plug from his own beer. "It also means you'll be seeing Summer again."

Darius didn't say anything. Yes, that meant he would probably see Summer again today. No telling how many more times he'd see her before he finished up what needed to be done at the shelter.

Because of the nature of what went on at women's shelters, Helping Hands needed top security twenty-four hours a day, seven days a week. The TCC had decided to upgrade all the computers to eliminate the risk of getting hacked. The majority of the women seeking refuge at the shelter were the victims of domestic violence, women whose lives could be placed in danger if their batterers discovered their whereabouts.

"Tell me about her, Darius."

Darius met Lance's gaze. "I've practically told you everything about how we met and how things ended. She went to college and got a degree, and now works for the shelter."

"Did you mention anything to her about being a member of TCC?"

"No. She thinks my company was hired to handle security at the shelter."

Lance smiled. "In a way, that's true."

"Yes, which is why she doesn't need to know any different." Darius felt his face harden when he said, "There can never be anything between me and Summer again."

Yet he knew making sure of that wouldn't be easy. Summer was the type of woman who easily got under a man's skin. Just the memory of walking into that office and finding her sitting behind the desk had the power to make him feel weak and vulnerable.

And that was the one thing he could not let happen. He did not have a special woman in his life and preferred keeping it that way. Desire for anything more had died seven years ago with Summer's betrayal.

Chapter 2

"Mr. Franklin wanted me to let you know he left for lunch but will be coming back, Ms. Martindale."

"Oh. Thanks, Marcy," Summer said, trying to keep her voice as normal as she could. After taking a file off Marcy's top tray, she went into her office and closed the door behind her.

Today she had taken an extra-long lunch, hoping by the time she returned Darius would have finished what he'd come to do. But it seemed that would not be the case. Summer bit her lip, deciding she would be professional as well as mature about the matter. He had a job to do and so did she, and as long as they each knew where the other stood, there was no reason they couldn't at least be decent to each other. But then what right did he have to be upset with her since she was the injured party? He was the one who'd left town after discussing their night together with his partner. He probably didn't know Walt had told her the truth, and he was upset because she had left town when he'd returned. It was crazy how men thought sometimes, but it didn't matter now. He had made it quite clear what he thought of her and she hoped she'd left no doubt in his mind just what she thought of him. So there. That was that.

She dropped down in her chair thinking, no, that wasn't that at all. Not as long as the sight of him could send sensations oozing up her spine. Whenever he looked at her, even with anger flaring in the dark depths of his eyes, she felt stirrings in places she didn't want to think about. He'd always had that effect on her. In the past she'd welcomed it, but now she despised it.

She drew in a deep breath and for the first time in years, she felt like the world was closing in on her. It had taken her a while after leaving Houston to pull herself together and decide that no man—Tyrone or Darius—was worth that much pain. But she had moved on with her life. She was proud of her accomplishment and intended to obtain her doctorate after working in her field a few years.

"Don't you have anything to do?"

Summer blinked and saw Darius standing in her doorway. She glared at him—so much for thinking they could be decent to each other. "You should have knocked before entering my office."

He shrugged. "The door was open."

"And that gives you the right to just walk in? I could have been with a client."

"In that case, I would hope you'd be professional enough to shut the door for privacy. But you aren't with a client *and* you knew I was coming back, so stop making a big deal out of it," he said, stepping into her office and closing the door behind him.

Summer just stared at him for a moment, wondering how on earth the two of them were supposed to get along. Of course, whoever hired him had no idea they knew each other, and there was no way she could go to anyone at the TCC and request that they swap security companies without a valid reason.

"Look, Darius. You have a job to do and so do I. Evidently, I'm the last person you expected to see today. However, we're professionals and are mature enough to make the best of it. It shouldn't take you more than a day at the most to finish up here and—"

"Wrong."

She lifted her brow. "Excuse me?"

He crossed his arms over his chest. "I said you're wrong. Finishing up things here will take me every bit of a week. Possibly two."

His words hit her like a ton of bricks. "You've got to be kidding."

"I don't kid."

She pressed her lips together to keep from saying, *No, but you do kiss and tell.* Instead, she asked, "Why will it take *that* long to install a security system?"

There was a pause. A long pause. And for a moment, she wasn't sure he was going to answer her.

"The reason it will take so long is because in addition to installing a new security system on all the computers in this building, I'll be setting up a billing system for the Texas Cattleman's Club. I'm getting paid well to do a good job and I don't intend to do otherwise by rushing through things just to make your life less miserable."

"My life isn't miserable," she all but snapped.

"Sorry. It was foolish of me to assume that it was. And I see you're not wearing a ring so I guess you didn't get a rich husband after all."

Summer wondered what he was talking about and decided she really didn't want to know. "Look, Darius—"

He moved to her desk so quickly she jerked back in her chair. He placed his palms down on her desk and leaned over, his face within inches of hers. "No, you look, Summer. You're right, we are two professionals. Two adults who just happened to have had an affair that led to nowhere. I'm over it and so are you. So let's move on."

"Fine," she snapped.

"Great." He straightened his tall form, moved away from her desk and looked at a closet door across the room. "Unfortunately, the mainframe is in this office so I'll be spending more time in here than any other place. You might be inconvenienced a few times."

"If I'm scheduled to meet with clients, I'll use one of the vacant conference rooms," she said, trying to keep her voice civil.

He nodded. "And if you're not scheduled to meet with a client?"

"I have the ability to work through distractions."

He lifted a brow and held her gaze for a moment. "Do you?"

"Yes."

"Then we don't have anything to worry about," he said, looking at his watch. "Are you meeting with a client sometime today?"

"No, I just have paperwork to do. Will you be shutting down my computer?" She could tell they were both trying to be courteous and hold a decent conversation in less-than-biting tones. But in spite of everything, she couldn't stop the sensations that stirred inside of her every time she looked into his eyes.

"No, but if that changes I'll give you advanced warning."

"Thank you."

He moved to the other side of the room. "Right now I need to get into this closet."

She swallowed as she stared at him under her lashes. His hands were on his hips, unconsciously drawing emphasis to his jean-clad hips and thighs. Tapered. Perfectly honed.

Deciding she had seen enough—probably too much—she picked up a file off her desk, leaned back in her chair and began reading. She tried like heck to concentrate on the document in front of her, but every so often she would look up and glance over at Darius. He was standing in front of a huge unit that had a bunch of wires running from it. He was concentrating on the computer's mainframe but her eyes were concentrated on him, drinking him in with feminine appreciation. He might be an arrogant ass but he was a good-looking one.

And as if he could feel her eyes on him, he looked up and met her gaze. Their eyes held for a moment longer than necessary before she dropped hers back to the document in front of her, thinking, *so much for working through distractions.*

Darius stared at Summer. Although he wished he were anyplace else other than here, he couldn't stop looking at her and remembering. She had gone back to reading, so he let his gaze travel over her, noticing the way her shoulder-length hair had fallen in her face. She absently brushed it back, giving him a view of her face once again. It was a face that had been his downfall the first time he'd seen it.

He could vividly recall just when that had been. After crawling through her bathroom window, she had seen him before Whitman had known he was in the house. With eye contact, Darius had encouraged her to stay calm and not give him away. Using the training he'd acquired, it had taken only a couple of quick kicks to bring Whitman down. He hit the ground before he'd realized what had happened to him.

It was then that a nearly traumatized Summer had rushed into his arms, holding on to him as if her life depended on it. Even after the police officers had rushed in and handcuffed Whitman, she had still held on to him, like she was too shaken to let him out of her sight. Since it had been almost quitting time, he had followed the squad car that had taken her to the hospital to get checked out. He'd also dropped by her place the next day to repair her broken window.

During the weeks that followed, he would find some excuse or other to see her, and when he'd learned that her ex had been let out on bail, he had made it a point to drive by her house a couple of times a night just to make sure she was okay. Most of the time they would sit in her living room and talk.

During that time Summer had shared a lot about her life. He knew she had been raised by an aunt and that she had left her hometown of Birmingham, Alabama, for California with dreams of becoming an actress or, better yet, to find a rich older man to marry. At the time he'd thought she was teasing, but he'd discovered a few months later she'd been dead serious.

He'd found out the hard way that while he had been falling in love with her, she had been looking for a man with a lot more money than he'd had.

He fought back the anger that tried consuming him all over again, anger that seven years hadn't erased. He must have muttered something under his breath because she looked up and again their eyes met.

He tried looking away but couldn't. And when he moved to close the closet he told himself to head straight for the door and walk out. However, he couldn't do that, either.

Instead, he found himself crossing the room to where she was sitting. Although he had tried to forget it, he was still bothered by the fact that she had left him for another man. A man who had been old enough to be her father from what he'd heard.

By the time he reached her, she was standing. "What is wrong with you?" she asked, backing away from him until her back hit a solid wall and she couldn't go any farther.

His lips curved into a forced smile. "There's nothing wrong with me, Summer."

"Then what do you think you're doing?" she asked in a whisper.

"You still ask too many questions," he murmured, just seconds before leaning in and capturing her mouth with his.

The instant their mouths touched it registered in Summer's brain that she didn't have to accept his kiss. She could outright refuse it. However, any thoughts of doing so tumbled from her mind as he expertly took control of her mouth in a way she remembered so well.

His tongue surged between her parted lips and the moment it tangled with hers, she was a goner. Instead of being swamped with memories of the past, she was overtaken by sensations from the present, where he was causing a stir within her so effortlessly.

And it wasn't just about tongue play; it was a lot more than that. It was about body heat and the way she felt pressed against him, with his arms wrapped firmly around her waist and hers finding their way around his neck.

And then it was about a need. She could not characterize his, but she could certainly define her own. It had been seven years since she had been kissed by a man. Seven years of denying herself this one particular pleasure as well as numerous others. Those denials, especially the primal ones, were coming back to haunt her in the worst kind of way, thanks to him.

And then, she thought, when he pulled her body closer to his, closer to his heat, there was the idea, the very fact, that after all this time she was still attracted to him and he to her. Some things couldn't change. There was the chemistry, physical attraction, sexual tension. Lust was a strong benefactor, especially when motivated and fueled by sexual need.

He changed the angle of his mouth to deepen the kiss and tightened his hold around her waist. And then he used his tongue to taste her in a way he'd never done before. It was as if he were trying to get reacquainted with her flavor, sliding his tongue from one side of her mouth to the other.

Then, in a move she could only deem as sensuously

strategic, he captured her tongue with his and began mating with it in a way that nearly brought her to her knees. He was building desire within her, slowly escalating their fiery exchange. Her hands moved from his neck to his shoulders, and then she spread her palms over his back as he elicited a response from her that she felt in every pore of her body.

Despite the greedy protest of her lips, he finally pulled his mouth away from hers. She drew in a much-needed breath. The kiss had been totally unexpected—completely without warning—and had managed to leave her breathless, speechless, with her senses heightened to their full capacity.

And then reality returned. She stiffened, determined that he would not assume the kiss would be the first of many, or that he was on the verge of finding his way back into her heart with the sole purpose of finding his way back into her bed.

Too late she began berating herself for letting the kiss last as long as it had. He was staring at her and she wondered if the kiss—especially the intensity of it—had been some kind of point he'd wanted to make. Probably, but she had news for him.

"If you want to keep your job, Darius, I would advise you to never do that again," she said in a cutting tone. "If you do, I will report your actions to the Texas Cattleman's Club. I'm sure there are other security companies they could use to do what you were hired to do."

She thought she saw a smile touch his lips before his gaze narrowed slightly. "Does it matter that you kissed me back? Moaned in my ear? Rubbed your body against mine?" he asked with a hint of scorn in his voice.

Summer felt heat flush her cheeks. Had she actually

done all those things while they'd been kissing? Okay, she had returned his kiss, possibly even moaned a few times in his ear, but had she really rubbed her body against his? Due to the intensity of the exchange, that may very well have been a possibility. But that didn't mean she'd given him free rein to enjoy her mouth anytime the mood suited him. She needed to make sure he understood that.

"Fair warning, Darius. Kevin Novak of the TCC will be meeting with me this week to see how things are going at the shelter, and we'll be discussing ways that things around here can be improved. I'm sure getting this job was a feather in your cap and I'd hate to ask that you be replaced, but I will if you don't keep your hands to yourself."

His gaze locked on to hers for longer than necessary, and then he stepped back. Evidently, he realized she hadn't just made an idle threat. There was a long silence as they stood there staring at each other and then to her surprise, he smiled and said, "You enjoyed that kiss just as much as I did and I will bring up that fact to Mr. Novak if he questions me about anything. If you're thinking about putting me on the hot seat, then be ready to join me there. The TCC hired you to do a job, just like they hired me."

His dark eyes hardened. "And need I remind you that I've been living in Somerset a lot longer than you have? People around here know I'm a professional who's selective when it comes to friends. I have a tarnish-free reputation. This is a nice town, close-knit. You're the stranger here, Summer, not me. But I will heed your wishes. The next kiss, you'll initiate. Until then, you're safe with me."

She lifted her chin, wondering when he had become so arrogant, so sure of himself. For him to assume she would make a move on him was outright preposterous. "That won't happen."

He smiled. "Then I guess that means you're safe with me."

She was about to give him a blistering retort when his cell phone rang. "Excuse me," he said, and Summer watched as he quickly pulled it from his belt clip. She figured it was probably some woman calling him.

He muttered a few words to the caller and then glanced back at her and said, "I need to take this call. Remember what I said." And then he turned and walked out of her office.

Darius strolled into the lobby of the shelter, a safe distance from Summer's office, yet close enough so he could see if she left. He pulled in a deep breath and then remembered he had Kevin holding on the phone.

"Okay, Kev, I can talk now. What's up?"

"Just a reminder we're meeting at the TCC's game room Thursday night to shoot pool."

Darius couldn't help but grin. If Kev was calling to remind everyone, that meant he was feeling lucky. "I won't forget."

"Where are you?" Kevin asked.

"At Helping Hands. I decided to install the security system myself since I'm the one who's going to set up TCC's billing account for the shelter. Besides, all my men are handling other projects."

Darius then remembered something. "Your name came up in a conversation I had with the social worker here, Summer Martindale. You're supposed to meet with her sometime this week."

"Yeah, don't remind me. That was something Huntington was supposed to do and he delegated it to me like he's the king and I'm one of his lowly subjects. That man really grates on my last nerve."

Darius understood just how Kevin felt. He, Lance, Mitch and Justin all felt the same way. The five of them, along with Alex Montoya, were the most recent inductees into the Texas Cattleman's Club. This didn't sit well with some of the club's old guards—namely Sebastian Huntington and his stuffy cohorts—who for some reason felt the younger men really weren't deserving of membership in what was known as the most exclusive social club in the state of Texas.

"Hey, man, I thought all of us agreed to just overlook Huntington and his band of fools," Darius reminded his friend.

"Yeah, but he just rubs me the wrong way at times. He doesn't want to put his full support behind the shelter since the funding of it was our idea and not his."

"But he was outvoted, so eventually he'll get over it," Darius said. "And if he doesn't, then that's too bad. Maybe it's a good thing that he's having you do it instead of him. He wouldn't do anything but find fault with everything anyway."

"You're probably right. So, you've met Ms. Martindale?"

"Yes. She's the Summer I was involved with before moving here to Somerset."

"Damn, man, she's *that* Summer?"

"Yes, she is *that* Summer." Kevin didn't know as much about what had happened as Lance, but both of his best friends knew Summer had screwed him over in a bad way, which was the reason he'd wanted to leave Houston and start a new life here in Somerset.

"I need you to do me a favor," he said to Kevin.

"Sure. What do you need?"

It had always been this way between him, Lance and Kevin since their college days. Kevin had agreed to the favor without even knowing what would be required of him. The three trusted each other implicitly. "I'll go into full details when I see you Thursday night, but when you meet with Summer Martindale, if my name comes up, I don't want it mentioned that I'm affiliated with the TCC."

"No problem."

Darius had made the decision to tell Summer the truth when he was good and ready. He couldn't wait to see her face when she realized he was probably just as wealthy as the old man she had left him for.

He and Kevin began talking about the update he'd gotten on the fire at the Brody refinery. Darius was listening to Kevin's take on why he thought Alex Montoya was responsible when he heard footsteps on the tile floor. He glanced up to see Summer walking out of her office. He was standing behind a pillar, so she didn't have a full view of him, which to his way of thinking was a good thing. That way he could check her out at his leisure.

She walked over to a row of file cabinets and he quickly recalled that he'd always thought her walk was a turn-on. There was a sexy sway to her hips with every step she took. She was wearing a pair of brown slacks and a light blue blouse. The lush curves of her hips and the firm swell of her breasts were outlined to perfection by her outfit. He couldn't help standing there staring, taking in everything about her. He easily picked up on the differences in her, differences that, considering everything, he still couldn't help but appreciate.

She seemed a lot more self-assured, had taken ownership of her life and didn't easily back down from a fight. She certainly didn't have any problems trying to put him in his place earlier. The key word was *trying.* As far as he was concerned, when it came to her, he didn't have a place, especially not one she could put him in.

He should not have kissed her. But in all honesty, he could not have *not* kissed her. And now that he had, he wanted to kiss her again. Hold her in his arms. Take her to bed.

Darius tightened his hand in a fist at his side, not liking the way his thoughts were going and liking even less that he wanted to do those things with the same woman who had crushed his heart. But her response to the kiss had caught him off guard—her complete surrender had made him hard in a way he hadn't been in years.

He had forced himself to end the kiss before he'd taken a mind to do something stupid like take her on her desk. He had been that far gone and she had been right there with him, although she'd gotten a little hot behind the collar later.

"Darius? You still there?"

His concentration was pulled back into the phone conversation, and he was trying like heck to recall what Kevin had just said. "Look, Kev, I'll get back with you later. There's something I need to do before it gets too late."

"Sure, man."

After snapping the phone shut, Darius walked toward

Summer. She glanced in his direction with a surprised look on her face. "I thought you had left."

He forced a smile. "I'm sure you were hoping so, but I'm not the type who takes off without letting a person know why, unless there is reason outside of my control. Not like some people."

She glared at him. "And just what is that supposed to mean?"

"Think about it. When you do, it won't take you long to figure things out. I'll be back tomorrow."

Without giving her a chance to say anything else, he walked away.

Darius tried to keep his composure as he eased his long legs into his car. Moments later, after he'd driven away from the shelter and was headed toward home, he let out the expletive that he'd been holding back. Summer was certainly playing the innocent act well, having the gall to pretend she hadn't a clue what he was talking about when he'd thrown out his dig. He couldn't help but wonder what else she was concealing. For all he knew she could very well know about his vast wealth or his membership in the TCC.

He tightened his grip on the steering wheel. Despite the deep animosity he was feeling toward her, his body refused to deny that it wanted her. She could stir embers of passion within him without saying a word. All it took was a look, her presence or her scent to bring his libido to full awareness. He had to do something about her. She had invaded his comfort zone. His space.

For six years he'd been living in Somerset, enjoying peace and harmony. Of all the cities for her to relocate to, why Somerset? Avoiding her wasn't an option, although it would make his life a whole heck of a lot easier. Her very presence unsettled him in the worst way.

He breathed in deeply and fought back the anger that was getting him riled all over again. If she wanted to pretend, then two could play that game. He was in a position to teach her the very lesson she deserved to learn. She'd wanted a rich husband and in his own way, he would let her know just how she'd lost out on one. He would bide his time, get on her good side and then, when she assumed things were going great between them, after he'd gotten her back in his bed, he would do the very same thing to her that she had done to him.

Walk away without looking back.

Chapter 3

The following morning, with butterflies floating around in her stomach, Summer swiped her security card through the scanner before stepping into the shelter, hoping she was early enough to have arrived before Darius. He was the last person she wanted to see. She hadn't gotten much sleep last night and he was the reason. She'd been unable to get the kiss they'd shared yesterday out of her head.

As she made her way toward her office, she refused to even consider the reason why she'd taken more time getting dressed this morning than she usually did. Why she had spent a good ten minutes more putting on her makeup and why had she pulled out the curling iron for the first time in weeks.

When she stopped at Marcy's desk, she checked her watch. Marcy wasn't due in for another hour or so. Summer unlocked Marcy's desk to retrieve a clipboard that listed all her appointments and meetings for that day. Perusing the clipboard, she began to see what her day was going to be like.

"You look nice today."

Summer didn't bother to turn around. She didn't have to. She had left home with a made-up mind that no matter what, she was not going to let Darius rattle her. She was not going to allow him to make her come unglued and she would not look for condescension in his every word. So with that resolve, she would take his compliment in stride and assume he meant no more by it than what was said.

She turned around and her hands automatically tightened on the clipboard the moment she did so. She then swallowed deeply as the nervous sensations stirring in her stomach escalated. How was it possible that he looked even better today than yesterday? He was casually but impeccably dressed. A different pair of jeans and a different shirt, but the utterly breathtaking look was still there. All lean. Well-defined muscles. Perfect abs. And with the tan-colored Stetson sitting on his head, tilted at an angle that shadowed his dark brows, she couldn't help but admit he was truly a fine, handsome specimen of a man.

"Thank you for the compliment. You look nice, also," she heard herself say, determined not to get in a sparring match with him. "Will you need to be in my office today?"

"No, I'll be working in the other offices the majority of the day, other than when I start setting up the accounting for the TCC. It will be a while before I start on that."

She nodded, not wanting to prolong her time with him. "Then I guess I need to let you get started."

"How about lunch?"

She stared up at him, certain she had misunderstood. "Excuse me?"

He smiled and she felt a semblance of heat stirring in her blood, through her veins, in a number of other places she didn't want to think about. "I asked if you wanted to do lunch with me."

"Why?" She couldn't help but ask.

"Why not? You gotta eat and so do I."

"But that doesn't mean we have to share a meal," she pointed out.

His smile widened and the heat stirring in her blood intensified. "No, but it would mean that we're trying to put the past behind us and move on," he said. "It's not like we're going to become bosom buddies, because we aren't. But I'll be hanging around here for the next couple of weeks, so we might as well learn how to get along. I'm not going anywhere and I doubt you are, either. So, what about lunch?"

"I'm not sure that would be a good idea, Darius."

"What was it that you said yesterday? Oh, yes, your very words were, 'We're professionals and are mature enough to make the best of it.'"

Summer breathed in deeply. Yes, those had been her very words.

"I promise not to bite."

She opened her mouth to say something and changed her mind, quickly shutting it. A twist of emotions rumbled in her chest and she knew why. Darius was offering the olive branch, the chance to move on and put what they'd once shared behind them since there was no way it could ever happen again. And deep down she knew she needed that.

She couldn't continue carrying the bitterness of the last seven years. If they were doomed to live in the same town and would be running into each other on occasion, at least they could be civil to each other. But there was no chance of them ever getting back together. For her, the pain had gone too deep.

"Lunch will be fine," she heard herself say, hoping she didn't live to regret it.

"Great. You pick the place, just as long as they sell good hamburgers."

She couldn't help the smile that touched her lips. Some things evidently never changed and his love for hamburgers was one of them. "Too much ground beef isn't good for you," she said, quoting what she'd told him over a hundred times in the past.

And as expected, he rolled his eyes. "Yeah, yeah, I know, and the key words are *too much.* I've become a physical fitness addict, so I don't indulge in too many things that aren't good for me, but there's nothing wrong with enjoying a big, juicy hamburger every once in a while."

Summer decided not to say anything more on the matter. It was evident by his perfect body that he was into physical fitness. "I guess not. I'll be in the lobby at noon."

Darius stretched his neck to work out the kinks as he leaned back in the chair, away from the computer. He glanced up at the clock. It was almost noon.

He stood and stretched his entire body, refusing to acknowledge the anticipation he felt over joining Summer for lunch. Instead, he tried convincing himself that his nerves were the result of knowing he was slowly but surely breaking down her defenses and in good time, he would have the upper hand.

He was leaving the small office when his ears picked up the sound of commotion coming from the front of the building, near the lobby. He quickened his stride and when he rounded the corner, he saw a man standing outside the building with a baseball bat in his hand, threatening to break the glass door if he wasn't allowed to come in to get his wife and children. Summer, Darius saw, was talking to the man on the intercom, trying to reason with him.

He watched her, amazed at how calmly she was speaking to the man, clearly determined not to get ruffled by the vulgar language he was using and the threats he was making.

He glanced over at Marcy, who was sitting at her desk. "Have the police been called?" he asked, shifting his attention back to the scene being played out a few feet away. "And where the hell is security?" he continued, keeping his gaze fixed on Summer. She continued to appear composed as she tried to settle the man down and convince him to go away.

"The police are on their way. Our security guard called in sick this morning."

Darius looked at Marcy. "They didn't send a replacement?"

"Not yet."

Darius frowned. Huntington and his group had voted against the idea of Darius's firm being in charge of all the security for the shelter. Instead, Huntington had recommended a security company the TCC had used in the past, claiming it was top-notch. The majority of the members had gone along with him except for Lance, Kevin, Mitch and Justin. When they had been outvoted, as a compromise, they had pushed for the club to consider Darius to handle the security for all the computers and to set up the billing system.

Huntington had fought hard against it, saying Darius was too new to the club to take on such tasks, but he had lost the fight when Alex Montoya had sided with them instead of Huntington's group. Darius got the feeling that in addition to the bad blood between Alex and the Brodys, there was bad blood between Alex and Huntington. But then it seemed Huntington had a beef against anyone under the age of forty who joined the club.

The sound of breaking glass recaptured Darius's attention and in a flash he raced forward and placed himself in front of Summer just as the man who was wielding the bat forced his way through the broken glass toward her.

"Be a man and hit me instead of a woman. I dare you," Darius snarled through gritted teeth, not trying to hide the searing rage coursing through him.

The man evidently thought twice about following through on Darius's offer and dropped the bat, taking a step back. Within seconds, the shelter was swarming with police officers. Two of them quickly came through the broken glass door to apprehend the man, who didn't put up a fight.

Darius turned to Summer. "Are you all right?" he asked in a low voice. He hadn't realized just how angry he was until now. If that man had harmed a single strand of hair on her head, Darius would have gone ballistic.

In a way, Darius wished the man had taken him up on his offer. That would have given him the excuse he needed to flatten him. The man had just proven what a coward he was. He was willing to take a bat to a woman, but had wasted no time backing away instead of squaring off with a man equal to his size and weight.

He watched Summer breathe in deeply. "Yes, I'm fine. It's not unusual for a husband to show up wanting to see his wife and children, and when we tell them they can't, most move on. Once in a while, we get someone like Mr. Green who refuses to abide by our rules and causes problems. Usually when that happens, security handles it."

Darius nodded. He would be calling a special meeting of the TCC to make sure something like this didn't happen again. He didn't want to think what could have happened had he not been there. There was no doubt in his mind that the man intended to use that bat on someone.

Before he could say anything, a police officer approached them to obtain their statements. After recording all the facts, the officer advised Summer that she would need to go down to police headquarters so formal charges against the man could be filed.

No sooner had the officer walked away than a woman Darius recognized as a staff member walked up. "Excuse me, Ms. Martindale, but some of the women are upset. They heard a man was trying to force his way inside."

Summer nodded. "Okay, I'm on my way to meet with them."

She then turned back to Darius. "Thanks for your help. I really didn't think he would go so far as to break down the glass. I was hoping that I'd be able to talk some sense into him."

She glanced at her watch. "I need to calm down the women and then go to the police station. I guess lunch is off now."

He shook his head. "No, it's not. Go meet with the women and then I'll drive you to headquarters. Afterward, on the way back, we'll grab something to eat."

"Okay. Thanks." She started to walk away and then glanced at all the glass around the door.

"Go on. I'll make sure this mess is cleaned up and get the glass replaced," he said.

She gave him an appreciative smile before hurrying off with the staff member.

When she'd rounded the corner, Darius released a curse and pulled the cell phone from his belt, hitting the speed dial for Lance's number. His best friend answered on the first ring. "Hey, what's up, Darius?"

"There was an incident here at the shelter and security was not in place. We need to call a TCC meeting."

"I thought we were never going to get out of there," Summer said as they left police headquarters. Darius led her over to his car.

After calming down the women and children, she'd had to meet personally with Gail Green to let her know what her husband had done. Then Summer had to assure Gail that the shelter wouldn't be putting her and her two children out because of the incident.

Gail and her two little boys had arrived at the shelter three days ago after fleeing from their home in the middle of the night. The bruises on her body were evidence enough that she'd been in an abusive situation, but like a number of other women who sought refuge at the shelter, she had refused to press charges.

"I thought they handled everything in a timely manner," Darius said, smiling faintly as he opened the car door for her.

She rolled her eyes. "Spoken like a true ex-cop."

He chuckled before closing her door and moving around the car to the other side. The clock on his console indicated it was after three and they still hadn't eaten lunch.

"Where to?" he asked when he got settled behind the wheel with his seat belt in place. "And don't say back to the shelter because it won't happen. I'm taking you somewhere so we can grab something to eat. I'm hungry even if you're not."

As if on cue, her stomach growled and Summer couldn't help but grin. "Sorry. I guess that means I'm hungry, too. Have you tried that café around the corner from the shelter? The Red Sky."

"No. I've passed by it a few times but have never eaten there."

"Then I guess this is your lucky day because that's where I want to go."

"All I want to know is do they make good hamburgers?" he asked, easing his car into traffic.

"I've never eaten one of their burgers. I'm a salad girl."

He glanced over at her and grinned. "So, you haven't kicked that habit?"

"You want to consult Dr. Oz to determine which of us is eating healthier?"

"No."

She couldn't help but laugh. "I figured as much."

It felt good to laugh. She would never admit it to anyone, especially to Darius, but Samuel Green had truly frightened her and she was glad Darius had been there. When Mr. Green had burst through that door after breaking the glass, she'd had flashbacks to that time with Tyrone when she'd been exposed to his true colors. She had seen his anger out of control, and that anger had been directed at her. A backhand blow had sent her sprawling across the room but she had been quick enough to make it to the door before he could do anything else.

That had been the one and only time Tyrone had raised a hand to her, and she made sure it was the last. A courier had returned her engagement ring to him in the same box it had come in and later that same day, he'd been notified of the restraining order she'd filed. Thinking about it now, she appreciated the fact that she'd gotten out of an abusive situation. She had known when it was time to part ways even if Tyrone hadn't.

She glanced over at Darius. "Did you get much work done today?"

He shrugged. "Not as much as I would have liked, but that's okay. Typically, a job of this sort wouldn't take a whole lot of time, but security is a concern at the shelter, as it should be."

There was no way she would argue with that.

"And as far as the billing system goes," he continued, "I understand the TCC has money, but they want a firm accounting of how their money is being spent."

"Yes, and rightly so," she said, wondering if he thought she felt otherwise. "This shelter is fortunate to be funded by such a distinguished group of men. Do you know any of them?"

He lifted a brow. “Any of whom?”

“Members of the TCC?”

“Why would I know any of them?”

She noted that he sounded offended by her question. “I didn’t mean if you knew them personally. I was just wondering if you’ve ever met any of them. After all, you were hired by them.”

He didn’t say anything for a moment. “Yes, I’ve met some of them. They’re okay for a bunch of rich guys, and I respect the club for all the things they do in the community. It’s my understanding that some of the members prefer not having their identities known. They like doing things behind the scenes without any recognition.”

Summer nodded. She could respect that, knowing there were a number of wealthy people who preferred being anonymous donors. She appreciated everything the TCC had done so far and all the things they planned to do. She was definitely looking forward to her meeting with Mr. Novak on Friday. Presently, Helping Hands could accommodate up to fifteen women and children that needed shelter care. Already the TCC had plans in the works to expand the shelter’s facilities to triple that amount.

“You’ve gotten quiet,” he said.

She glanced over at Darius and couldn’t help but feel a rush of gratitude. He had stood back and let her handle things until the situation had gotten out of control. She appreciated his intervening when he did, playing the role of knight in shining armor once again.

She continued looking at him. His eyes were on the road and her mind couldn’t help but shift to another time when he’d been driving her someplace. It had been their first official date. They had gone out for pizza and afterward he had taken her home. She had invited him inside and later, sitting beside him on the sofa, the kissing had begun. A short while later she had been lying beneath him in her bed as he made love to her in a way she hadn't known was possible. The intensity of the memories of that night was almost enough to push everything that had happened over the past seven years into the background.

Almost, but not quite.

"Summer?"

She blinked when she realized they had come to a traffic light and he had glanced over at her, catching her staring. "Yes?"

"Are you sure you're okay? I guess incidents such as what happened earlier are expected to some degree, which is the reason I'm installing state-of-the-art security software on all the computers—to reduce the risk that the location of the women seeking refuge is discovered. But still, it has to be unnerving when one of the husbands or boyfriends shows up."

If you only knew. "Yes, and what's really sad is the fact that the women have to go into hiding at all. The Greens have two beautiful little boys and today their father showed up demanding them back with, of all things, one of their baseball bats. The person we saw today was not a loving father or husband but a violent and dangerous man."

Summer frowned and then she sighed deeply. Tonight she would get a good night's sleep and try to forget the incident ever happened. Fat chance. She would remember it and she would imagine what could have happened had Darius not been there.

"Here we are."

She looked around. Darius had pulled into the café's parking lot and brought the car to a stop. She glanced over at him. He was staring at her with an intensity that sent shivers of awareness through her body.

Sexual chemistry was brewing between them again. She could feel his body heat emanating from across the car. Summer forced the thought to the back of her mind.

"Umm, I guess we should go on inside," she forced her mouth to say. The way he was looking at her made her want to suggest that they go somewhere else, but she fought the temptation and held tight to her common sense.

She decided now was as good a time as any to thank him. "I really do appreciate what you did today, Darius, and I want to—"

"No, don't thank me."

His words stopped her short. "Why?"

"Because I didn't do any more than what was needed. No more than any other man would have done."

She contemplated his words. He was a man of action. Twice she had seen him in full swing and neither time had he accepted her words of gratitude. "I *will* thank you, Darius Franklin, because you deserve to be thanked."

And before he could respond, she got out of the car.

"Hey, Ms. Martindale, do you want your usual spot?" Tina asked when Summer walked in.

"Whatever is available," Summer answered, feeling the heat of Darius's chest close to her back. His nearness was almost unsettling.

"You must come here often," he said, moving to stand at her side.

She glanced over at him and smiled. "Practically every day. It's not far from the shelter and I enjoy the walk. And I like their grilled chicken salads."

Moments later they were being escorted to a table in the rear. Darius shifted his full attention to the people whose tables they passed. They either greeted her by name or smiled a hello. "You're pretty popular, I see," he said when they had taken their seats.

She shrugged. "Most are regulars who know that I work at the shelter. They believe it benefits the community and appreciate our presence."

They halted conversation for a while to scan the menu. Darius was the one deciding what he wanted since Summer was getting her usual. However, she was inclined to check out the soup of the day, or at least pretend that she was doing so. It was hard concentrating on anything, even food, while sitting across from Darius. As he studied his menu, she studied him over the top of hers.

She almost laughed out loud at the intense expression on his face. Deciding what hamburger he wanted couldn't be all that serious. But then Darius had always been a very serious man. Especially when it came to making love.

For a heart-flipping moment she wondered why a memory like that had crossed her mind, but she knew. Darius was the kind of man that oozed sexuality as potent as it could get, making those incredible urges consume the lower part of her body. They'd only had one night together, but it had been incredible. No matter what had happened after that, she could not discount how he'd made her feel.

He was the most gifted of lovers. Pleasing her had seemed to be the most natural thing in the world to Darius. She hadn't realized just how selfish Tyrone had been in the bedroom until after she'd made love to Darius. How could she have realized when Tyrone had been her first? No matter what her sexual experience had been with Tyrone, one time with Darius had made everything just fine.

Darius glanced up and she took in a lungful of air. The intensity of his gaze—she wanted to look away, but she couldn't. It was as if she were held captive by his deep, dark eyes.

"Here are your waters."

Summer almost jumped when Tina appeared with two glasses of water. "Thanks." Barely giving her a chance to set the glass down in front of her, Summer picked it up and took a long gulp, feeling the need for the ice-cold water to cool her down.

Tina hung around long enough to take their food and drink order before moving on again.

"So, what do you like about your job?"

She glanced over at him to answer his question, making an attempt to keep her gaze trained on his nose instead of his eyes. "Everything, but mostly the satisfaction I get from helping women in distress, those who might feel broken up because of what has happened. I like letting them know they aren't alone and somebody cares."

What she didn't add was that she enjoyed giving them the same support he had given her during those first crucial days, when she had begun doubting herself, second-guessing the situation and believing that maybe she had been the cause of Tyrone's problems instead of the other way around.

"I notice there's not a director at the shelter," he said.

Her gaze drifted down from his nose to his lips. Focusing on his mouth was just as bad as looking into his eyes. He had a sexy mouth. It was a mouth that could move with agonizing slowness when talking…or when being used for other things. She swallowed before responding.

"When I was hired by the TCC it was decided that I could handle it all for now. When they complete the proposed expansions and decide to fill the position, I'm hoping I'll be considered for the job."

Darius nodded. He had not been a part of the TCC committee that had done the hiring for Helping Hands, which was one of the reasons he'd been surprised to discover her working there. He would have recognized her name the second it came across his desk.

"The shelter is pretty full now. How do you manage it all?" he asked.

She shrugged. "It's not so bad. I think the most challenging times are when I'm called in the middle of the night to a police station or hospital to comfort a woman who's been beaten or raped."

Darius's jaw twitched at the thought of anyone treating a woman so cruelly. Mistreatment of a woman was one thing he could not tolerate.

"It's also difficult at times when manning the abuse hotline. Someone is there to take calls twenty-four hours a day—usually a volunteer trained to do so. Every once in a while, a call will come through that I need to handle. Those are the ones that can get pretty emotional, depending on the circumstances."

Darius could tell from her voice that she was dedicated to what she did every day. To stay on safe ground and not stray on to a topic neither of them wanted to deal with, he decided to keep her talking about her work at the shelter.

For the first time since seeing her again, he was lowering his guard a little.

When the waitress finally delivered their order, he had to admit the food looked good. And after a bite into his hamburger, he had to own up that it tasted good, too. One of his uncles in Charleston once owned a sandwich shop that used to make the best burgers around. As a kid, he enjoyed the summers he spent there and the older he got, he found himself comparing every hamburger he ate to his uncle Donald's. None could compare, but he had to admit this one came pretty close.

"How does it taste?"

He glanced over at Summer and could only smile and nod, since he couldn't talk with a mouth full of hamburger.

A half hour later, on the drive back to the shelter, he reflected on a number of things he hadn't expected. Mainly, he hadn't figured on sitting across from her for almost an hour and enjoying her company without animosity or anger seeping in. However, what couldn't be helped was the sexual tension. Although they had tried to downplay it with a lot of conversation, it was there nonetheless.

There was a lot about her he could barely resist. Her scent topped the list. Whatever perfume she was wearing filled his nostrils with a luscious fragrance that seemed to get absorbed right into his skin. And then there were her eyes. He was fully aware that she'd tried to avoid looking at him, which had been hard to do since they were sitting directly across from each other. Each time he would catch her staring at him, he would feel a pull in his stomach.

Thankfully, his hands were gripping the steering wheel because at that moment, it wouldn't take much for him to reach over and touch her, stroke that part of her thigh exposed beneath her skirt. Seeing her flesh peeking at him was making his mind spin, so he tried focusing on the road and decided to get her talking again. Anything to keep his mind off taking her.

"So, where do you live?" he asked.

He kept his gaze glued to the road. She didn't need to see the heat in his eyes, a telltale sign that although he wished otherwise, she was getting to him.

"I bought a house a block from the post office," she said.

He noted she didn't provide him with the name of her street. There were a couple of new communities sprouting up near the post office, as well as a number of newly renovated older homes that had been for sale. "Nice area," he heard himself say.

"I like it. My neighborhood's pretty quiet. Most of the people on my street are a lot older and are in bed before eight at night."

He nodded. From the information she had just shared he could safely assume that she had purchased one of the renovated homes in the older, established communities. Doing so had been a smart move on her part; they were a good investment.

She then opened up and began telling him about it,

saying she was having a lot of fun decorating the house. He didn't find that hard to believe. When she'd lived in Houston, her apartment had been small but nice and he'd been surprised to learn she had done most of the decorating herself.

All too soon he was pulling into the parking lot of the shelter. "Thanks for taking me to lunch," she said, reaching to unsnap her seat belt even before he could bring the car to a complete stop. "Although I have to admit, riding in the car instead of walking only means I have to get my daily physical activity some other way," she added.

He came close to saying that he knew another way she could get her physical activity, and it would be something she would enjoy—he would make sure of it. Instead, he decided it would be best to keep his mouth shut.

"But since it will probably be dark when I leave today, I'll take the day off from exercise," she tacked on, getting out of the car.

He glanced over at her. "Why are you staying late?"

"Because I have a lot of work and can't leave until I'm finished. I'm meeting with Mr. Novak on Friday and there are a number of reports I have to run. More than likely, the TCC will have heard about the incident today and will want a full report on what happened."

He tightened his mouth after almost telling her that he'd already given them one. While at police headquarters, he had gotten a call from Mitch, Justin and Kevin. Lance had told them what had happened. Minor details had been given on television—since it was a women's shelter, no television crews or reporters were allowed to show up in order to protect the women staying there.

He knew if Summer stayed beyond five o'clock, she'd be pulling a long day. But for some reason, he had a feeling that was probably the norm for her. "Isn't there someone who can help you with those reports?"

"Afraid not. Besides, I'd rather run them myself, especially since I plan on pleading my case to Mr. Novak for an expansion of the shelter sooner rather than later."

Darius didn't say anything, but considering what had happened earlier that day, he wasn't crazy about her walking out to her car alone. Although the parking lot was well lit, he still didn't like it. Two security guards had shown up after the incident. He decided that before he left for the day, he would talk to the guards and make sure one of them walked Summer to her car.

When they reached the door he decided that unlike her, he intended to leave at a decent time. He had a meeting with the fire chief later, and it was a meeting he didn't want to miss. And besides, the last thing he needed was to end up in the office late at night with Summer—alone.

Chapter 4

Darius grabbed a beer out of the refrigerator and popped the top before tilting the can to his mouth, appreciating the cool brew that flowed down his throat. When the can was empty, he scowled before crushing the aluminum and tossing it into the recycling bin.

His frown deepened as he sat down at the kitchen table, thinking that today had certainly not gone like he'd planned. He was convinced that the incident at the shelter was the prime reason his protective instincts toward Summer had kicked in. He had been ready to do bodily harm to anyone who even thought of hurting her. And he could admit that the reason he had driven her to police headquarters and then later to lunch was because he hadn't wanted her out of his sight. He was becoming attached again, and that wasn't good.

He rubbed a hand down his face. Maybe he needed

to rethink the notion of exacting some sort of revenge on her and instead, just put distance between them and let it go at that, treating her the way he would other groupies or gold diggers whenever they crossed his path.

But he wasn't able to do that. If anything, today proved that when it came to Summer, he didn't think straight or logically. Right now, the only thing he should be thinking about was hurting her the way she had hurt him. Therefore, regardless of any protective instincts he might have, he would continue with his plan to make her think something special was going on between them. Then, at the right time, he'd drop the bomb that she meant nothing to him, and she'd discover she had gotten played, just like he had.

When his cell phone went off, he stood and pulled it off his belt. "What's up, Lance?" After his meeting with Chief Ingle, he had stopped by the TCC Café and had dinner with Kevin and Justin. Lance and his wife had driven to Houston to attend some sort of function there.

"I got your message. So Ingle thinks the fire was started with some sort of petroleum-based product?" Lance asked.

"He's pretty sure of it. But it wasn't one that could easily be detected, which is the reason the investigation took so long. They're trying to narrow the components down. However, he believes it's the same kind found in lubricating oils used for ranch equipment," Darius responded.

"Something that Montoya could easily get his hands on, since he owns that cattle ranch," Lance was quick to point out.

Darius shook his head. "His men are the ones working his ranch the majority of the time, Lance. Montoya's heavily involved in his import/export business."

"For crying out loud, Darius, you just don't want to believe he's responsible for that fire, do you?" Lance asked with frustration in his voice.

"What I don't want is for you to be so convinced Montoya is behind the fire that you start overlooking any other possible suspects."

"There aren't any other possible suspects, Darius. Montoya is the only one who hates me and Mitch bad enough to do such a thing. At the end of your investigation, you'll see that all the evidence points in Montoya's direction."

A few hours later, the fire investigation was the last thing on Darius's mind when he finally eased into bed, determined to get a good night's sleep. Moments later, after a number of tosses and turns, he discovered doing so wouldn't be easy when thoughts of Summer filled his mind. When he thought of what could have possibly happened had he not been there today. Even now he was worried that she was still at the center working, and he was tempted to go check for himself to make sure she was all right. But then he quickly recalled he had spoken with security to make sure someone escorted her to her car whenever she did work late.

He breathed in deeply, getting angry with himself that his concern for her, this feeling stirring deep within him, was making him weak. He refused to let that happen. But each time he closed his eyes, he saw her, remembered a better time between them, a time when she had been his whole world.

He stared up at the ceiling, determined to remember that she was not his whole world any longer, would never be it again. It was something he couldn't lose sight of. He would keep up his guard with her, no matter what.

"Thank you for walking me to my car, Barney, but it really wasn't necessary."

"No problem, ma'am. Besides, it was Mr. Franklin's orders."

Summer raised a brow at the uniformed guard. "Was it?"

"Yes."

Summer pondered that. How could Darius give an order to a guard who didn't work for him? Evidently, Barney had no problem following an order from someone who wasn't his boss.

"Well, good night," she said, opening her car door and getting inside.

"Just a minute, Ms. Martindale. This was pinned to your windshield beneath the wipers," he said, handing the piece of paper to her.

Summer tossed the flyer onto the seat beside her. "Good night."

"Good night."

Summer drove off, noticing Barney was still standing there, watching her pull out of the parking lot. No doubt he was still following Darius's orders. After what happened today, she could understand his concern and appreciated him wanting to make sure she was all right. Just like she had appreciated him taking her to lunch.

There had been something strange about sitting across from a man who had once undressed her, rubbed his hands all over her naked body and made love to her in a way that thinking about it took her breath away.

A man who'd shown her that foreplay was an art form that could be taken to many levels, and that a person's mouth was just as lethal as his hands when making love.

When her car came to a stop at a traffic light, she turned on the radio, hoping the sound of music would drown out her thoughts of Darius. That wasn't going to happen, she thought, when she recalled how long after she'd left Houston she would lie in bed and think of him.

Her stomach growled and she remembered she'd missed dinner. When she got home she would make a sandwich and a glass of iced tea. It was one of those hot August nights.

As she waited for the light to change, she glanced over at the flyer she'd thrown on the seat and picked it up. Her breath caught in her throat and chills ran up her spine when she read the words, "I take care of my own."

The light turned green but she didn't realize it until the driver behind her blasted his horn. She accelerated, wondering which husband or boyfriend had placed the note on her car. It wouldn't be the first time one of the abusers of the women at the shelter blamed the staff for keeping his family from him. Mr. Green had taken the same position earlier that day. She wouldn't be surprised if it had been Mr. Green who had placed the note there, since her car had been parked in one of the spaces reserved for shelter personnel.

Summer tossed the paper aside, thinking of Mr. Green and the baseball bat, and his terrified wife. She sighed. She had long ago stopped trying to figure out why some men could treat a woman they claimed to love so shabbily.

The next day, Darius studied the computer screen in front of him and tried not to think about the woman a few doors down. She had been holed up in her office all morning and it was almost noon. He would bet any amount of money she would not be stopping for lunch.

A part of him knew it was really none of his business whether she ate or not, but another part decided to make it his business. Just as well, since he hadn't been able to concentrate worth a damn anyway.

Before arriving at the shelter, he had dropped by the refinery to take a look around the area damaged by the fire, hoping he would find something that had been overlooked previously. He hated admitting it, but Lance was right. All the evidence accumulated so far was pointing at Montoya, especially since the man didn't have an alibi for that night and he'd been seen in the vicinity of the refinery. However, the evidence was too cut-and-dried to suit Darius—way too pat. As far as he was concerned, if Montoya wasn't guilty, then someone who knew about the feud between Montoya and the Brodys was certainly making it look that way.

Darius stood as he checked his watch, deciding it was time to feed his stomach and satisfy his desire to see Summer again. He had fought the impulse to drop by her office and say hello when he had arrived at the shelter. But he couldn't fight it anymore.

Her office door had been closed, which meant she was either counseling someone or buried knee-deep in work. She had mentioned getting ready for that meeting tomorrow with Kev. But still, she had to eat, and he kind of enjoyed that café where they had eaten yesterday. The hamburger had been delicious.

Walking down the corridor, he went to the secretary's desk. "Is Ms. Martindale in a meeting with someone?" he asked Marcy.

Marcy stopped thumbing through a bunch of folders on her desk long enough to look up and smile at him. "No, she's going over some papers. If you need to talk with her about something, just knock on her door."

He returned her smile. "I think I will. Thanks."

Strolling back the way he'd come, he came to a stop in front of her door, hesitating a moment before knocking, convincing himself he was only pretending to be a nice guy when in fact, she really didn't deserve his kindness.

"Come in."

He opened the door and walked into her office, closing it behind him. She didn't look up. "Ready for lunch?" he asked.

She lifted her gaze from the document she'd been reading to fix it on him. The moment their eyes met, a slight tremor touched him. And if that weren't bad enough, he could feel a deep stirring in his gut. He stood there, fully conscious of the effect she was having on him and not liking it, but unable to do anything but stand there and take it like a man who wanted a woman, a woman he should have gotten from under his skin long ago. She broke eye contact with him and looked back down at the document she'd been reading. "I can't today."

You can't or you won't? Instead of asking, he said, "Yes, you can. You'll think better on a full stomach."

When she looked back up at him without saying anything, as if giving his words some serious thought, he decided to add, "Besides, that hamburger I ate yesterday was pretty good and—"

"And you probably don't need another one today. Too

much beef," she finished for him, pushing her papers aside. "Why don't you try a salad?"

He chuckled. "That's rabbit food."

She rolled her eyes. "That's healthy." And then she said. "Okay, I'll have lunch with you, but only if we walk to the café."

He felt the amusement leave his face. "Walk?"

"Yes. Walk."

He noticed she was watching him intently, probably expecting him to back down. He couldn't help the smile that touched the corners of his lips when he said, "Fine. We'll walk."

"You really didn't expect me to do it, did you?"

Summer glanced over at Darius. They had been walking for the past few minutes in silence, which gave her the chance to wonder how, for the third day in a row, she'd been in his presence. He was right. She hadn't expected him to agree to walk to the café with her. Not that she thought he wasn't in any kind of shape to do so, but mainly because he didn't have a pair of walking shoes tucked away in a desk like she had. He was wearing cowboy boots, and they complemented his jeans and chambray shirt. And he had grabbed his Stetson off the rack to put on his head, which, considering the heat of the sun, had been a good idea. He looked good in his Western attire, too good to be walking with her on the dusty sidewalk. Every so often when someone needed to squeeze by them, Darius's denim-clad thigh would brush up against hers, making her very aware of the strength of his masculinity.

"No, I really didn't," she said finally. "But you have

to admit it's a beautiful day outside. A perfect day to walk."

She couldn't help remembering the last time they had taken a walk together, late one afternoon when he'd shown up at her place after getting off work. They had strolled to the neighborhood park and on the way back had stopped at a corner store for ice-cream cones. That had been a perfect day to walk, too.

She breathed in deeply in an attempt to erase the memory from her mind. For three days, she had allowed him to invade her personal space and she wasn't exactly happy with the fact that he'd done so. She had appreciated his help yesterday, but somehow she needed to get him to understand that being cordial to each other didn't mean they had to share lunch every day.

"How is Aunt Joanne?"

She nearly missed a step and felt his hand on her elbow, reaching out to steady her, keeping her from falling. She stopped walking and glanced up at him. He was standing a scarce few inches in front of her and met her gaze. Darius had met Aunt Joanne when she had come to Houston to give Summer much-needed support during Tyrone's trial. Her aunt had liked Darius, and Summer wanted to believe that Darius had liked her aunt, as well, that his feelings toward Aunt Jo had been genuine and not fake—like the ones he'd displayed toward her.

"Summer, what's wrong?"

She swallowed and fought back the tears that threatened every time she thought of losing her aunt. "Aunt Jo died two years ago."

She saw surprise and then sorrow in his eyes. "I'm sorry. What happened? Was she ill?" he asked. He moved his hands from her elbow to her hand, and she could feel him wrapping his fingers around hers.

She shook her head. "No, in fact she'd had a physical the day before and had called to tell me how well it went, and that the doctor had even joked about her being fifty-five and would probably live well past ninety-five because she was in such good shape."

Summer paused a moment and then continued. "On her way home from work one night, she stopped at an ATM. A guy came up, demanding her money. She emptied her account and gave him all she had, but he shot and killed her anyway."

"Oh, Summer, I'm sorry to hear that," he said, pulling her into his arms. And she went without hesitation, ignoring the fact they were standing in the middle of the sidewalk. She was being given the shoulder to cry on that she had needed so badly two years ago. Burying her aunt had been the hardest thing she'd ever had to do. Less than a year after graduating from college, she'd lost the only person who'd been there for her consistently.

"That's it, Summer, get it all out," Darius urged gently in her ear. "Let it go." She felt the strength of his arms wrap around her shoulders, drawing her close.

Summer wasn't sure just how long she stood there, on a public street, being comforted by the only man she had ever loved—and who had done her wrong. She wasn't sure if she could ever forgive him for breaking her heart.

Pulling herself together, she eased back out of his arms, breaking all physical contact with him. "Sorry about that," she said softly.

"Don't apologize. Are you okay?"

"Yes, I'm fine." She nudged her hands into the pockets of her slacks and glanced down at the pavement. "It's still hard for me sometimes."

"I imagine that it would be, and I really meant it when I said that I'm sorry, Summer."

The sincerity in his voice as well as the warmth of his tone touched her in a way that it should not have. She lifted her head to glance back up at him. "Thank you."

"You're welcome."

As they continued their walk toward the café, Summer's head was spinning with confusion over whether she could trust this man who had crushed her heart once before but seemed filled with pure compassion for her. Should she listen to her head, her heart…her body? She suddenly felt like she was nineteen again, and she didn't like it at all. Not at all.

Chapter 5

"You haven't been listening to a thing I've said," Justin Dupree complained while eyeing Darius curiously. The two men were enjoying a meal at one of the exclusive restaurants in town with plans to drop by the TCC later and play pool with Lance, Mitch and Kevin.

Darius took another sip of his beer and gave his friend an apologetic smile. "Sorry, what did you say?"

A smile touched the corners of Justin's lips. "I said Monica Cooper has been giving you the eye all night."

Darius raised a brow. "Who?"

Justin rolled his eyes. "Monica. You know. Sultry lips Monica."

Darius couldn't help but grin as he leaned back in his chair and took another sip of his beer. "No, I don't know her, but I'm sure you do."

There weren't too many single women with sultry

lips that Justin didn't know. He had a reputation of being Somerset's number one jet-setting playboy. Heir to his family's multimillion-dollar shipping company, Justin could probably talk a nun out of her clothes. He could also close any business deal he wanted—he had a reputation of being a tough-as-nails, ruthless businessman. Darius was proud to consider him a friend.

Justin smiled. "Yes, I know her. Her dad owns a nice spread outside of Austin. She comes to Somerset every summer to visit her aunt. She seems taken with you."

Darius didn't even bother looking over his shoulder at the woman. Instead, he said, "That's nice." He knew Justin had to be wondering why he wasn't showing Monica, or any woman for that matter, any interest tonight. Even their waitress had given him a flirty smile. But the only woman he could think about at the moment was the one he'd had lunch with today. The one he couldn't get out of his mind.

The one he had held in his arms while she'd cried.

"Okay, Darius, what's going on in that brain of yours? Lance said you still don't want to believe that Montoya was behind that fire."

Darius studied the contents of his beer bottle before glancing over at Justin. The two of them were best friends to the Brodys. Justin was Mitch's best friend like he was Lance's.

In a way, Darius felt guilty. He hadn't been thinking about Montoya and the fire, and he really should be. He had been thinking about Summer. But now that Justin had brought it up…

"I'm just not as convinced as everyone seems to be. Like you, Montoya is a shrewd businessman. Always on top of his game. Smart as a whip. I can't see him being stupid enough to set fire to his enemy's refinery, not when all fingers would point his way. He has no motive."

Justin shook his head. "Sure he does. You just said it. He and Lance are enemies."

"But that's just it, Justin. They have been enemies for years. That's nothing new. According to Lance, that goes as far back as high school. Competing against each other every chance they got."

"Yes," Justin said, "and they are still competing against each other today, in practically everything. The only reason Montoya decided to join the TCC was to be a deliberate thorn in Lance's side. On top of that, Montoya is friends with Paulo Ruiz, and everyone knows that guy has underworld connections and is as shady as they come. For all we know, Ruiz may have been the one to arrange the fire for Montoya."

Darius nodded, but he still wasn't convinced. "Well, all we got now is circumstantial evidence that wouldn't hold up in court. Unless there is valid proof, then—"

"I'll get it," Justin said, interrupting Darius.

Darius raised a dark brow. "And just how do you plan to do that?"

Justin smiled. "You'll find out when I lay all the evidence you need at your feet."

Hours later on the drive away from the TCC, Darius couldn't help but reflect on what Justin had said over dinner. Granted, he didn't know Montoya as well as the others since he hadn't lived in Somerset all his life, but he couldn't help but admire someone who had worked hard to propel himself from rags to riches. He'd heard that Montoya had once been a groundskeeper at the club.

And Darius had a hard time believing that someone that driven to succeed would risk losing it all in a situation where he would automatically be labeled the guilty party. Darius was convinced that if Montoya had been involved in the fire, he would have done a better job of covering his tracks. The man didn't even have a valid alibi, for crying out loud. Definitely not the stance of a guilty arsonist.

Darius decided that before going to bed he would go back over the information he had collected so far, especially his interviews with a number of employees who had left the company within the past couple of years on bad terms. He then cursed under his breath when he realized he'd left the file with his notes back at the shelter.

Darius turned on the radio, deciding he needed to hear some music. He let out a deep breath as he recognized the song as one that had been playing earlier today at the café while he and Summer had shared lunch.

The image of Summer sitting across from him as she tried to put the pain of losing her aunt behind her flooded his mind. He'd liked her aunt and thought it was tragic how the woman had lost her life. He could just imagine what Summer had gone through during that time. But he really didn't want to think about that. Then why was he? Why did he have to constantly remind himself that he couldn't—and shouldn't—care?

He glanced at the clock on his car's console. It was close to ten. Tomorrow he would spend the day at the refinery, checking out a few things and questioning a number of the employees, including one who claimed he saw someone fitting Montoya's description in the refinery's parking lot the night of the fire.

The moment he stopped at a traffic light, his cell phone went off. He quickly slid it open. "Yes?"

"Darius, this is Walt. I got a message that you called."

Darius smiled. Hearing his old partner's voice reminded him of working as a detective in Houston. They'd had some good times together, despite Walt's miserable attitude. "Yes, Walt, how are things going?"

"Pretty much the same. I'm sure you heard that Smothers finally retired. We were all glad about that."

"Yes, I heard." John Smothers was a tough detective who should have retired ages ago.

"So, what's up? You said you needed my help with something," Walt said.

"I'm investigating a case of arson here in Somerset and need you to do a background check on one of the company's employees. I heard from another employee that the man used to work for a company that burned to the ground a few years ago in Houston."

"Sure, what's the employee's name?"

"Quincy Cummings," Darius said, hoping Walt would be able to obtain information about the guy.

"I'll let you know something in a day or so," Walt said.

"Thanks, I appreciate it."

"So, what's been going on with you, Darius? The last time we talked was over a year ago. I thought you were calling to let me know you had gotten married or something," Walt said in a joking tone. But for some reason Darius was annoyed by Walt's words—they had definitely hit a nerve. It could be because Walt had been the one to tell him about Summer and the things she had said about him.

"Not hardly. I plan to stay single for the rest of my days," Darius said, wondering why each and every time he talked to Walt, his marital status came up.

"Same here, man. Women are nothing but liars. None of them can be trusted. Hey, remember that good-looking broad you had the hots for when we were partners? The one who dumped you for some rich old man when you were out of town? I don't recall her name but I—"

"Summer," Darius cut in, trying to keep his tone from showing the irritation he felt.

"What?"

"I said her name was Summer. Summer Martindale," Darius said, ready to end the call.

"Oh, yeah, that's right. I wonder what happened to her after she left Houston. If she and that old man she ran off with are still together."

"I wouldn't know," Darius said shortly, deciding not to mention that Summer was now living in Somerset and he had not only run into her but had kissed her again. "Look, Walt. I appreciate you calling me back. Let me know if you find something out on that employee."

"Sure thing, pal."

Darius hung up the phone. Walt was the kind of man who believed misery loved company and had always seemed miserable, mainly because he'd had a tough time when it came to women.

Deciding he needed that file he'd left back at the shelter, he made a turn at the next traffic light. A few moments later, he was pulling into the parking lot and was surprised to see Summer's car in the usual spot. Why was she still here?

It didn't take him long to get out of his car and walk toward the shelter's entrance. The security guy named Barney recognized him but followed security procedures before allowing him entry.

"Is Ms. Martindale in her office?" he asked the man as he stuffed his ID back into his wallet.

"Yes, sir, and I did as you asked and walked her to her car last night."

"Thanks. I appreciate it."

Walking toward Summer's office, he stopped at the night-duty secretary's station. He had met the older woman, Raycine Bradley, the evening before. "Good evening, Ms. Bradley, is Ms. Martindale meeting with someone?" he asked.

The woman smiled at him. "No. I think she's packing up to call it a night. Finally."

Darius nodded, thinking Summer should have done that long ago. "I think I'll go hurry her along," he said, heading to the corridor that led to Summer's office.

Moments later he knocked on her door.

"Come in."

He stepped into her office and closed the door behind him. She was standing at a table with her back to him sorting out papers. Without looking his way, she said, "I promise I'll be leaving in a few minutes, Raycine."

Darius crossed his arms over his chest and leaned against the closed door. "That's good to hear. I intend to do everything in my power to make sure that you do."

Summer swirled around and stared at Darius in surprise. From the look on his face, he wasn't a happy camper. "What are you doing here?" she asked.

"I need to ask you that same thing," he said in a curt

tone, moving away from the door to stand in the middle of her office with his hands braced on his hips.

Now she knew what had him upset. He didn't like the fact she was still there. She couldn't help wondering why he was making it his business. "I had a lot to do for tomorrow's meeting with Mr. Novak. In addition to that, a new woman checked into our facilities today."

She saw the look of concern that immediately showed on his face. "How is she?"

"She was a lot better once we got her settled in and assured her that if her husband showed up here, we wouldn't let him near her."

Darius shook his head. "It's sad that any woman has to worry about something like that."

Summer sighed deeply. "Yes. Been there. Done that."

But she didn't have to remind him of that since he'd been a part of that particular drama in her past. She had truly believed a restraining order would keep Tyrone away from her. He had proven her wrong. She didn't want to think about what might have happened if Darius hadn't shown up when he did, putting his life on the line for her.

Not wanting to think about Tyrone any longer, she asked, "So, are you going to tell me why you're here?" His gaze stroked her like a physical caress she couldn't ignore.

"I left something I need for tomorrow. I forgot to mention that I won't be back here until next week, when I start setting up the billing account."

"Oh." She should have been thrilled that she wouldn't be seeing him for the fourth day in a row but a barrage of emotions she couldn't explain tried to engulf her. She fought them back.

"I'm working on a case that requires my attention elsewhere," he added.

She wanted to tell him that he owed her no explanation. Instead, she said, "Sounds real serious."

"It's a case involving arson. You probably read about it in the papers a few weeks back. A fire at the Brody Oil and Gas refinery."

"Yes, I do recall reading about it," she said, leaning against the table. "And you think it was deliberately set?"

"It looks that way. I've been asked by the Brody brothers to find out who did it."

Summer eyed Darius. She recalled how much he'd enjoyed his job as a detective. Once in a while he would tell her about a particular case he was trying to solve. "Got any leads?" she asked.

"Not enough to suit me, which is the reason I need to spend a day at the refinery." He moved over toward her. "So, what do you need me to do?"

She straightened her stance. "About what?"

"About helping you pack up and get out of here, like you should have done hours ago."

"I told you why I'm still here."

"But your reason isn't good enough. I can see you staying over for an hour or so, but damn it Summer, it's going on eleven o'clock and knowing you, you'll be back here first thing in the morning."

"Of course. My meeting is at eight."

Darius wondered how she would feel knowing he had just finished playing a game of pool with the man she would be meeting with. And now Kev knew she was someone from his past, someone who had once meant a lot to him. His friend knew how much she had hurt him, as well. "So, what can I do to help?" he asked.

When Darius came to a stop in front of her, Summer released a resigned sigh. It wouldn't do any good to argue with him. Besides, she was too tired. "I guess you can help by stapling these papers that I've already sorted."

"Okay."

She tried to scoot over when he joined her at the table but their arms touched nonetheless, and she felt it—a spark of sensations that swept through her. She inhaled a sharp breath.

He glanced over at her. "You're all right?"

She breathed in deeply before saying, "Yes, I'm fine. Why wouldn't I be?"

"No reason."

There was a reason and they both knew it. Memories filtered through her mind of a night she just couldn't forget. There was no way she could deny that over the years she had lain in bed missing a warm, hard body beside her, and being awakened by the taste of a desire so potent it could blind you.

"If you're meeting just with Kevin Novak, why are you making all of these handouts?"

His question cut into her thoughts and she glanced over at him. "For the other members of the TCC, for him to share with them. I want everyone to know what's going on here at the shelter, that we're benefiting the community and that I'm competent enough to handle things."

Darius reached out and touched her arm. "You're worried for nothing. If they thought you weren't competent enough to handle things, you wouldn't be here."

"But what if—"

He reached for her. "For crying out loud, woman, you worry too much."

She should have seen it coming and backed away from him. But the moment his mouth touched hers she knew she could not have moved an inch. And now that her stomach was contracting with desire, there was no way she wasn't going to enjoy it while it lasted.

That was one thing she was truthful about, the fact that Darius knew how to kiss, even during those times when he should be doing something else. Like now. He had offered to help her, not seduce her. Awareness, bold and daring, raced through her, made her acknowledge that Darius was the only man who could ever make her purr in his arms. The only man who'd made her feel she'd been cheated out of many more nights with him.

If only...

She didn't want to think about if only. She only wanted to think about now, not what did or didn't happen seven years ago and during the years in between. She didn't even want to think about why being in his arms felt natural, like a place she should be. A place she belonged. His mouth felt in sync with hers, also totally natural, connected to hers while kissing her so perfectly.

When he finally ended the kiss, she couldn't do anything but pull in a deep breath, still tasting him on her lips. She didn't bother giving herself a mental shake and questioning why she had let him kiss her. She knew very well why. She wouldn't do as she'd done the last time, pretending she hadn't wanted any part of it since, like before, she hadn't resisted. She doubted that she could have even if she'd wanted to.

But she didn't want to talk about it. Without saying

anything, she turned back to the table and gathered up what was left of the papers she had sorted. She was fully aware that he was watching her, but following her lead, he didn't say anything, either. Out of the corner of her eye, she could see him neatly stacking the handouts she'd made. They turned at the same time and their gazes locked for a mere second before simultaneously, they stepped into each other's arms again.

It seemed what was happening at the moment was Summer's mind was refusing to remember the bad times, only the good. And there had been good times, as good as good could get. They had only shared a bed once but before then, they had shared companionship, although she'd found out later he'd had an ulterior motive for doing so. But she wouldn't dwell on that now. The only thing she wanted to dwell on was the way his mouth was taking hers, with a hunger she could feel all the way to her toes, with an intensity that had her stomach churning as they were enjoying this kiss to the fullest.

It didn't even bother her that he was holding her in a possessive and intimate way, with his hands cradling her backside to fit her pelvis snugly against the front of him. She could feel the muscled tone of his body and his erection, hard and strong, pressed against her.

Taking his cue, she wrapped her arms around his neck as he sank deeper into her mouth, sending points of pleasure all through her. She felt sensations in her fingers as she caressed the back part of his neck, and through the material of her skirt where she was making contact with his denim-clad thigh. And she was very well aware of when he changed the angle of his mouth to position hers more to his advantage.

His efforts had her mind reeling, filling her with an urgent need to recognize and accept what was taking place, giving her the resolve to simply stand there, indulge and take it like a woman. And she was. She was taking it like a woman who needed every stroke of his tongue, every bit of his taste and every mind-blowing, tantalizing sensation his mouth was making her feel.

When the kiss ended moments later, she couldn't resist placing a lingering heated kiss on his jawline. Nor could she resist taking the tip of her tongue and tracing along his upper lip before finally taking a step back.

Darius drew in a deep breath and fought the urge to pull her back into his arms again, ask if he could follow her home and make love to her with the same intensity that he had made love to her that night. But this time, his heart wouldn't come into play, only his lust.

He wished the kiss could have wiped away all the wrongs of the past and he could move on without feeling animosity in his heart. Unfortunately, it hadn't. What it had done was make him fully aware of how vulnerable his heart still was when it came to Summer, and just how hot and strong his desire for her still burned within every part of his body.

"Finish up in here so I can walk you to your car," he heard himself say in a deep, throaty voice. A yearning for her was stirring his insides, thundering all the way through his veins, making him want to say the hell with it and take her on that very table.

But he couldn't. He wouldn't.

"I'll be fine, Darius. I don't need you to walk me to my car."

As he studied her, he saw the way her eyes glowed

in a seductive lure. He doubted she even realized it. He needed to act accordingly and not give in to what she was asking for without even knowing she was doing so.

"I'm walking you out anyway, Summer."

He saw the lure in her eyes quicken to a sharp edge and he wouldn't be surprised if she stood her ground. Then it would become a standoff, since he had every intention of walking her out. In fact, he intended to follow her home to make sure she got inside her house safely.

"Fine. Suit yourself, Darius."

Her words ripped through the air. He could tell by her tone that she wasn't happy, but that didn't bother him. When it came to her safety there was no compromising. He moved from the table to stand in front of her desk, convincing himself that it was his protective instincts kicking in where she was concerned, and nothing more.

Darius watched as Summer grabbed her purse and then he followed her out the door, pausing in the hall while she locked up her office. The shelter was quiet since most of the people in residence were probably in bed, asleep. "What did you have for dinner?" he asked when they began walking down the corridor toward the lobby.

"I worked through dinner."

Darius pressed his lips together to keep from saying a word that might have burned her ears. Knowing she had missed a meal bothered him a lot more than he cared to admit.

"And please, Darius, no sermons. I'm too beat to listen."

He glanced over at her. "I don't do sermons."

"Could have fooled me."

He halted his steps and brought her to a stop before

rounding the corner that led to the lobby. She might be too beat to listen to what he had to say, but there was no doubt in his mind that she had plenty of energy for an argument and was gearing up for one. However, he had no intention of obliging her.

He leaned forward and placed a light kiss on her lips. "You're much prettier when you're not trying to be difficult."

She frowned up at him, clearly caught off guard. "I'm not trying to be difficult."

He couldn't help but smile. "Could have fooled me."

He didn't even try to hold back a chuckle when she narrowed her gaze at him. Ignoring the look, his hand took hold of her elbow. "Come on, Summer, let me grab that file off my desk and then get you home before you fall flat on your face from exhaustion."

Summer glanced over her shoulder before opening the door to her house. She had been fully aware that Darius had followed her home. She could have been nice and invited him in, but she'd decided not to. There was only so much Darius Franklin she could take, and after the kisses they'd shared in her office tonight, she had reached her limit for today.

She didn't have to wonder what there was about him that made her feel so raw and exposed yet at the same time so well protected. Whenever they kissed, she couldn't help but recall the passion. And then there were the memories of the hopes and dreams that had blossomed in her heart of what she'd assumed was a promising future between them. She had even allowed her dreams to include marriage and babies.

She headed for the bathroom to take her shower,

wondering if at any time during the past seven years Darius had regretted bragging about their night together in such a degrading manner to his partner, Walt Stewart. She appreciated the fact that Walt felt she needed to know just what Darius had said.

Pain tore into her heart every time she realized just how wrong she had been about him, and that made her determined not to make another mistake by giving him her heart a second time. But she *had* enjoyed their kiss. In her mind, one didn't have to do with the other, just as long as she knew where she stood with him and where he stood with her.

He was now a dedicated businessman who seemed to enjoy what he did for a living and she had a new life, a new career and was no longer looking over her shoulder, fearful of seeing Tyrone. The past seven years had been good for her, although lonely. When it came to men she had learned the hard way to play it safe, and she would continue to do so.

And one sure way to do that was to make sure she didn't assume anything where Darius was concerned.

Darius needed a shower to relax. After making sure Summer had gotten home okay, he had driven straight home with memories of their kisses running all through his mind. Having her in his arms had felt natural, like that was where she belonged. Considering what she'd done to him seven years ago, was that weird or what?

When he had reluctantly ended their kiss, she had taken her tongue and swept it across his lips. He still felt a stirring deep in his gut just thinking about it. It had been unexpected. It had felt good.

And now he knew where she lived and would make

it his business to get her to invite him over to her place one night. It might take a while to work up to that, but he would get there. He wouldn't see her again until Monday, which was just as well since he of all people knew Summer was the type of woman who could grow on a man.

She was the type of woman who could easily get under a man's skin. And he had to admit that she had gotten under his tonight. She had made sensations he hadn't felt in years rush through him, reminding him what it was like to lose control with a woman.

Darius headed toward the shower with a deep frown on his face. No matter what Summer evoked within him, he was determined to remain immune to her charms. He had no intentions of making the same mistake twice.

Chapter 6

"How did your meeting go on Friday?"

Summer glanced up and met Darius's gaze. She had wondered if he would be dropping by the shelter today. She hadn't expected to see him Friday, but she hadn't known for sure when he would be back to complete the project he'd been hired by the TCC to do.

"I think the meeting went great. Mr. Novak appreciated the handouts and was very attentive to what I had to say. He agreed that based on our occupancy log, it would be a good idea to consider expanding the facilities sooner than later. He said he'd take his recommendations back to the other members of the TCC."

Darius nodded. "And how was your weekend?"

"Busy as usual. And yours?" she asked, watching him carefully. She used to have the ability to read his thoughts, but now his expressions were unrevealing and she didn't have a clue as to what he was thinking.

"It was okay. After spending Friday at the refinery, I had to follow up several leads," he said, stepping into the room.

She immediately felt his heat, breathed in his scent and admitted to herself that she had missed seeing him around. "And you're still certain the fire was intentionally set?"

She tried not to notice how good he looked standing in front of her desk with a cup of coffee in his hand. All it took was a glance at his mouth to remember their kisses right here in this office last week.

She refused to admit she had purposely left her office door open on the off chance he dropped by Helping Hands today. On a number of occasions he had caught her unaware and she didn't want that to happen this time. She also refused to admit that she had thought about him a lot over the weekend, wondering how he was spending his time—and with whom. The latter was something she had no right to concern herself with, but she couldn't help it.

"I'll pick up the official report from the fire marshal this week, but so far, all evidence still points to arson," he said.

"Then I'm sure you'll be the one to solve this case."

Darius didn't want to think about what effect her confidence had on him at that very moment. She'd always had a way of making him feel that he could leap tall buildings with a single bound if he had to. He used to tell himself the reason she felt that way was because he had been the one to save her from a dangerous situation, and he shouldn't put much stock into it. But he had anyway.

"So, what's next?"

That was another thing that had drawn him to Summer, her interest in his job. She would ask questions and seemed to understand his excitement about it as well as his frustrations. He would enjoy getting off work at the end of his shift and dropping by her place to tell her how his day had gone.

"I'll continue to conduct an investigation over at the refinery while working on the security and the accounting systems here. Since the TCC wants me to personally handle both, I've delegated my other projects."

There, he'd just told her his plans which meant, whether she liked it or not, he would be hanging around for a while. He wondered if she had assumed he would be moving on and assigning the shelter job to someone else, but he couldn't read her expression.

"Well, I'll let you get back to work. I'll see you at noon."

He watched as her brow lifted. "Noon?"

He smiled. "Yes. We're doing lunch."

She stared at him. "Are we?"

"Sure we are, and I'll even let you twist my arm into getting one of those salads you seem to like so much."

There was a pause, and Darius sensed she was trying to determine whether it was worth the effort to start an argument with him. When she began speaking, she spoke her words slowly as if to make sure they were understood. "I don't want you to assume we're going to lunch together every day, Darius."

"Don't you like my company?"

She hesitated, and he watched her nervously lick her top lip with her tongue before she answered. "Whether I like your company or not has nothing to do with it. We have issues we haven't yet resolved."

They had issues yet to be resolved? She made it sound like she had been the injured party and not the other way around. He hadn't been the one to skip town with a man old enough to be her father who could buy her all the things Darius couldn't afford on his detective salary. They would resolve things all right, but his way. Pretty soon she would see how it felt to have someone you assumed loved you turn around and leave you high and dry with a broken heart.

"Some things can't be resolved and are better left alone," he said. "And in our case, maybe that's the way things should be, Summer. What happened between us was seven years ago. People change and they grow to regret things they did when they were young and foolish."

Darius maintained eye contact with her, assuming she was thinking about what he'd said. He made it sound as if he was giving her a chance to redeem herself, and that he was willing to forgive her for what she had done. Little did she know how far from the truth that was.

"Maybe you have the right idea," she finally said. "It *was* seven years ago and we've grown a lot since then."

"I'd like to believe we have." Deciding he didn't want to discuss it any further, he asked, "So, do we have another date for lunch?"

She hesitated and then said, "Yes, we do."

After Darius walked out of her office, Summer couldn't help wondering if she was making a mistake by agreeing to put the past behind them. He evidently found it easy to do so, but he hadn't been the one to get his heart broken. But then, on the other hand, she couldn't discount the fact that Darius had saved her life. And then another part of her wondered if perhaps she had put more stock in their affair, and had expected more from the relationship than he had.

She had gone a long time without getting involved with a man and she wasn't so sure if she could handle Darius—she wasn't even sure if she wanted to. She had gotten used to being by herself. Why was he determined to invade her space?

The only thing she was certain about was the way he made her feel whenever he touched her. To be honest, he didn't even have to touch her to make her hormones react. He could stand five feet away and she had the ability to feel how the tension in the air surrounding them seemed to vibrate, emitting all sorts of sensuous stirrings and longings. He had been in her office less than fifteen minutes and already her vital signs were at their highest peak.

But she was no longer concerned by the staggering degree of physical chemistry flowing between them. It had always been there, from the first. What she was concerned about was how easily she wanted to forgive him and believe that what Darius had said was true. Seven years ago, they had been different people with different values, at a different place in their lives. People change. And they come to regret decisions and actions of their past. Decisions and actions that they can't change.

She knew some men didn't like confrontation and Darius was probably of the mind that even if they hashed the issues out, it would not change anything. But still, was it too much to expect an apology for sharing something private and personal with his partner? Couldn't he see that doing so had degraded what they'd shared?

Even now she could vividly recall that day, after she and Darius had spent the night together. He had left her bed that morning seemingly in a good mood, making plans for them to spend the day together. But first he had to go home to get a change of clothes and stop by police headquarters to complete some paperwork, and she had to work a few hours at the restaurant where she was a part-time waitress.

When she'd returned home, she had waited for Darius. When hours passed, she had gotten worried. That evening, Walt had appeared on her doorstep with a message from Darius saying he'd had to leave town unexpectedly on police business. After delivering that message, Walt had asked if he could talk to her privately. That is when he'd told her how Darius had come to the station that day and bragged about finally sleeping with her. He had made a bet with Walt that it would take less than a month to share her bed. Discovering their one night together hadn't been anything more than a chance for him to win a bet had hurt her deeply. And then to know he'd gone back and told his friend had been another crushing blow.

While listening to Walt level with her about what Darius had done, she had barely been able to maintain her composure. Only after Walt had left did she break down and let it all out. She knew she had to leave Houston immediately and did not want to see Darius again, ever. It had been bad enough with Tyrone, but the hurt Darius had inflicted was even worse because in just a short time, she had fallen in love with him.

She had been too ashamed to call her aunt to tell her what had happened, so in the days that followed, she'd made some quick decisions. One of her regular customers at the restaurant, an author of academic books named Jack Lindsey, would be spending a year in Florida with his wife while he penned his next book. Jack had offered her the chance to accompany them as his assistant, to organize and edit all of his notes. He had made the offer before, but she had turned him down because of Tyrone's threats regarding what he would do if she ever left town. But with no future for her in Houston, she had quickly packed up and left town with the Lindseys.

The Lindseys had been wonderful and she had enjoyed the year she had spent with them on their beach property in Miami. She had buried herself in her work, determined to put Darius out of her mind and go about healing her heart. When she hadn't heard from him in over two weeks, that had only verified everything Walt had said. Their night together had been a conquest for him and nothing more.

Since both Mr. and Mrs. Lindsey were former teachers, they had encouraged Summer to pursue a college degree, and Mrs. Lindsey had even tutored her on those subjects Summer had felt would hold her back from getting accepted to any college. Using the money she'd made working for the Lindseys, along with a very nice bonus they had given her at the end of the year, she had remained in Miami to attend college there. She had poured all her time and energy into her classes, determined to reach every goal she had established for herself and refusing to wallow in the hurt and pain Darius had caused her.

Summer got up from her desk and looked out the window, not sure how she would handle the one man she thought she would never see again.

What she was up against now was how he could make her feel. Whenever she was around him, he was capable of bringing out feelings and desires that she wished would stay buried. In seven years, no man had made her remember how it felt to be a woman. A desired woman. It was something Darius could do so effortlessly.

When he met her gaze, she could see the desire in his eyes, and on most occasions he wasn't trying to mask it. It was as if he knew exactly what he was doing to her, what buttons to push, what words to say.

She had thought about him a lot over the weekend, wondering how and what he was doing. And, she thought as she bit her lower lip, with whom. She wished she could claim she didn't care, but she did. She couldn't help but notice how ladies would glance their way whenever they walked into the café together. There was feminine interest in their eyes and she couldn't very well blame them for it. After all, she was a woman, too.

She sighed deeply before checking her watch. It was time to make her rounds and greet everyone. She would keep herself busy until lunchtime.

Darius stared long and hard at the computer screen, thinking he must have missed something while setting up the billing system. He needed to go back and recheck. Or better yet, he thought, leaning back in the chair and rubbing the bridge of his nose, it would probably be a good idea if he kept his mind on what he was doing and stopped thinking about Summer. Having her on his mind was probably the reason he'd thought he'd found a number of irregularities in the TCC's accounting.

Deciding to give both his eyes and his mind a break,

he pushed away from the desk and stood, needing to stretch his body. He had been sitting at the computer practically all morning and the limited space under the desk had been murder on his long legs.

He glanced at his watch. He had another hour to go before lunch and he couldn't deny he was looking forward to dining with Summer again. He tried convincing himself that spending time with her meant absolutely nothing, and was just a part of his plan for revenge. There was no reason to think it was anything more than that.

He breathed in deeply, truly wishing he believed that. But he knew if he wasn't careful, he would be succumbing to Summer's charms all over again. And he didn't want that. He had given his heart to her once and what she'd done had almost destroyed him, made him unable to put his complete trust in another woman.

He had asked her how her meeting with Kev had gone, but he'd already been privy to that information. To say she had impressed Kev was an understatement. Besides stating the obvious about what a good-looking woman she was, Kev had been taken with her keen sense of intelligence as well as her concern for the women who sought refuge at the shelter. Kev also felt she had a lot of good ideas that the TCC should definitely take under consideration.

Sitting back down at the computer, he resumed setting up the Helping Hands account, trying to push thoughts of Summer to the back of his mind. However, once again a few discrepancies within TCC's accounting system popped up.

He pulled back when his cell phone went off. It was Lance. "Yeah, Lance, what's up?"

"Kate's fixing dinner tonight and wants you to come eat with us."

Darius smiled. He liked Kate and would be the first to say she was just what Lance needed. "I'd love to."

"Great. I'll let her know."

"Lance?"

"Yeah?"

Darius paused, not sure if he should mention anything about the discrepancies he'd found in TCC's accounting. Huntington and his band of tightwads managed the accounting for the club—namely the money they got from fundraisers and endowments. And everybody knew his group kept a tight squeeze on TCC's money supply. If there was anything wrong with the club's funds, they would know it. But still…

"Darius? What is it?"

Darius breathed in deeply. "Nothing," he finally said, deciding not to jump to any conclusions about the discrepancies until he'd had a chance to look at them more carefully.

"How are things going with you and Summer Martindale?"

Darius frowned. "You talk as if we're a couple."

"Aren't you?" Lance countered.

"Not yet."

There must have been something in his voice that gave him away.

"I don't know what your plans are regarding her, Darius, but be careful. They can backfire on you. If you're going to pursue her, then you need to forget about what happened seven years ago and move on."

Darius didn't say anything for a moment and then admitted, "I can't."

"You should try, man. When the shit blows up in your face, don't say I didn't warn you."

"Today I came prepared," Darius said, glancing down at his feet.

Summer followed his gaze and noted he had removed his boots and was now wearing a pair of leather loafers. That meant he had come to the shelter today prepared to walk over to the café, and *had* assumed she would have lunch with him. She wasn't sure whether she liked the fact that he'd known she would give in.

She returned her gaze to his face. "So I see. You're ready?"

"I'm always ready, Summer."

She had absolute confidence in the truth of that statement. "Excuse me for a second. I need to let Marcy know I'm leaving."

She walked over to Marcy's desk. Marcy was in her late fifties and was someone Summer had become close to since working at the shelter. "I'm going to lunch now, Marcy."

Marcy smiled. "Okay. Did you ever get that dripping faucet at your house fixed?"

Summer shook her head. "Not yet, but I better do so soon, since it's keeping me from getting a good night's sleep." She then turned to rejoin Darius and together they left the building to walk over to the café for lunch. Her morning had been busy and she needed time away from the shelter. She always enjoyed her lunch, at least whenever she could make time for it.

It was a beautiful day and for some reason, Summer couldn't push aside the pleasurable sensations she was feeling with Darius beside her. She felt lucky today.

She had counseled two women that morning and after listening to their stories, a part of her felt blessed that she had cut her ties with Tyrone when she had, otherwise she could have been one of them. And although Tyrone had caused unnecessary drama that had landed him behind bars for twenty years, she was free to make choices about her life. Now it was her job to convince those two women they could make choices about their lives, as well.

"So, how has your day been so far?" Darius asked.

She began sharing bits and pieces of how busy she'd been as they continued their walk to the café. Although his legs were a lot longer than hers, he adjusted his steps to keep in line with hers. More than once, while sharing her ideas about a number of things she would like to see happen at the shelter, she would glance up and see how absorbed he was in what she was saying. They were ideas she hadn't shared with Kevin Novak for not wanting to overwhelm the man since everything she had in mind included a hefty price tag. But they were expenditures she felt would greatly benefit the women who sought refuge at the shelter.

Then, while it was on her mind, she asked about his brother, something she should have done long before now since she knew how close the two of them were. Like her, he had lost his parents at an early age, and he and his brother had been raised by their grandmother.

"Ethan is doing fine now."

She opened her mouth to ask what he meant by that when suddenly a warm, masculine arm snaked around her waist to stop her from stepping in a rut in the cement sidewalk. "Thank you."

"Don't mention it," he said, releasing her.

Summer tried to ignore the sensations that raced through her veins at his touch. When they reached the café and he opened the door, she quickly moved past him, wondering how she was going to get through her meal.

Kate Thornton Brody smiled up at Darius. "You need a woman in your life," she said.

Darius lifted a brow, wondering where that had come from. He glanced across the living room and shot Lance a questioning look, but all his friend did was smile and shrug his shoulders. Damn, he hadn't been in the house five minutes and already Kate was on him about being single.

Seeing that Lance wouldn't be giving him much help, Darius reached out and placed a friendly arm around Kate's shoulder. "Sweetheart, you know I prefer being single."

She gave him one of her sidelong looks that said she'd taken what he'd said with a grain of salt. "So did Lance at one time."

"But now he has you and he's a lucky man," Darius said truthfully. He had known Kate ever since she began working for Lance as his very competent administrative assistant when he took over Brody Oil and Gas a few years back, and had always liked her.

"What's for dinner? I'm starving," he quickly said, before Kate could make another comment about the state of his affairs or lack of them.

"Didn't you eat lunch?" Lance asked, finally moving off the sofa.

Lance's question reminded him of Summer…not that he could forget. He hated admitting that whenever he had lunch with her, it was a pleasant experience. She was a great conversationalist. Always had been. And today she'd seemed more relaxed with him, more at ease. And as usual, she had looked beautiful sitting across from him.

"Yes, I had lunch," he finally said. "A salad."

Humor lit Lance's eyes. "A salad? What kind of foolishness is that?"

"Don't let Lance tease you, Darius. There's nothing wrong with eating a salad," Kate said, walking back toward the kitchen.

When she was gone, Lance looked at him and chuckled. "I take it you had lunch with Summer."

Darius met Lance's amused look. "What makes you think that?"

"She's the salad girl."

Darius couldn't help but smile. When he'd left Houston because of Ethan's accident, Lance had shown up in Charleston to give him the support he needed. It was during that time that he had told Lance all about Summer, even how much she liked eating salads.

"I'd like to meet her. Invite her over one—"

"It's not that kind of relationship, Lance, and you know it," he said quickly, deciding to squash any foolish ideas that might be floating around in his best friend's head.

"Whatever you say," Lance said, smiling.

"I'm serious, Lance."

"Of course you are. I believe you."

Darius frowned. He could tell his friend really didn't believe him. "It's hard to love someone who has hurt you deeply," he said.

The amusement disappeared from Lance's face.

"I'm glad everyone doesn't feel that way, Darius, or I wouldn't have Kate as my wife. If you recall, I almost lost her when I announced my engagement to another woman. But she still found it in her heart to give me another chance."

Darius's frown deepened. "So, what are you trying to say?"

Lance held his friend's gaze. "What I'm trying to say is that if you love someone, there can always be forgiveness."

"I really appreciate you walking me out to my car again, Barney, but it's really not necessary," Summer said to the security guard at her side.

"No problem, Ms. Martindale. Besides, it's Mr. Franklin's orders."

Summer shook her head, still not sure how Darius could give orders when he wasn't paying the man's salary. She was just about to ask Barney how that was possible when he suddenly said, "Someone has slashed your tires."

"What?"

"Your tires," he said, pointing his flashlight on her car. "They've been slashed."

Summer followed the beam of light and saw what he was talking about. She hauled in a deep breath, recalling the last time her tires had been slashed and who had been responsible. She forced herself to calm down as old fears tried to resurface.

That was all seven years ago. Tyrone was locked up and couldn't touch her. More than likely, the husband or significant other of one of the women at the shelter was venting his anger on her since the shelter was standing in the way of the person he really wanted to take it out on. But it couldn't be Samuel Green, since he was still locked up, held without bond.

"I need to follow procedures and report this to the police, Ms. Martindale," Barney was saying, interrupting her thoughts. "Please come back inside while I contact the authorities and complete an incident report."

Summer turned her attention away from her tires. "Yes, of course."

She moved to follow him back inside. She'd heard reports of acts of revenge being directed at staff members who work with victims of violence. Incidents of rock throwing, drive-by shootings and even bomb threats had been reported. As far as she was concerned, the person who damaged her tires was nothing but a bully.

"Are you all right, Ms. Martindale?" Barney asked with concern when they had reached the door to go back inside.

She forced a smile on her lips. "Yes, I'm fine." She heard the words she'd just spoken, but wasn't sure she believed them herself.

Chapter 7

"What's this about your tires getting slashed last night?"

Summer glanced up and saw Darius leaning in her office doorway. News had spread quickly. The evening crew from last night had a lot to share with the staffers that had arrived that morning. She'd figured he would hear about the incident sooner or later. She wished it had been later, since she really didn't want to talk about it right now.

"I'm sure you've heard the story, Darius, and I'm not in the mood to rehash it."

"Humor me," he said, crossing the threshold and closing the door behind him. She couldn't help but study his features. There was something different about his eyes. Their darkness was still striking, but now they contained an element of hardness she hadn't seen since that first day he had discovered her working at the shelter. And his lips were pressed together in a tight line. On most days, it wouldn't take much to look at his lips and remember how they had introduced her to pleasures of the most decadent kind in a single night.

"I'm listening."

Summer blinked. While she had been staring at him, probably like a lust-crazed woman, he had taken a seat in the chair in front of her desk. She leaned back, trying to relax under the intensity of his direct gaze, but found it difficult to do so.

"What you've already heard is probably correct," she started. "Barney walked me out to the car like he's been doing since that incident with Samuel Green and noticed my tires had been slashed. We came back inside, called the police to report it and he filled out an incident report. End of story."

"I don't think so."

She heard the near growl in his voice. He was angry, she could tell. And she knew his anger was not directed at her but at whomever had slashed her tires. Given his mood, that was a comforting thought.

"I want to find out who did it," he said in the same tone of voice. "What did the police say?"

She shrugged. "Not much. They would have liked a list of the women residing here to check out the names of husbands and boyfriends, but because of our confidentiality policy, we couldn't provide it for them. I contacted the TCC earlier today to see if we could have two guards here at night instead of one."

"I thought there were two guards here since the night of that incident with Green."

"That lasted all but two days before one of them was

pulled. Evidently, the TCC rehashed the idea and felt only one was needed. That's why I called them—to see if they would reconsider since the staff members around here were beginning to get nervous. However, the man I spoke with at the TCC said adding an additional guard wasn't going to happen."

"Who did you talk to?"

"I asked for Kevin Novak but the person I talked to was an older gentleman by the name of Sebastian Huntington." She saw his jaw twitch. "You know him."

"Yes, I know him."

Summer noticed that he'd said the words in a tight voice with more than a little distaste. "He wasn't very friendly," she added. "Nothing at all like Mr. Novak."

He didn't say anything but from the way he was looking at her, she knew he was taking it all in. And then he asked, "Is there anything else?"

She shook her head. "No, nothing other than the piece of paper that had been placed on my car, which I also mentioned to the police last night."

He lifted a brow, his posture on full alert. "What paper?"

"One night last week someone placed a note under the wiper blade. Barney had walked me to my car, and he pulled it off and gave it to me, thinking it was some kind of sales flyer. It wasn't until I stopped at a traffic light and glanced at it did I notice what it said."

"And what did it say?" he asked, leaning closer and moving toward the edge of his seat.

She swallowed, remembering precisely what was written in bold letters on the paper. "It said, 'I take care of my own.'"

* * *

The moment Darius left Summer's office he darted into an empty conference room and called Kevin. He picked up on the second ring. "This is Kevin."

"Kev, were you informed that Huntington had reduced the number of security guards at Helping Hands?"

"No."

An angry Darius went on to tell Kevin about the incident that had occurred last night.

"Huntington has no right to make those kinds of decisions without discussing it with the committee first, and I am part of that committee," Kevin said, almost livid.

"The man's been a part of the TCC for so long I believe he thinks he owns it, which is why he constantly overlooks anything the younger members have to say," Darius said.

"And how is Summer Martindale?"

"She's a little shaken up, although she was trying not to show it. The staff here is nervous—first Green breaking doors down and now this tire-slashing incident. It doesn't bode well. There have been revenge-type incidents reported in various cities around the country, and they are aware of it. We need to make sure they feel protected."

Darius tried to convince himself that his concern for Summer was no different than his concern for any other woman he'd once been involved with, but deep down a part of him knew that wasn't true. He would even go so far as to admit missing her whenever he spent time away from Helping Hands.

They were feelings that he didn't want to feel. One way to remedy that was to start keeping his distance, but then he wouldn't be able to make her feel the way he had felt when she'd left. He just needed to make sure he kept things in perspective.

"I totally agree," Kevin said, bringing Darius's attention back to the matter at hand. "I'll confront Huntington myself, and if I have to, I'll call a special meeting of the board."

Moments later, Darius hung up the phone feeling a lot better than he had before making the call to Kev. He knew his friend wouldn't like the "executive" decision Huntington had made regarding the security at the shelter any more than he did. As usual, the man was trying to throw his weight around, fighting for power he really didn't have. But Darius relaxed a bit, knowing Kev was on it.

He glanced at his watch. He needed to leave for a while to attend to business concerning the fire at the refinery—he had to talk to several guys who had been off work the day he'd met with the employees the last time. But he intended to return to the shelter before Summer left for lunch. The thought of her walking anywhere alone troubled his mind.

From now on, he would make sure that she was well protected. At all costs.

Three days later, Summer glanced over at Darius before looking down at her watch. It was a little past eight in the evening. She had volunteered to stay for a few hours to help man the abuse hotline, and he had surprised her when he volunteered to assist her.

At first, she hadn't been sure whether women on the other line would want to unload their pain and anguish to a man, but from overhearing bits and pieces of his conversations, she could tell he was handling things quite nicely. She would be the first to admit that he had a good demeanor for assisting those who called in, male or female.

"What time are you leaving?" she asked him. Since the night her tires had gotten slashed, he had made it his business to return to the shelter every day after being at the refinery in the mornings, to walk her to the café for lunch. And if she remained late in the evenings, he did so, as well. Then he would not only walk her to her car, but would follow her home to make sure she got in safely.

"I'll leave when you leave," he said, glancing over at her.

In a way, his protectiveness irked her. She didn't want him to feel like she needed him in any way. "There are two security guards now, so I'll be all right." She really hadn't been surprised when, the day after the tire-slashing incident, two guards were on duty. There was no doubt in her mind that Darius had had something to do with it, although what exactly, she wasn't sure.

"I plan to leave in a few minutes," she said.

He smiled over at her. "Then so will I."

And he did. After she had handled the last call she would take, she gathered up her belongings and headed for the door with him by her side. He nodded to the guards on duty as they passed.

"Nice night," he said.

She looked up at the sky and saw the full moon and the stars, and how they illuminated the otherwise dark sky. He was right. It was a nice night.

"I'll be following you home again."

She glanced over at him. "It's your gas."

She said nothing as they continued walking. When he opened the car door for her, she slid inside, noticing how his gaze shifted to her legs when her skirt accidentally showed a little bit of flesh. She started to say something about his wandering eyes and decided not to. It probably wouldn't do any good anyway.

The drive to her place was uneventful and whenever she glanced in her rearview mirror, he was there. She would admit that, considering the incidents of the past two weeks, she felt a semblance of security knowing he was near, just like the days and nights following that episode with Tyrone.

She parked her car in the driveway and was surprised when he parked behind her and got out of his vehicle. The other times he had followed her home, he had stayed in the car while she went inside and then left. She wondered why he had changed the routine, and she didn't like the way her skin seemed to feel warm all over as he came closer.

"You have a two-car garage. Any reason you aren't parking in it?" he asked, coming to a stop in front of her.

"It's full of boxes. I haven't unpacked everything yet." She paused. "Why did you get out of the car?"

She appreciated him seeing her home, but she had no intentions of asking him inside. Her house was her place. Her own private space. When she had moved to Somerset and found what she thought was the perfect neighborhood along with the perfect house, she had moved in, determined to keep bad memories from past experiences outside. Darius was a reminder of a bad past experience.

"I overheard you mention to Marcy that you had a

dripping bathroom faucet that was keeping you awake at night. I thought I'd take care of it for you."

"Now?"

"I don't have anything else I have to do."

Summer sighed. She did. She wanted to take a shower and go to bed. "Thanks for the offer, but I'll get around to calling a plumber later this week."

"No need. It will only take a minute. Then I'll be out of here."

Standing in the shadows, she could barely see the features of his face in the moonlight. But what she did see was a man who had first been her friend and then her lover. She didn't know what he was now, aside from very determined to look out for her.

From the look of things, his mind was made up. She really wanted the faucet fixed. Since he *had* volunteered, she might as well take him up on his offer. "All right, then. Thanks."

"I've told you more than once that you don't ever have to thank me for doing what I do when it involves you, Summer."

She swallowed. Yes, he had said that more than once. Most times had been when they were sitting on a sofa, hugged up while watching television. She'd enjoyed those nights when they would sit curled up with a movie, sharing a bowl of popcorn in her living room, talking.

Another thing she had appreciated about him was that he had never tried pressuring her into sex. That night when they had finally made love, it was because it was something they both wanted, not something he had pushed her into doing.

"Yes, I know you don't need my thanks, but I don't want you to think I don't appreciate it," she finally said.

"Fine. Let me grab my toolbox out of the car."

She waited while he went back to his car. Moments later, she grabbed her mail out of the box and opened the door, hoping she wasn't making a mistake letting him inside.

He followed her and closed the door behind them. The click of the lock made her fully aware that they were alone, totally and completely. Trying to ignore her nerves, she threw the mail on the table. Since she paid most of her bills online, she knew the majority of it was nothing but junk mail anyway.

"Nice place," he complimented, glancing around. She knew he was taking stock of her place.

She tried to ignore how at home he looked in her living room. Like he belonged there. "Thanks."

This house was a lot more spacious than her apartment had been, and since she had a job that paid well, she could afford nice furniture.

"Which bathroom has the dripping faucet?"

"The one in my bedroom." Too late she realized that he was going to go into her most private room.

"Which way?"

"Down the hall to your right."

When he disappeared around the corner, she inhaled deeply, deciding she needed to do something other than just stand there while he repaired the faucet. She needed to at least appear busy. Unfortunately, there weren't any plants she had to water, nor were there dishes in her sink that she needed to wash. Her gaze lit on the junk mail that she had placed on the table and she decided now was as good a time as any to go through it.

* * *

Darius moved down the hall toward Summer's bedroom, thinking she had a lovely home. It was an old house, but very well cared for and maintained. He also liked the vibrant colors that suited her decor and the furnishings that blended in so well. And she was still neat as a pin, he thought, entering her bedroom and glancing around. His gaze came to a stop on the queen-size bed and he couldn't help but wonder what man had probably shared it with her. A rich, older man, no doubt.

Overhearing the conversation about her dripping faucet had given him the perfect excuse to invite himself in. For some reason, he had wanted to see the house that she was living in without him. Although they'd never actually discussed marriage seven years ago, as far as he was concerned, it had been the next thing on the agenda for them. He'd known that after what Whitman had put her through, it would be hard for her to put her trust in any man, but he had been willing to be patient and give her whatever amount of time she needed to learn to trust a man again. She'd needed to know that he was someone she could depend on. Someone who would always be there for her. Too bad she hadn't given them a chance.

Forcing those thoughts from his mind, he headed toward her bathroom. He had just stepped over the threshold and placed the toolbox on the floor when she frantically called out his name.

He rushed to the living room and saw total shock on her face. "Summer? What's wrong?"

She stared up at him, barely able to force words past her lips. But he did hear the one single name she said.

"Tyrone."

He looked at her, confused, not sure why she was bringing up the man who'd caused her nothing but grief. "What about Whitman, Summer?"

She glanced down and he followed her gaze to the mail sprawled at her feet. He quickly figured that something in one of the letters must have upset her.

He bent down, picked up the envelopes and flipped through them. Then he saw a letter from the Texas Parole Board. From the look of the envelope—specifically, all the stamp marks all over it—the post office had made several attempts to deliver it to her.

He pulled out the letter and read it, and then took a deep breath. As a former police officer, he was familiar with Texas law regarding those who'd been victims of violent crimes. A standard letter was issued to notify victims of the parole board's decision to release an inmate.

Darius glanced up at the date of the letter. It had been sent over a month ago. Tyrone Whitman was now a free man.

"I want you to drink this and please don't tell me that you don't need it because you do," Darius said, walking over to where Summer sat on the sofa with a cup of coffee laced with brandy in his hand.

Something had had him on edge all day, and he hadn't been able to figure out what. But now he knew. The thought that the man who had caused Summer so much grief had only served seven years of a twenty-year sentence made him very angry. But right now, Summer didn't need his anger. More than anything, she needed his support.

Surprisingly, she took the cup without giving him a

hard time and took a sip. A frown appeared on her face and he knew why—he had made it a little too strong but if anything, it would help her sleep.

"I can't believe it," she said, breaking the quiet stillness of the room and leaning forward to place the cup on the coffee table. "How can Tyrone be out of prison? That makes no sense."

Darius had to agree with her. It definitely made no sense given the man's crime. They should have put him in jail and thrown away the key. There was no way Whitman should be free to walk around. At least not on this planet. How could they have done such a thing?

He cringed whenever he thought about the final days of the trial and the threats Whitman had shouted out to Summer, saying what he would do to her if he ever got out. He wondered if Summer was remembering those days. He doubted she could forget. She stood and began pacing the floor. He watched her. He of all people knew how she felt, how upset she had to be.

"Tomorrow I'll make a few calls and try to pinpoint his whereabouts," he said, trying to make her feel secure. "Usually when someone who has committed a serious crime is paroled, they're released with a number of restrictions. I bet Whitman can't leave Houston."

She stopped pacing and glanced over at him with blatant hope in her gaze. "You think so?"

"I'll find out tomorrow."

Seeing the panic she was fighting to control gave him pause. At that moment she was no longer the confident, self-assured woman he had watched over the past two weeks. Now there was real fear in her eyes and a sign of helplessness in her voice, and he didn't like it.

Crossing the room he pulled her into his arms. And

when she began to tremble while he held her close, whatever hard casting surrounding his heart began to crumble. She needed him and there was no way he could not be there for her.

As if she was relieved to be able to hold on to something solid, she wrapped her arms around him. He was unprepared for the slew of emotions that rushed through him. He would protect her with his life if he had to, and would never let Whitman get close to her again.

He pulled back slightly, wanting to look at her, to make sure she was okay, and when his gaze settled on her lips, he was drawn to them like a magnet. Without any control, he lowered his mouth to hers.

The moment he drew her tongue into his mouth and began feasting on it, he felt sensations all the way to his toes and couldn't do anything but shiver with the pleasure of their intimacy. He drew his arms around her, tightening his hold to bring her body flush with his.

Summer felt his hardness, firm and rigid, pressing against her and marveled that his body was letting her know how much he wanted her. The only times she'd ever been kissed with such heat and passion was when he did the kissing.

He shifted the angle of his head, which caused her to follow as she tilted the curve of her mouth to his and nearly moaned out loud when his tongue took hold of hers with an intensity that made her weak in the knees.

When he finally released her lips, she leaned into him and sighed deeply. She had needed that kiss. She had needed the connection.

He felt firm, warm and solid—everything she needed at that moment. And in his arms she felt safe and secure. Protected. The thought that Tyrone was no longer locked up behind bars sent real fear through her, fear she was trying hard not to show. But every time she remembered those threats he'd yelled out in the courtroom while being taken away, she couldn't ignore the real panic that wanted to overtake her entire being.

"I don't want you to stay here tonight. You should come home with me, Summer."

She leaned back in his arms and met his gaze. "I can't do that, Darius. I'll be okay and—"

"No, Summer, think about it. I don't want to scare you, but until we know for sure that Whitman is in Houston, I don't want you here alone. What if those two incidents at the shelter had nothing to do with a disgruntled husband or boyfriend? What if Whitman is in violation of his parole and is not in Houston but here in Somerset and responsible for leaving that note on your windshield as well as slashing your tires?"

Darius saw the glint of real fear in her eyes when she considered those possibilities. What he'd said was true. He was not deliberately trying to scare her but she had to face the facts. And until he checked to see just where Whitman was and what he was doing, he would not let her feel safe. Hell, as far as he was concerned, as long as Whitman walked the streets he wouldn't advise Summer to feel safe. She had become an obsession to the man. In Whitman's eyes, she had betrayed him and he intended to teach her a lesson for doing so. He had made that threat in the courtroom with a crazed look in his eyes. Darius would never forget it.

"I'll go back to the shelter and sleep on the sofa in my office, and—"

"And what if word gets around to the women at Helping Hands that you, the woman who counsels them, is in the same predicament they are? Will that offer them any real hope for a brighter future when the man who disrupted your life seven years ago is still doing so?"

Summer's throat tightened as she stared up at him. She wished she could go anywhere but home with him. Being in such close quarters when she was feeling so vulnerable would be temptation she wasn't sure she could handle.

"Go on and pack an overnight bag for now, at least until I find out a few things tomorrow. If I get information indicating Whitman is in Houston behaving himself under the watchful eye of a parole officer, then I'll bring you back here tomorrow. Until then, you're going to be with me, Summer."

Summer breathed in deeply. A part of her wanted to scream out that this had all been a mistake, a nasty nightmare, and she would wake up any minute snuggled in Darius's arms for another reason, one that didn't have anything to do with Tyrone.

Darius released her, dropping his arms. "Get your bag so we can go. I'll wait here."

Summer looked at Darius, knowing his mind was set about her going home with him. There was nothing she could say to make him consider leaving her here tonight. But a part of her didn't want to be here tonight, the part that vividly recalled Tyrone's threats. She was well aware of what the man was capable of.

Because she hadn't lived in town for long, she hadn't gotten to know her neighbors. There were elderly couples that lived on either side of her that she would see on occasion. But other than the staff at the shelter, Darius was the only person she knew in Somerset. She had planned to join some community organizations but hadn't gotten around to doing so.

Making a decision, she said, "All right. It won't take me long to get my things."

A faint smile touched his eyes. "Take your time. I'm not going anywhere."

Her heart felt full. Some things had changed, but Darius was Darius, the man who'd always been and forever would be her knight in shining armor. The one person she could always depend on to be there for her.

Without saying anything else, she rushed off to her bedroom to pack.

Chapter 8

Summer fell in love with Darius's home the moment she walked through the door. Although it was too dark outside for her to see everything, she knew he had taken her to a sprawling two-story ranch house. When she stepped into his living room, she felt a sense of comfort. She knew it was strange for her to feel that way, but she couldn't help it. During the short drive he had made her feel safe, assuring her that he would find out everything he could about Tyrone's whereabouts and that until he did, she would stay with him.

She glanced around and wondered if he'd hired an interior designer to decorate his home. Everything was color coordinated perfectly, and the furniture complemented the decor. A huge brick fireplace took up one entire wall and a bevy of windows guaranteed sunshine deep in the house during the daylight hours.

To shield the foyer from the interior rooms, a glass-blocked wall was erected between the main living area and the front door. The furniture in the living room was dark, rich leather and looked comfortable as well as sturdy.

"You have a beautiful home, Darius," she said when he followed her inside, carrying her overnight case.

"Thanks. Come on and let me get you settled in the guest room. It's past midnight and you have to be tired."

She was, and couldn't wait to get a good night's sleep, or at least try, she thought. But then she figured that he had to be tired, as well. He had spent the day at both the shelter and the refinery.

Moments later, after following him up a flight of stairs, she stepped into the guest bedroom. She glanced around in total awe. The spacious room had a high roof beam with Old Hickory decor. The king-size bed appeared massive, and the bedspread was a colorful patchwork that matched the country curtains.

"Evidently, your security company is doing well," she said.

When he didn't respond, she glanced over at him and saw a hardness that had formed around his mouth. What had she said to irritate him?

"Darius?"

"Yes, it's doing well," he finally replied in a somewhat biting tone. "There's a guest bath over there with a Jacuzzi tub," he said, pointing across the room. "My bedroom is at the end of the hall if you need anything. Good night."

Summer held her composure as she watched him quickly leave, closing the door behind him. Again she wondered what she had said that had hit a nerve with him. Why had commenting on his success bothered him?

She moved toward the bed and decided that when she saw him in the morning, she would find out.

Darius lay in bed wide awake, staring up at the ceiling. After he'd left Summer, he had made his rounds, making sure everything was locked and secured before going to his bedroom. There he had continued to stew over her comment, which had reminded him that a man's wealth was all she cared about.

He rubbed a hand down his face, not wanting to think that, but what else was he supposed to think? Now that she knew he had a little money, would her attitude toward him change?

He had brought her to his home to protect her, but that didn't mean he had to forgive her for all her past deeds. He wasn't sure that he could. His hands tightened into fists. He heard a sound and glanced over at the illuminated clock on the nightstand. It was almost two in the morning. Since his state-of-the-art security system hadn't sounded to alert him of an intruder, he guessed that Summer was up and moving around in his home. Evidently, she couldn't sleep, either.

Easing out of the bed, he slipped on a pair of jeans. He walked out of his bedroom and immediately saw a light shining downstairs.

When he reached the living room, he didn't see her anywhere. He gently pushed open the kitchen door. She was sitting at the kitchen table drinking what appeared to be a cup of tea, wearing a silk bathrobe belted around the waist. And although he had a feeling she was fighting hard not to do so, he could tell by the trembling of her shoulders that she was crying. Tears from any woman were his downfall—and when they came from Summer, doubly so.

Crossing the room, he fought the tightening of his heart. Hearing his movement, she whipped her head around and met his gaze. But she hadn't been quick enough to wipe away her tears. Without asking what the tears were for, he reached out his arms. "Come here, Summer."

She stared at him for a moment and he wasn't sure exactly what she would do. Then she rose to her feet and crossed the distance separating them. He pulled her into his arms and when he did so, she buried her face in his chest.

"Shh. It's okay, sweetheart. Things are going to be okay."

She shook her head and wiped her eyes, pulling back slightly to look up at him. "No, they're not. I've gotten you upset with me and I don't know why."

At that moment, he felt like a total ass and wished there was a way he could take back his earlier behavior, but he couldn't. So he stood there and held her in his arms, remembering times past when he would hold her the same way just moments before he would claim her mouth with his.

He knew at that moment that his desire for her was just as keen as it had ever been and, unable to fight what he was feeling, he gazed into her face just seconds before using the tip of his tongue to trace a line across her lips.

He heard the catch in her breath and tried to ignore it. He eased closer, unable to stop his body from responding to it. His hard erection pressed against her, warming him in a way he hadn't been warmed in a long time. His tongue left the corners of her mouth to glide over her bottom lip before pulling it into his mouth to suck on it a little. And then there was the feel of her nipples pressing into his bare chest like hardened tips.

He released her bottom lip, but only long enough to press his mouth fully onto hers, needing this taste of her, liking how she trembled in his arms not from fear but from his safekeeping. He had thought about this part of their relationship many times, the moments when he would capture her mouth and take them both to another level. Then one night their kissing had driven them to lose control and they had made love. He continued to kiss her deeply, wanting to lose himself in the kiss again like he had that night. And wanting to lose himself inside of her. He couldn't for the life of him remember connecting to any woman and feeling this way.

"Darius."

The sound of his name sent shudders of arousal through him. It was spoken in a breathless tone, a voice barely able to do anything but purr out a sexy timbre. It made the heat within him rise to a temperature that could easily cause him to boil over.

He shifted his hips and thighs to plaster them closer to the juncture of hers. Every cell within his body felt vibrantly alive, sensitized to her. His mind was finally in sync with what the rest of his body already knew. He wanted her.

He had to have her.

There was no question about his wants and his needs, only about how long he could last without having them satisfied. He pulled back, separating their mouths, but his gaze held hers and he knew she saw in his features the desire he could not hide. His entire being was ruled by an urge to mate with her, to share a physical intimacy to a degree he hadn't had since the last time they'd been together.

While her eyes continued to hold his, she brushed the back of her hand across his cheek and the caress sent shivers through him. He let out the breath he'd been holding, and his hands dropped from her waist to cup her backside, bringing her snug against him.

He could feel the fluttering in her stomach stirring against his erection, making it throb. His nostrils picked up her scent and blood pounded through his veins. He felt himself losing what little control he had and fought to rein it back in. Then she did something he hadn't expected. She made a move he couldn't combat.

She reached out and eased down his zipper before inserting her hands through the opening to cup him, as if she needed to touch, stroke and massage his aroused body part, getting reacquainted with its size and thickness. She didn't break eye contact with him, and he grew even more aroused with her bold ministrations. The more she stroked, the more his body vibrated, making blood rush through his veins, all going directly to that throbbing part of his body.

Minutes ticked by as he continued to stand there and stare at her while she literally drove him over the edge with her hand. He studied her face, saw the intent look in her eyes, the need to touch him this way. There was a feminine glow in her gaze that stirred everything male within him, and then once again, catching him off guard, she leaned in closer, stood on tiptoes and slid her tongue all around his lips, leaving a wet path in its wake. She caressed his mouth with the tip of her tongue the same way her fingertips were now stroking his aroused shaft.

He heard himself groan at the pleasure easing up his spine and he knew if he didn't stop her now, he would embarrass himself in her hands when he preferred being inside of her body.

Now it was his turn to catch her off guard. He gently pushed her hand away seconds before sweeping her into his arms. He leaned down and kissed her with a voraciousness that had her moaning in his mouth.

When he finally pulled away, he took in a deep breath and knew he had to get completely submerged inside her body before he lost it. He stared down at her kiss-swollen lips as he held her in his arms.

"Do you know what you've asked for?" He wanted to make sure they were on the same page.

She held his gaze. "Yes. I know."

"You sure it's what you want?" He had to make doubly sure.

She shifted in his arms and ran her wet, warm tongue across his bare chest. The muscles in his stomach tightened and he knew, without her uttering a single word, he had gotten his answer.

Without saying anything else, he carried her upstairs to his bedroom.

Summer felt hot.

And when Darius placed her on his bed and joined her there, she felt passion that had been bottled up inside of her, ready to boldly claim its freedom. Every bone in her body seemed to vibrate, needing a release.

Her head began spinning when Darius removed her clothes with a swiftness that sent pieces flying everywhere. Then he stood and in record time, dropped his jeans and put on a condom he'd taken out of the nightstand drawer. Moments later, when she lay flat on her back, naked, he towered over her and she felt her thighs quiver with a yearning she hadn't felt in years.

He leaned back to slowly peruse her body and she felt heat every place his eyes touched, especially around her feminine core where his gaze seemed to linger, making sensations stir deep within her. The look in his eyes gave her more than an inkling of what he was thinking, and when he reached out and lifted her hips, placing her legs across his shoulders, she literally cried out before his mouth had a chance to touch her.

She cried out again when his mouth did touch her. He pushed his tongue inside, working it around in her with a greed that sent sparks shooting off in her, scorching everywhere it touched and weakening every bone in her body, turning her muscles to mush.

He spread her legs wider as his mouth continued to inflict upon her torment that was unyielding. What he was doing had captured her senses, totally wrecked her brain cells and fractured all rational thought. Physically, she was beginning to feel herself break into pieces and she grasped the strong arms on each side of her, trying to let him know there was no way she could take any more.

As if determined to prove to her that she could, he continued his torment on her body, tightening his grip on her thighs as his tongue dived deeper inside of her. When he flicked across a sensitive part of her, she shattered, and helplessly screamed his name as an onslaught of sensations ripped into her.

It was only then that he pulled back and straddled her, and before her lungs could fill with more air, he entered her in one deep thrust as he captured one of her breasts into his mouth, sucking deeply on a nipple.

The joining had been so perfect it nearly brought tears to her eyes. She grabbed hold of his head to hold him to her breast and wrapped her legs around him to keep him inside of her. But the movement of his body told her he wasn't going anywhere.

He began moving, retreating and then pushing back in. Over and over again. Harder. Deeper. Faster. She felt every hard inch of him, felt the strong veins of his erection throb deep inside of her and push her over an edge that had her moaning yet again.

And when he shifted his mouth to her other breast and began the same mind-wrecking torment, her moan turned into another scream. She felt every nerve in her body explode, and she began riding a wave that took her across the top of anything and everything. When his body stiffened and bucked mercilessly while he tightly gripped her hips, she knew this was the fusing of not only their bodies, but their minds and souls.

And at that moment, nothing else existed in her world but the man who continued to push in and out of her while screaming her name. This was the same man who'd first shown her how beautiful the joining of a man and woman could be. The same man who moments later slumped down on the bed beside her and pulled her into his arms, holding her as if he never, ever wanted to let her go.

Summer awoke with the sunlight shining on her face and a strong, hard body plastered to her own. She shifted slightly and looked over at the man sleeping beside her, the man whose strong masculine leg was thrown over hers and whose arms, even in sleep, were wrapped around her.

Memories of last night flowed through her mind. It was the first time she had made love in seven years and it had been everything that she had remembered and more. Same man. Same passion. Same love.

She closed her eyes thinking that by rights, she should be upset with herself for still loving him and for the weakness that allowed her to tumble back into bed with him, especially after the way he had cheapened their first night together. But then she couldn't feel remorse when every part of her body was rejuvenated, like it had been awakened from a long sleep by pure pleasure. It had been making love with Darius the last time that had made her appreciate the fact she'd been born a woman, and it was his lovemaking now that was deepening that appreciation.

But still…memories of her pain, her humiliation wouldn't completely go away. How could a man who was so caring when it came to her so easily dishonor her the way he had? She had fallen in love with him completely and when he had made love to her that night, that love had intensified to a point that totally overwhelmed her.

He hadn't said the word *love* to her, but she had been certain of his feelings and had felt he'd displayed with his actions what he hadn't spoken. But she'd discovered her assumptions had been wrong. She did not intend to make the same mistake twice. All she and Darius had just shared was a sexual release. For her, it was a long time coming. She would not assume anything about their relationship ever again. She would accept it for what it was.

He shifted in bed and she tilted her head to look over at him. Before she could say a word, he leaned over and kissed her with a tenderness that made her groan. She didn't have to mull over what they were about to do again, this time in the brightness of the sunlight. And when he eased his body over hers, she wrapped her arms around his neck and eagerly gave him the mouth he seemed so intent to claim.

Summer stood at the window in her office. She kept replaying in her mind what had transpired last night and this morning. Although Darius had made love to her with an intensity and passion that nearly brought tears to her eyes, on the drive back over to her place this morning, she could sense him withdrawing. Why? Was he afraid she might assume just because they had slept together that she would think he wanted her back in his life? If that was the case, then he didn't know how wrong he was about it. She knew better than to think that way. She had learned her lesson well.

He had insisted on driving her to the office after he'd taken her home to dress, and he hadn't had a lot to say about what they had shared last night. Instead, he'd kept the conversation centered on Tyrone and all the things he would be checking on, saying he would take a trip to Houston if he had to.

He was still displaying those protective tendencies, but she could feel him putting up his guard, shielding emotions from her, keeping them out of her reach. More than once while in his arms last night and this morning, she had been tempted to ask him why he had done what he did seven years ago. But then she would decide to leave well enough alone. What happened was no longer a threat as long as she kept her heart out of the mix. Besides, she had bigger fish to fry. Tyrone Whitman and his whereabouts were what she needed to stay focused on. It was the only thing she should care about, the only thing that mattered.

The thought of Tyrone being free made her skin crawl, but she refused to allow him to make her live in total fear. More than ever she was convinced he was the one who'd left that note on her windshield and slashed her tires, mainly because those were things Tyrone would do. Saying he took care of his own was something he'd said to her more than once. The reason she hadn't made the connection before was because she had assumed he was still locked up in prison. But now she knew that was not the case.

She glanced up at the clock on the wall. Darius said he would be coming back to walk her over to the café for lunch, and not to leave without him. This would be one time she did what he asked without any hesitation.

The phone on her desk rang and she immediately went to pick it up, hoping it was Darius with good news. "Hello?"

The person on the other end didn't say anything. "Hello?" she repeated. Chills ran down her spine when the person finally hung up. She tried to convince herself it was probably just a misdialed number. But deep down she had a feeling that wasn't true.

Darius's hands tightened on the steering wheel as he turned down the street that would take him to Helping Hands. Already he was regretting the news he was about to deliver to Summer.

He had made a call to the Houston Police Department as soon as he'd dropped Summer off at work. He'd been told Walt was out of town on an investigation, so he had spoken with Manny, another detective he knew. It had taken Manny less than an hour to find out what he wanted to know.

Manny had verified Whitman was out on parole with an order not to leave Houston. However, according to Manny, Whitman could not be found at what should have been his current address, and his landlord hadn't seen him in weeks. Since Whitman had a week or so left before they could haul him in for violating parole, so far he hadn't broken any laws…unless it could be proven he had left Houston.

There was no doubt in Darius's mind that Whitman had been in Somerset and was possibly still around. Since Somerset was such a small town, it would be easy for Whitman to find out where Summer worked—as well as where she lived. The thought of her being at Whitman's mercy again was enough to make every fiber of his being roar in anger.

He shifted his thoughts to last night and this morning. While making love to her, he had tried holding himself back but he hadn't been able to control his emotions. Never had he been so affected by making love to a woman. It was as if the last seven years hadn't existed and there had never been a wedge between them. Last night and this morning fit perfectly into his plans. After this morning, he was supposed to take her back home, tell her about all the wealth he had accumulated over the years, that he was a member of the TCC and that not only did he know Kevin Novak but that Kevin was one of his closest friends. He had wanted to see the hurt in her eyes.

But Whitman's parole made that impossible—at least that's what he told himself. If it was determined the man was a threat to Summer, that would mean she'd stay with him for a while. She wouldn't like the idea, but he was determined to protect her at all costs.

Summer had been hoping, praying that the last seven years in jail would have changed Tyrone and she would no longer matter to him. It was disheartening to know she had been wrong and there was a strong chance he was stalking her again.

She told Darius about the strange phone call she had gotten that morning, and he, too, was convinced it had been Tyrone.

"Come on, let's go to lunch."

During lunch at the café Darius received a call. After the conversation ended, Summer knew from the look on his face that she was not going to like what he had to say.

He proved her right. "Before coming to the shelter I stopped at police headquarters to alert them that Whitman might be in the area. I provided them with a description of how he looked the last time I saw him, figuring his looks hadn't changed much over the years. But even if they had, Somerset is a small enough town that a stranger would stick out like a sore thumb."

He stopped talking, but she could tell there was more.

"And?" she prompted.

"And they think he's been seen. A couple of the police officers who were cruising the area a few blocks from the shelter got suspicious of a guy who met Whitman's description. When they tried to approach him to question him, he ran."

Summer didn't say anything for a moment. "I refuse to let Tyrone scare me again, Darius. Although it didn't work the last time, I'm going to get another restraining order."

"That's a good idea. If he is taken into custody here in Somerset for any reason, his parole will automatically be revoked."

Darius hesitated a moment and then said, "Although

you're refusing to let Tyrone scare you, I'm hoping you'll continue to stay with me until this issue with him is resolved. It will only be a matter of time before he finds out where you live, if he doesn't know already. Alarm or no alarm, if he ever breaks inside your home again, depending on his frame of mind, there's no telling what he will do. If knowing he will go back to jail and serve out the rest of his sentence hasn't deterred him, that can only mean he doesn't care. And people who don't care will do just about anything to get back at the person they think has betrayed them."

Summer knew what Darius said was true. Tyrone had held a gun to her head, willing and ready to end her life as well as his own. She really didn't want to go home with Darius again, but she didn't have a choice. Even after what they had shared last night and this morning, she could still feel tension between them. She could tell he still had his guard up.

"Summer?"

She met his gaze, felt the heat in the dark depths of his eyes. He wanted to keep her safe. And he wanted her. Summer knew that no matter how guarded he was being, he couldn't deny he enjoyed having her back in his bed, and she would admit she enjoyed being there. Intimacy between them wasn't just good, it was off the charts. Sexual tension was always oozing between them, even when she didn't want it to, like now.

Knowing he was waiting on an answer, she said, "Okay, I'll move in with you for the time being if you think it will be for the best."

Chapter 9

A week later, as Darius sat in the TCC café waiting to meet with Lance, he was convinced that Summer moving in with him had been the best thing to keep her safe. Although he wasn't sure just what her being underfoot was doing to his peace of mind.

At first, he had put up his guard, finding excuses to work outdoors in the evenings to stay away from the house. But living under the same roof made it difficult to deny his desire for her when she was near.

Evidently, she hadn't been sure just where she should sleep the night she had returned to his place. They had stopped by her house to get more of her things, and after she had gotten settled at his place and taken a shower, she had gone to sleep in the guest bedroom.

He had stayed outside deliberately talking to his ranch foreman, and when he had come inside and found her asleep in the guest bedroom, he tried to convince himself that her sleeping arrangements were fine with him.

He'd taken a shower and crawled into his own bed. But knowing that she was asleep in another bedroom didn't suit him. However, his stubbornness, the cold hard casting around his heart, just wouldn't thaw any.

After the third night, he realized that he had finally reached his limit. He got out of bed and went into the guest bedroom to discover her wide awake. She had been unable to sleep those nights, too.

He could vividly recall that particular night, and how he had stood in the doorway and stared at her across the room, wanting so much to despise her, and also his weakness for her. Without saying a word, he had reached out his hand to her and she had eased out of bed, crossing the room to place her hand in his.

Darius sighed deeply thinking it had been at that particular moment that he could no longer deny that she was and would always be a part of him. He had faced the truth that the reason he was so determined to protect her was because he still cared for her. Deeply.

Since then she had shared his bed every night and he'd enjoyed waking up with her beside him each morning. And he was getting used to her being in his home, in his space. Being under the same roof with her gave him a chance to get to know the new Summer, the one that had grown up without him. And he couldn't help but admire the woman she had become, the dedicated social worker who understood what it was like to be a woman in jeopardy. A woman who had been abused.

In the evenings he no longer found reasons to stay away from his home. Together they would prepare meals, clean up the kitchen and talk about the day's events, only bringing up Whitman when they needed to. He had been sighted several more times in Somerset. Darius had even approached the Texas Rangers about Whitman informing them that he had violated parole. Although he had yet to be apprehended, Darius was convinced that eventually he would be, and was glad, in the meantime, that he was keeping Summer safe.

"Sorry I'm late. I sort of got detained," Lance said, breaking into his thoughts and sliding into the chair across from him.

Darius couldn't help but laugh. Based on the satisfied smile on his best friend's face, he could only assume Kate was the reason he was late, and now he understood what it was like to have a woman under your skin and close at hand.

"No problem. I just wanted to give you a copy of the official fire department report and provide an update on my investigation. I checked out all your employees who were questionable and was able to rule out each and every one of them."

Lance nodded. "I figured you would. I told you who I suspect."

Yes, Lance had told him, Darius thought, several times. But Darius still wasn't convinced. Something didn't sit right with him.

Darius checked his watch. It had become a routine for him to drive Summer to work every morning and pick her up in the afternoon, and he did not want to be late. It was a routine he was beginning to get accustomed to. And it was one he liked, whether he wanted to admit it or not. Business would have to wait.

* * *

Summer came down the stairs and looked around, not seeing Darius anywhere. She went into the kitchen, deciding to make a cup of tea. It wasn't unusual for him to go outside and spend time with the men who ran his ranch in the afternoons, and she had been fully aware that when she'd first come to stay with him he had used that as an excuse to put distance between them.

Now that had changed. He no longer avoided her in his home and she spent every night in his bed. She still wasn't assuming anything and knew once Tyrone had been captured, Darius would expect her to leave and return to her home. She wouldn't be doing herself any favors if she became attached to his beautiful home, which she already loved. It was far enough from town to offer peace and quiet that anyone would cherish, yet at the same time it was a place where a family could be raised.

She shook her head, determined to get such foolish thoughts out of it. What she and Darius were sharing was physical and nothing more. She turned at the sound of footsteps and knew it was him.

He walked through the back door, saw her and smiled. He might not love her but there was no doubt in her mind that he enjoyed having her around. He closed the door behind him, locked it and just stood there, staring at her. When he had brought her home from work she had gone upstairs to take a shower. Now she felt refreshed but at the same time, hot. And the way he was looking at her was making her feel even hotter.

Without a word, she crossed the kitchen floor and wrapped her arms around his neck. Then, leaning upward she captured his mouth with hers. His response was immediate and he didn't waste any time letting her know it, or letting her feel it. His thick erection was throbbing against her, making her senses come unglued and sending sensations rushing through her veins and all over her skin.

Moments later she pulled back and met his gaze. "We need to prepare dinner," she said in a ragged voice, barely able to breathe.

"Later." And then he swept her off her feet and headed upstairs to his bedroom.

Bodies joined. Summer moved with Darius as his lips brushed a kiss beneath her ear and whispered just how much he enjoyed being inside of her, making love to her, being one with her.

The rhythm he had established was perfect, and floated them toward fulfillment. The air surrounding them was charged and the more he thrust into her body, the more her senses seemed whipped with a pleasure so profound it took her breath away.

"Now!"

As if on cue, her body began convulsing right along with his, endlessly, as shivers tore through them, pulling them down yet at the same time building them up. And when she cried out in pleasure, every pull of her feminine muscles was regulated by his steady yet rapid strokes into her body, making her lift her hips and use her thighs to squeeze him tight, clench him for all she was worth.

She tossed her head back when he surged even deeper inside of her, gripping her thighs and taking her all over again, pushing her toward another orgasm and doing everything in his power to make sure they both got there.

They did.

Instead of letting up, the heat was on yet again, and the workings of her inner muscles signified that such a notion made perfect sense, given the depth of their desire, their passion and their sexual hunger. It was as if they were making up for lost time and then some, filling a drought, satisfying a yearning, soothing an ache.

And when he began moving inside of her in quick, rapid successions, she cried out his name as shivers of pleasure tore through her once again.

"Do you know how beautiful you are? And you're even more beautiful after making love."

Summer glanced over and saw Darius had awakened. He was smiling, and the look in his eyes was filled with the same heat she still felt on some parts of her body. "Thank you."

She knew at that moment she would have to broach the subject she had tried putting behind her since seeing him again.

His betrayal.

"And you are a very handsome man, making love or not," she said softly. Truthfully. She paused a moment and then asked the one question she needed answered. One she could not put off asking any longer. "Why did you make that bet?"

A confused look appeared on his face. "What bet?"

Summer was certain there was no way he could not know what bet she was referring to. But if he wanted to pretend to have a loss of memory, she could remedy that. "I'm talking about the bet you made with Walt about how quick you could take me to bed."

In an instant, he was up, leaning over her. The look on his face was one of incredulous fury. "What the hell are you talking about? I never made a bet like that."

She wondered why he was not going to own up to it now. "That's all right, Darius. It doesn't matter."

"Yes, it does matter," he said in a hard voice. "Especially if you believed it."

She frowned. "Why are you denying it?"

"Because I never did such a thing. How could you have believed something like that?"

She drew in a deep breath and held his gaze. "Because Walt told me what you did. He felt that I had a right to know."

His face hardened. "Walt!" he all but roared.

"Yes," she countered in a voice filled with just as much conviction. "Yes, Walt Stewart. He was your partner at the time. Or have you forgotten about him, as well?"

"No, I haven't forgotten about Walt. In fact, I spoke with him just last week about that arson case I'm investigating. What you're saying doesn't make sense, Summer, because Walt knew how I felt about you. There's no way he could have told you something like that."

Summer's head began spinning and it took her a second to find steady ground. *Walt knew how I felt about you...*

Could he be saying that he had cared as deeply about her as she had about him? She continued to stare at Darius and noted the way he was looking back at her. Then he asked slowly, with disbelief, "And Walt actually told you that?"

"Yes."

Darius released her and eased out of bed, seemingly barely able to keep the lid on raging anger. She swallowed, slowly realizing the impact of what now appeared to be a blatant lie. But why?

"Put on some clothes. We need to talk, and this is not the place for us to do it," he said, interrupting her thoughts. He picked up his jeans and eased into them. "Please meet me in the living room."

Summer stared at his back as he walked out the room.

Darius paced his living room with his hands in tight fists. Why in the hell had Walt told Summer something like that? How could he have told her?

He could vividly remember sharing a beer with Walt one night after their shift had ended and telling him just how much Summer had come to mean to him. Walt had sat there listening, not saying anything, mainly because Darius hadn't given him a chance to say anything. His heart had been filled with love, and he had wanted to share those emotions with someone he had considered a friend.

He and Walt had gotten hired around the same time and had easily become friends. He was well aware of Walt's issues with the opposite sex because of his ex-wife's betrayal, but Darius had overlooked them because it hadn't been his issue or concern.

Now he had to wonder just how deep Walt's deception went. He knew what Summer had been told, but what about what Walt had told him about Summer, and the message she had supposedly left for him? According to Walt, Summer had left town with an older man. A rich man.

"I'm here now."

Darius stopped his pacing and turned around. She stood there, not in the shorts and blouse he had taken off her earlier that night, but in one of his T-shirts that had been thrown across a chair in his room. Whether it was her intent or not, her wearing his shirt meant something to him. It was as if she was giving him an unspoken acknowledgment of their connection, a connection that had started seven years ago and by some work of miracle was back in full force.

Making love to her over the past weeks had closed old wounds. But now he was discovering that those wounds were self-inflicted due to his belief of Walt's lies. "Let's sit and discuss this, please. I'm beginning to think we've been played."

He watched as she took a seat on the sofa, trying not to notice that his shirt hit her mid-thigh, and how sexy she looked in it. More than anything, he had to keep his mind on the issues at hand, issues they needed to dissect and resolve. After she was seated, instead of sitting beside her on the sofa, he took the leather wing chair that sat not far away.

"To take up the conversation we started in bed, I want you to know, I want you to believe, that at no time did I discuss sleeping with you with Walt. There was no bet."

He watched her features. She held his gaze as intensely as he was holding hers. He saw in her eyes a desire to believe what he said. But…

"Then how did he know about that night?" she asked. "He knew that you had spent the night over at my place."

Darius thought about her words. "He must have driven by your apartment and seen my car parked out front."

He could tell from her expression that she was taking his explanation into consideration, agreeing that it was possible. However, there was still lingering doubt in her eyes.

"Why didn't you contact me?" she then asked him. "He told me you left town and would be gone for a few days, but I never heard from you again. It was like you *had* scored and put me out of your life."

Darius leaned back in his chair. "Did he not tell you why I had to leave immediately or where I had gone?"

"He didn't go into any details. He just said you'd been called away on police business and would be gone a few days."

Darius jaw tightened. "The reason I had to leave when I did was because I got a call that Ethan had been critically injured in a car accident and was being wheeled into surgery. Since I'm his only family, I had to get to Charleston. For a while, I wasn't sure Ethan was going to make it. I was by his bedside day and night and did not have use of my cell phone. And when I did call, I got a message that you had gotten your cell number changed."

He saw the shock in Summer's gaze and before she could say anything, he knew she hadn't known. "Walt didn't tell me that," she said angrily, getting to her feet. "I didn't know."

Connecting his fingers in a steeple, he placed them under his chin. "When I returned to town almost two weeks later, after Ethan's condition had stabilized, I went straight to your place from the airport, only to be told by your landlord that you had moved out a few days earlier, and that an older man in a Mercedes had picked you up and that you had left with him."

She nodded. "Yes, that was Karl Lindsey."

He paused for a second and then said, "Walt is the one who told me why you had left."

She shifted in her seat and his gaze was drawn to a flash of her thigh. His attention went back to her face when she said, "Yes, Walt just happened to drop by that day Karl was there, and just on the off chance you cared enough to ask, I told him that I had taken a job with Karl and would be moving to Florida for a year."

Darius raised a brow. "A job?"

"Yes, Karl had been one of my regulars at the restaurant. He's a writer. He offered me a job as his assistant, editing and organizing his notes. He had offered me the same job before but Tyrone had forced me to turn it down. When I hadn't heard anything from you, and after Walt told me what you did, I decided to take Mr. Lindsey's offer and moved to Florida with him and his wife and—"

"His wife?"

Summer didn't say anything for a moment as she studied his expression. Then she said, "Yes, Lola, his wife. You sound surprised."

Darius stared at her as a deep sharp pain ripped through him. For the first time he was seeing that trust on both sides had been shattered because he and Summer had been quick to believe the lies of others. He had been so quick to believe the worst of her and she of him. Not because they thought of each other as devious people, but because their relationship had been in the early stages, at a very delicate period when trust, faith and love was building. He didn't want to think of how strong their relationship would be if it had been given a chance to grow.

"Darius?"

He hated telling her what he'd thought, what he'd assumed, but knew that he had to do so. "The message Walt gave me, the one he claimed you left, was that you had met this old, rich man and that you couldn't waste your time with someone who was nothing but a college-educated cop with no aspirations of being anything else."

She stared at him. He saw the hurt and pain in her eyes and knew why. Just like she had believed Walt's lies about him, he had believed the man's lies about her.

"Why were we so quick to believe the worst of each other?" she asked in a whisper that he could barely hear. "We played right into Walt's hands," she added. "That's sad."

As far as he was concerned, it was worse than sad. It was pathetic. Seven years wasted. He then said the only thing that he could say at that moment. "I'm sorry."

She breathed in deeply. "And I'm sorry, as well."

Darius could only sit there silently for a moment, wondering how one went about repairing a love that had been destroyed by lies. Lies that had been so easy to accept. Inside of him, a voice said, *One day at a time.*

"Summer, I—"

"No, Darius, I think we both need time to come to terms with what happened, the lies that were told and why we were so quick to believe them. I haven't been in a relationship with anyone since you, serious or otherwise. I've grown accustomed to being by myself, not wanting a man to share my life. I don't trust easily anymore. I'm more cautious. I really don't know if that can change."

He could read between the lines. She was letting him know when it was all said and done, regardless of the fact that they had lived together for the last few weeks or so, getting along marvelously, complementing each other's personalities, she was not all that certain that she wanted to give them another chance because of their lack of faith and trust in each other. From what she was saying, she still didn't want a man in her life. Things had changed. She had changed. In a way, he understood.

Over the years he had kept most women at bay, being selective about who he wanted to spend his time with and not allowing himself to get serious about anyone. But he could see all that changing and wondered if she could. Their relationship—and he considered them to be in a relationship—had to undergo some serious repairs. Major repairs. But he thought they could do it.

They had uncovered a lot tonight. But he still had something else to come clean about—his association with the TCC.

"Summer. I—"

"Will you contact the authorities to see if anyone has seen Tyrone again?" she cut in to ask.

He knew she was trying to get off the subject. He would let her do so for now since tonight had been overwhelming, to say the least, and he wasn't sure how she would handle the unveiling of another lie. One that had been his own, as a way to hurt her. He would tell her another time. Soon. Tomorrow.

"Yes, I'll do that."

There was no need to tell her that he planned on killing two birds with one stone by driving to Houston tomorrow to meet with Tyrone's parole officer and that he would also be paying a visit to Walt.

He studied her, wondering if she knew the significance of what she had admitted moments ago. He was the last man she had made love with. She hadn't wanted a man in her life in seven years, yet she had shared herself with him.

At that moment, all he could think about was what they had shared. The heat. The passion.

"I guess we could sit here and stare at each other all night," she finally said, "but I prefer going back to bed."

He rose to his feet, accepting the gravity of the mistakes they'd both made. But he also accepted that she needed him now like he needed her. "Then I don't plan to keep you up any longer."

He crossed the room to her. They had a lot left to talk about, still more truths to tell. But at that moment, they needed to be together and they both knew it.

Darius held his hand out to her and she took it. Together, they returned to his bedroom.

While en route to the shelter the next morning, Darius received a call. "This is Darius."

He listened attentively to what the caller was saying and then he said, "That's good news and I appreciate you calling to let me know. I'll pass the information on to Ms. Martindale."

He clicked off the phone and glanced over at Summer. "That was a Texas Ranger friend of mine. He was calling to let me know that they picked up Whitman this morning."

Darius saw a wave of relief pass through her. "Where?" she asked.

They had come to a stop at the traffic light and Darius glanced over at her. "Less than a block from your house."

He hated telling her the next part but knew that he had to. "He had a gun and a rope in his possession."

Summer stiffened and Darius understood why. Chances were Whitman had discovered where she lived, and a good possibility existed that he had planned on using that information for no good. Since he had violated parole in more ways than one, Darius knew he would return to prison and serve his entire sentence.

She didn't say anything, staring straight ahead, out the windshield.

"You okay?" he asked.

She turned to him. "Yes, I'm okay."

She might be okay, but he wasn't. How could he have been so wrong about her? He couldn't wait to confront Walt about the lies he'd told. "I have something to take care of this morning and won't be back in time to join you for lunch."

"All right."

She didn't seem to be in a talkative mood and he figured she needed time to digest everything he had told her about Whitman.

"Since Tyrone is in police custody, there's no reason I can't return home now, is there?"

None other than I don't want you to go. I've gotten used to having you around. I've fallen in love with you all over again. "No, there's no reason you can't," he said.

He breathed in deeply and at that moment, he knew there was no use denying what he'd known all along. He loved her. He had not stopped loving her.

And all this time he had tried convincing himself that he would seek revenge for what she had done, when he knew he couldn't have gone through with that plan no matter how much he'd thought he wanted to hurt her.

From the first moment she had turned her eyes on him he had been a goner, and although he'd convinced himself over the years that he had gotten over her, the simple truth was, he hadn't. Coming to terms with his love for her was a monumental release of the hold he'd placed on his emotions. All the built-up tension and anger he'd felt since seeing her again left his body, flowed out of his muscles. It strengthened his heart, propelling him to do whatever he had to do to make her his again.

Chapter 10

A few hours later, Summer slipped into her walking shoes to go to the café for lunch, reflecting that this was the first time in quite a while that she would be doing so without Darius by her side.

She drew in a huge breath of profound relief, knowing what could have been another nightmare with Tyrone was now over. She shivered when she thought of the items that had been in his possession. There was no doubt in her mind he intended to do her harm, and she was grateful yet again to Darius for keeping her out of harm's way.

Darius. The man she still loved.

She wondered if she'd sounded convincing when she told him that she didn't want a man in her life. A part of her did want to belong to him, totally and completely, but was afraid to get her hopes up again. Even though she knew the truth now, it couldn't erase the pain she had felt for seven years.

Besides, there was nothing Darius had said to make her think that he wanted to renew what they'd once shared. When she'd mentioned returning to her place now that the threat with Tyrone was over, he hadn't said anything to talk her out of it, he hadn't said that he didn't want her to leave.

He had apologized for believing the lies Walt had told him. And she had apologized to him, as well. Later, they had made love but no promises had been made. There had been no discussion of a future together. Although he hadn't said as much, she had a feeling that he didn't want a woman in his life.

That left her with the same life she'd been living since leaving Houston. The kind of life she had gotten used to. It was somewhat lonely but safe. She would continue to live it without the man she loved.

The anger within Darius told him to strike out the moment he saw Walt walking toward him. But he fought to hold his rage in check. There was only one thing he wanted from the man and that was for him to explain why he'd done what he did.

Without telling Walt why, he had called and requested to meet with him in Laverne Square, a newly developed area of Houston near the Madaris Office Park. He rose from the bench when he saw the curious look in Walt's eyes.

"Darius, didn't you get my message that the guy you wanted me to check out was clean? I left it on your voice mail last week."

"That's not why I asked you to meet with me," Darius answered, trying to keep the bitterness out of his voice.

Walt lifted a brow. "Oh. Then what's up?"

Darius looked directly into his eyes. "I'm here about the lie you told me about Summer Martindale."

Walt held his gaze for an instant before shifting his eyes to look out over the pond in the square. Time stretched on and for a moment, Darius wondered if he was going to say anything. Then Walt turned his gaze to Darius.

"She came with a lot of baggage and was trouble with that crazy boyfriend of hers. You didn't need her."

His words, spoken as if he'd had a right to make that decision, slithered down Darius's spine. "You were wrong, Walt. She wasn't trouble and you knew how I felt about her. I not only needed her but I loved her."

"You have a lot to learn about women, Darius. You can never let one get under your skin, and you can never admit to loving one."

Darius stared at him for a moment. "Actually," he said in a deep, cutting tone, "there's a lot that *you* need to learn about them, and recognizing a good one when you meet her is at the top of the list."

A deep frown settled on Walt's face. "There aren't any good ones."

Walt had extreme issues, but Darius couldn't concern himself with that right now. As far as he was concerned, what Walt had done was unforgivable. When he thought about all those wasted years when he and Summer could have been together, years when he had loathed her very name, he practically wanted to kill the man. It was all for nothing. All for lies.

Filled with total disgust and having nothing else to say, Darius started to leave.

"Hey, wait, man, we're okay, aren't we? We're still friends?" Walt asked in a lighthearted tone.

Darius stopped walking and looked over his shoulder. Their gazes locked. The message he was certain Walt saw in his eyes was blatantly clear.

"No. Our friendship died the day you lied to me. I loved her, but because I thought you were my friend, I believed you. A true friend would not have done what you did."

Without saying anything else, he walked off, leaving Walt standing there.

Summer was just about to go to the café when one of the security guards escorted a very well dressed, distinguished-looking older man through the entrance. It didn't take a rocket scientist to figure out from the way the man was carrying himself that he was someone of authority, someone of importance, which could only mean he was a member of the TCC. Kevin Novak had given her a heads-up that over the next few months, members of the TCC would probably be dropping by to check out the shelter since he had asked them for more money.

Putting on her brightest smile, Summer crossed the lobby to greet the man. "Welcome to Helping Hands," she said, extending her hand to him. "I'm Summer Martindale, a social worker here."

The man took her hand and looked at her. "So, you're the young woman who's been causing so much excitement."

Summer forced her smile to remain intact when she

recognized his voice. He was the person she had talked to on the phone when she'd called requesting additional security guards. "Am I?" she couldn't help but ask, not liking the way the man seemed to be staring down his nose at her.

"Yes. I'm Sebastian Huntington, a member of the Texas Cattleman's Club."

"Nice to meet you, Mr. Huntington."

He didn't say anything to indicate that the feelings were mutual. Instead, he glanced around. "Things seem calm enough around here. I really don't see why two guards are needed. But then, you've managed to convince Kevin Novak differently."

She was about to say the reason things appeared calm was because everyone felt safer with two guards when he once again looked down his nose at her and arrogantly said, "And then there's Darius Franklin, who's evidently quite taken with you. He's also been singing your praises at the TCC meetings." A sneer touched his lips as he studied her features. "Now I see why."

Surprise flickered in her eyes. "Darius?"

"Yes. He's one of our newest members."

Now she was confused. *Darius was a member of TCC?*

"How long has he been a member?"

The man frowned down at her like she'd asked a stupid question. "Not long enough for him and his friends to be throwing their weight around. He's only been a member for over a year."

Summer nodded. "Oh, I see." And the sad part of it was that she really did see. Darius had lied to her.

"Ready to go?"

Summer slowly lifted her gaze from the document at

the sound of the deep, husky voice. Had it been nearly three weeks ago when here in this office she had heard that voice again for the first time in seven years?

After Mr. Huntington left, instead of walking to the café, she had gone to the library. There she had researched information on the Texas Cattleman's Club branch that was located in Somerset. Darius was listed as a member, having joined the same day as Kevin Novak and several other men, and from the photographs she had seen, it was apparent that he and Mr. Novak knew each other very well. Why had he pretended otherwise when she'd told him of her meeting with Mr. Novak? Why had he deliberately kept his membership in the TCC from her?

Instead of answering his question, she asked one of her own.

"Why didn't you tell me you were a member of the Texas Cattleman's Club?"

She saw surprise light his eyes and knew he was probably wondering how she'd found out. "Mr. Huntington dropped by to check out the place and mentioned you're a member," she said, leaning back in her chair.

"So, my question is, why didn't you tell me, Darius? You had several chances to do so when I was preparing for my meeting with Mr. Novak, and many after that. Why didn't you tell me?"

A part of Darius wished he'd have told Summer everything last night. How would she react to finding out he had withheld the information because of his plan to hurt her?

Any chance of rebuilding a relationship with her would probably be destroyed now. But still, he had to be upfront and honest with her. Lies were the reason they were in the situation they were in now.

Sighing deeply, he entered her office and closed the door behind him, leaning against it. "The reason I didn't want to tell you is because I was still operating under the belief that you had left Houston with a rich man. A man you had chosen over me because of his wealth. With that belief festering in my mind as well as my heart over the years, I had grown to resent you for choosing wealth over love."

When she didn't say anything, he continued. "I figured that if that was true, once you found out about my wealth, the fact that I had become successful, I could get my revenge by seducing you, taking you to bed and then walking away from you the same way I thought you had walked away from me. I wanted to hurt you the way you had hurt me."

Summer still didn't say anything for a moment, and then in a low voice, she asked, "You hated me that much?"

Darius breathed in again, hearing the deep hurt in her voice. "I thought I did, but once I got to know what I thought was the new Summer Martindale, the one who's dedicated to the women at the shelter, the one who works tirelessly after hours when her shift is over, I realized that no matter how much I wanted revenge, I couldn't have gone through with it. And do you know why, Summer?"

"I have no idea," she said in a sharp tone.

He held her gaze. "Because I realized that although I'd tried over the years, I couldn't replace love with hate. Although I wanted to hurt you, I couldn't because I still love you."

Their gazes held and for a moment, he wondered if she believed him. He hoped and prayed for some sort of sign that she did. He had been wrong for wanting to get even with her, but at the time he'd felt it was something he had needed to do because of his pain.

"So many years have passed, Summer. We owe it to ourselves to try and rebuild the relationship that was destroyed because of our lack of faith and trust in each other. In Houston today, I made a point to see Walt. I had to know why he'd done what he did. His reason was he saw me falling for you and figured I'd get hurt. But the truth of the matter is that I was hurt in the end anyway. Not by you, but because I'd believed the worst about you."

He moved away from the door to stand in front of her desk. "I'm asking that you give me a chance to do what I wanted to do seven years ago and that is, love you the way a man is supposed to love a woman. Please allow me into your heart, Summer. Give me a chance to prove that I am the right man for you."

He took another step closer. "Will you put behind you all the hurt and lies of before and move forward in the way we should have years ago? Can you find it in your heart to love me as much as I love you? To work on rebuilding a relationship of love, trust and faith?"

He saw the single tear that fell from her eye and literally held his breath before she began speaking.

"Yes," she said slowly. "I can work on rebuilding our relationship because I love you, too, and I want you in my life. I want a future with you, not because of your wealth but because you are a man who's proven more than once that he can be there when I need someone, that he has my best interests at heart, and protects me when I need protecting."

She pushed her chair back and walked around her desk to him. "We have a lot of years to make up for, but I knew that night we made love again it was something I wanted. I was just afraid to hope for it."

Darius pulled her into his arms and held her tight, close to his heart. And then he lowered his mouth to hers. He wanted her with him always and from the intensity of their kiss, it seemed she wanted the very same thing.

Moments later, he pulled his mouth away from hers. "Ready to go home, sweetheart?" And to make sure she understood, he added, "Not to your place, but to mine. A place that you will one day consider ours, I hope."

She smiled up at him. "Yes, I'm ready."

He took her hand in his and they walked out of her office together. He knew there was a lot of work ahead, rebuilding their relationship into the kind they both wanted, the kind they deserved. Lies had destroyed their relationship, but love had restored it. Their love would make it all happen for them.

They would make sure of it. Together.

Epilogue

Three weeks later

Summer stepped outside on the porch and glanced around. It was a beautiful day and the smell of flowers was everywhere.

She felt butterflies move around in her stomach at the same time she saw the car pull into the yard. She smiled. Darius was home.

She glanced around again, thinking how easy it was to think of his ranch as home. She never returned to her place, and every week more and more of her things would show up here.

And then one night while they were busy unpacking some more of her boxes, he had got down on his knee and proposed to her. He asked her to be his wife, the mother of his babies and his best friend for life. Somehow through her tears she had accepted. The moment he had slipped the ring on her finger, more love and happiness than she'd ever thought possible filled her heart. They hadn't set a date yet, and had decided to take things one day at a time.

She had met his friends and could see the special friendship they shared. She liked them a lot. Tonight they would be joining Lance and Kate at the TCC for dinner.

As soon as the car came to a stop, she moved down the steps, and when Darius opened the door and got out, she was there waiting.

He pulled her into his arms and kissed her, making her feel wanted and loved. Things were so good between them that she would occasionally pinch herself to make sure it was real. And over and over he would prove to her that it was.

He pulled back and studied her face with concern. "Are you okay? I stopped by the shelter and Marcy said you had left early."

She smiled up at him. "Yes, I'm fine. I just wanted to be here when you got home. I thought that I would pamper you a little before we left for dinner."

A grin curved his lips and she could tell he liked the idea. "Pamper me?"

"Yes. Are you interested?"

Instead of answering, he swept her off her feet into his arms and carried her up the steps. *Yes,* she thought, *he was interested.*

She laughed, knowing once he got her inside the house he intended to show her just how interested he was.

* * * * *

Books by Olivia Gates

Harlequin Desire

Desert Knights

The Sheikh's Redemption
The Sheikh's Claim
The Sheikh's Destiny

Married by Royal Decree

Temporarily His Princess
Conveniently His Princess
Seducing His Princess

The Billionaires of Black Castle

From Enemy's Daughter to Expectant Bride
Scandalously Expecting His Child
Pregnant by the Sheikh
Claiming His Secret Son

Visit the Author Profile page
at Harlequin.com for more titles.

BILLIONAIRE, M.D.

Olivia Gates

To Natashya and Shane.
This one is definitely for you both.

Chapter 1

She opened her eyes to another world.

A world filled with grainy grayness, like a TV channel with no transmission. But she didn't care.

This world had an angel watching over her.

And not just any angel. An archangel. If archangels were the personification of beauty and power, were hewn out of living rock and bronze and unadulterated maleness.

His image floated in the jumble of light and shadow, making her wonder if this was a dream. Or a hallucination. Or worse.

Probably worse. In spite of the angel's presence. Or because of it. Angels didn't watch over anyone who wasn't in some serious trouble, did they?

Would be a shame if he turned out to be the angel of death. Why make him so breathtaking if he was just a life-force extractor? He was way overqualified. Such overkill was uncalled for, if you asked her. Or maybe his extreme attractiveness was designed to make his targets willing to go where he led?

She'd be more than willing. *If* she could move.

She couldn't. Gravity overwhelmed her, squashed her back onto something that suddenly felt like a bed of thorns. Every cell in her body started to squirm, every nerve firing impulses. But the cells had no connection to each other and the nerves were unable to muster one spark of voluntary movement. Distress bombarded her, noise rose in her ears, pounding, nauseating her….

His face came closer, stilled the vertigo, swept over the cacophony, stifling it.

Her turmoil subsided. She didn't have to fight the pull of gravity, didn't have to fear the paralysis.

He was here. And he'd take care of everything.

She had no idea how she knew that. But she knew it.

She knew *him*.

Not that she had any idea who he was.

But everything inside her told her that she was safe, that everything would be okay. Because he was here.

Now if only she could get any part of her to work.

She shouldn't feel so inert upon waking up. But was she waking up? Or was she dreaming? That would explain the detachment between brain and body. That would explain *him*. He was too much to be real.

But she knew he was real. She just knew she wasn't imaginative enough to have made him up.

She knew something else, too. This man was important. In general. And to her, he was more than important. Vital.

"Cybele?"

Was that his voice? That dark, fathomless caress?

It so suited the sheer magnificence of his face….

"Can you hear me?"

Boy, could she. She more than heard him. His voice spread across her skin, her pores soaking it up as if they were starved for nourishment. It permeated her with its richness, its every inflection sparking an inert nerve, restarting a vital process, reviving her.

"Cybele, if you can hear me, if you're awake this time, *por favor,* answer me."

Por favor? Spanish? Figured. So that's where the tinge of an accent came from—English intertwining with the sensuous music of the Latin tongue. She wanted to answer him. She wanted him to keep talking. Each syllable out of those works of art he had for lips, crooned in that intoxicating voice, was lulling her back to oblivion, this time a blissful one.

His face filled her field of vision. She could see every shard of gold among the emerald, moss and caramel that swirled into a luminous color she was certain she'd never seen except in his eyes.

She wanted to stab her fingers into the lushness of his raven mane, cup that leonine head, bring him even closer so she could pore over every strand's hue and radiance. She wanted to trace each groove and slash and plane that painted his face in complexity, wanted to touch each radiation of character.

This was a face mapped with anxiety and responsibility and distinction. She wanted to absorb the first, ease the second and marvel at the third. She wanted those lips against her own, mastering, filling her with the tongue that wrapped around those words and created such magic with them.

She knew she shouldn't be feeling anything like that now, that her body wasn't up to her desires. Her *body* knew that, but didn't acknowledge its incapacitation. It just needed him, close, all that maleness and bulk and power, all that tenderness and protection.

She craved this man. She'd always craved him.

"Cybele, *por Dios*, say something."

It was the raggedness, tearing at the power of his voice, that stirred her out of her hypnosis, forced her vocal cords to tauten, propelled air out of her lungs through them to produce the sound he demanded so anxiously.

"I c-can hear you…."

That came out an almost soundless rasp. From the way he tilted his ear toward her mouth, it was clear he wasn't sure whether she *had* produced sound or if he'd imagined it, whether it had been words or just a groan.

She tried again. "I'm a-awake… I think… I hope, a-and I h-hope you're r-real…."

She couldn't say anything more. Fire lanced in her throat, sealing it with a molten agony. She tried to cough up what felt like red-hot steel splinters before they burned through her larynx. Her sand-filled eyes gushed tears, ameliorating their burning dryness.

"Cybele!"

And he was all around her. He raised her, cradled her in the curve of a barricade of heat and support, seeping warmth into her frozen, quivering bones. She sank in his power, surrendered in relief as he cupped her head.

"Don't try to talk anymore. You were intubated for long hours during your surgery and your larynx must be sore."

Something cool touched her lips, then something

warm and spicily fragrant lapped at their parched seam. Not his lips or his tongue. A glass and a liquid. She instinctively parted her lips and the contents rushed in a gentle flow, filling her mouth.

When she didn't swallow, he angled her head more securely. "It's a brew of anise and sage. It will soothe your throat."

He'd anticipated her discomfort, had been ready with a remedy. But why was he explaining? She would swallow anything he gave her. If she could without feeling as if nails were being driven into her throat. But he wanted her to. She had to do what he wanted.

She squeezed her eyes against the pain, swallowed. The liquid slid through the rawness, its peppery tinge bringing more tears to her eyes. That lasted only seconds. The soreness subsided under the balmy taste and temperature.

She moaned with relief, feeling rejuvenated with every encouraging sweep of tenderness that his thumb brushed over her cheek as she finished the rest of the glass's contents.

"Better now?"

The solicitude in his voice, in his eyes, thundered through her. She shuddered under the impact of her gratitude, her need to hide inside him, dissolve in his care. She tried to answer him, but this time it was emotion that clogged her throat.

But she *had* to express her thankfulness.

His face was so close, clenched with concern, more magnificent in proximity, a study of perfection in slashes of strength and carvings of character. But haggardness had sunk redness into his eyes, iron into his jaw, and the unkemptness of a few days' growth of rough silk over that jaw and above those lips caused her heart to twist. The need to absorb his discomforts and worries as he had hers mushroomed inside her.

She turned her face, buried her lips into his hewn cheek. The bristle of his beard, the texture of his skin, the taste and scent of him tingled on her flesh, soaked into her senses. A gust of freshness and virility coursed through her, filled her lungs. His breath, rushing out on a ragged exhalation.

She opened her lips for more just as he jerked around to face her. It brought his lips brushing hers. And she knew.

This was the one thing she'd needed. This intimacy. With him.

Something she'd always had before and had missed? Something she'd had before and had lost? Something she'd never had and had long craved?

It didn't matter. She had it now.

She glided her lips against his, the flood of sensuality and sweetness of her flesh sweeping against his sizzling through her.

Then her lips were cold and bereft, the enclosure of muscle and maleness around her gone.

She slumped against what she now realized was a bed.

Where had he gone? Had it all been a hallucination? A side effect of emerging from a coma?

Her eyes teared up again with the loss. She turned her swimming head, searching for him, terrified she'd find only emptiness.

Far from emptiness, she registered her surroundings for the first time, the most luxurious and spacious hospital suite she'd ever seen. But if he wasn't there…

Her darting gaze and hurtling thoughts came to an abrupt halt.

He *was* there. Standing where he'd been when she'd first opened her eyes. But his image was distorted this time, turning him from an angel into a wrathful, inapproachable god who glowered down at her with disapproval.

She blinked once, then again, her heart shedding its sluggish rhythm for frantic pounding.

It was no use. His face remained cast in coldness. Instead of the angel she'd thought would do anything to protect her, this was the face of a man who'd stand aside and brood down at her as she drowned.

She stared up at him, something that felt as familiar as a second skin settling about her. Despondence.

It had been an illusion. Whatever she'd thought she'd seen on his face, whatever she'd felt flooding her in waves, had been her disorientation inventing what she wanted to see, to feel.

"It's clear you can move your head. Can you move everything else? Are you in any pain? Blink if it's too uncomfortable to talk. Once for yes, twice for no."

Tears surged into her eyes again. She blinked erratically. A low rumble unfurled from his depths. Must be frustration with her inability to follow such a simple direction.

But she couldn't help it. She now recognized his questions for what they were. Those asked of anyone whose consciousness had been compromised, as she was now certain hers had been. Ascertaining level of awareness, then sensory and motor functions, then pain level and site. But there was no personal worry behind the questions anymore, just clinical detachment.

She could barely breathe with missing his tenderness and anxiety for her well-being. Even if she'd imagined them.

"Cybele! Keep your eyes open, stay with me."

The urgency in his voice snapped through her, made her struggle to obey him. "I c-can't…."

He seemed to grow bigger, his hewn face etched with fierceness, frustration rippling off him. Then he exhaled. "Then just answer my questions, and I'll leave you to rest."

"I f-feel numb but…" She concentrated, sent signals to her toes. They wiggled. That meant everything in between them and her brain was in working order. "Seems…motor functions are…intact. Pain—not certain. I feel sore…like I've been flattened under a—a brick wall. B-but i-it's not pain indicating damage…"

Just as the last word was out, all aches seemed to seep from every inch of her body to coalesce in one area. Her left arm.

In seconds she shot beyond the threshold of containable pain into brain-shredding agony.

It spilled from her lips on a butchered keen. "M-my arm…"

She could swear he didn't move. But she found him beside her again, as if by magic, and cool relief splashed over the hot skewers of pain, putting them out.

She whimpered, realized what he'd done. She had an intravenous line in her right arm. He'd injected a drug—a narcotic analgesic from the instantaneous action—into the saline, flicked the drip to maximum.

"Are you still in pain?" She shook her head. He exhaled heavily. "That's good enough for now. I'll come back later…." He started to move away.

"No." Her good hand shot out without conscious volition, fueled by the dread that he'd disappear and she'd never see him again. This felt instinctive, engrained, the desperation that she could lose him. Or was it the resignation that he was already lost to her?

Her hand tightened around his, as if stronger contact would let her read his mind, reanimate hers, remind her what he'd been to her.

He relinquished her gaze, his incandescent one sweeping downward to where her hand was gripping his. "Your reflexes, motor power and coordination seem to be back to normal. All very good signs you're recovering better than my expectations."

From the way he said that, she guessed his expectations had ranged from pessimistic to dismal. "That… should be…a relief."

"Should be? You're not glad you're okay?"

"I am. I guess. Seems… I'm not…all there yet." The one thing that made her feel anything definite was him. And he could have been a mile away with the distance he'd placed between them. "So…what happened…to me?"

The hand beneath hers lurched. "You don't remember?"

"It's all a…a blank."

His own gaze went blank for an endless moment. Then it gradually focused on her face, until she felt it was penetrating her, like an X-ray that would let him scan her, decipher her condition.

"You're probably suffering from post-traumatic amnesia. It's common to forget the traumatic episode."

Spoken like a doctor. Everything he'd said and done so far had pointed to him being one.

Was that all he was to her? Her doctor? Was that how he knew her? He'd been her doctor before the "traumatic episode" and she'd had a crush on him? Or had he just read the vital statistics on her admission papers? Had she formed dependence on and fascination for him when she'd been drifting in and out of consciousness as he'd managed her condition? Had she kissed a man who was here only in his professional capacity? A man who could be in a relationship, maybe married with children?

The pain of her suppositions grew unbearable. And she just had to know. "Wh-who are you?"

The hand beneath hers went still. All of him seemed to become rock, as if her question had a Medusa effect.

When he finally spoke, his voice had dipped an octave lower, a bass, slowed-down rasp, "You don't know me?"

"Sh-should I?" She squeezed her eyes shut as soon as the words were out. She'd just kissed him. And she was telling him that she had no idea who he was. "I know I should…b-but I can't r-remember."

Another protracted moment. Then he muttered, "You've forgotten me?"

She gaped up at him, shook her head, as if the movement would slot some comprehension into her mind. "Uh… I may have forgotten…how to speak, too. I had this…distinct belief language skills…are the last to go… e-even in total…memory loss. I thought…saying I can't remember you…was the same as saying… I forgot who y-you are."

His gaze lengthened until she thought he wouldn't speak again. Ever. Then he let out a lung-deflating exhalation, raked his fingers through his gleaming wealth of hair. "I'm the one who's finding it hard to articulate.

Your language skills are in perfect condition. In fact, I've never heard you speak that much in one breath."

"M-many fractured…breaths…you mean."

He nodded, noting her difficulty, then shook his head, in wonder it seemed. "One word to one short sentence at a time was your norm."

"So you…*do* know me. E-extensively, it seems."

The wings of his thick eyebrows drew closer together. "I wouldn't label my knowledge of you extensive."

"I'd label it…en-encyclopedic."

Another interminable silence. Then another darkest-bass murmur poured from him, thrumming every neuron in her hypersensitive nervous system. "It seems your memory deficit is the only thing that's extensive here, Cybele."

She knew she should be alarmed at this verdict. She wasn't.

She sighed. "I love…the way…you say…my name."

And if she'd thought he'd frozen before, it was nothing compared to the stillness that snared him now. It was as if time and space had hit a pause button and caught him in their stasis field.

Then, in such a controlled move, as if he were afraid she was made of soap bubbles and she'd burst if he as much as rattled the air around her, he sat down beside her on her pristine white bed.

His weight dipped the mattress, rolling her slightly toward him. The side of her thigh touched his through the thickness of his denim pants, through her own layers of covering. Something slid through the mass of aches that constituted her body, originating from somewhere deep within her, uncoiling through her gut to pool into her loins.

She was barely functioning, and he could wrench that kind of response from her every depleted cell? What would he do to her if she were in top condition? What *had* he done? Because she was certain this response to him wasn't new.

"You really don't remember who I am at all."

"You really…are finding it hard…to get my words, aren't you?" Her lips tugged. She was sure there was no humor in this situation, that when it all sank in she'd be horrified about her memory loss and what it might signify of neurological damage.

But for now, she just found it so endearing that this man, who she didn't need memory to know was a powerhouse, was so shaken by the realization.

It also said he cared what happened to her, right? She could enjoy that belief now, even if it proved to be a delusion later.

She sighed again. "I thought it was clear…what I meant. At least it sounded…clear to me. But what would I know? When I called your…knowledge of me…encyclopedic, I should have added…compared to mine. I haven't only…forgotten who you are, I have no idea…who *I* am."

Chapter 2

Rodrigo adjusted the drip, looking anywhere but at Cybele.

Cybele. His forbidden fruit. His ultimate temptation.

The woman whose very existence had been like corrosive acid coursing through his arteries. The woman the memory of whom he would have given anything to wake up free of one day.

And it was she who'd woken up free of the memory of him.

It had been two days since she'd dropped this bomb on him.

He was still reverberating with the shock.

She'd told him she didn't remember the existence that was the bane of his. She'd forgotten the very identity that had been behind the destruction of one life. And the poisoning of his own.

And he shouldn't care. Shouldn't *have* cared. Not beyond the care he offered his other patients. By all testimonies, he went above and beyond the demands of duty and the dictates of compassion for each one. He shouldn't have neglected everyone and everything to remain by her side, to do everything for her when he could have delegated her care to the highly qualified professionals he'd painstakingly picked and trained, those he paid far more than money to keep doing the stellar job they did.

He hadn't. During the three interminable days after her surgery until she woke up, whenever he'd told himself to tend to his other duties, he couldn't. She'd been in danger, and it had been beyond him to leave her.

Her inert form, her closed eyes, had been what had ruled him. The drive to get her to move, to open her eyes and look at him with those endless inky skies that had been as inescapable as a black hole since they'd first had him in their focus, had been what motivated him.

Periodically she had opened them, but there had been no sight or comprehension in them, no trace of the woman who'd invaded and occupied his thoughts ever since he'd laid eyes on her.

Yet he'd prayed that, if she never came back, her body would keep on functioning, that she'd keep opening her eyes, even if it was just a mechanical movement with no sentience behind it.

Two days ago, she'd opened those eyes and the blankness had been replaced by the fog of confusion. His heart had nearly torn a hole in his ribs when coherence had dawned in her gaze. Then she'd looked at him and there had been more.

He should have known then that she was suffering

from something he hadn't factored in. Finding her distance and disdain replaced by warmth that had escalated to heat should have given him his first clue. Having her nuzzle him like a feline delighted at finding her owner, then that kiss that had rocked him to his foundations, should have clenched the diagnosis.

The Cybele Wilkinson he knew—his nemesis—would never have looked at or touched him that way if she were in her right mind. If she knew who he was.

It had still taken her saying that she wasn't and didn't to explain it all. And he'd thought *that* had explained it all.

But it was even worse. She didn't remember herself.

There was still something far worse. The temptation not to fill in the spaces that had consumed her memories, left her mind a blank slate. A slate that could be inscribed with anything that didn't mean they had to stay enemies.

But they had to. Now more than ever.

"I see you're still not talking to me."

Her voice, no longer raspy, but a smooth, rich, molten caress sweeping him from the inside out, forced him to turn his eyes to her against his will. "I've talked to you every time I came in."

"Yeah, two sentences every two hours for the past two days." She huffed something that bordered on amusement. "Feels like part of your medication regimen. Though the sparseness really contrasts with the intensiveness of your periodic checkups."

He could have relegated *those*, which hadn't needed to be so frequent, or so thorough, to nurses under his residents' supervision. But he hadn't let anyone come near her.

He turned his eyes away again, pretended to study her chart. "I've been giving you time to rest, for your throat to heal and for you to process the discovery of your amnesia."

She fidgeted, dragging his gaze back to her. "My throat has been perfectly fine since yesterday. It's a miracle what some soothing foods and drinks and talking to oneself can do. And I haven't given my amnesia any thought. I know I should be alarmed, but I'm not. Maybe it's a side effect of the trauma, and it will crash on me later as I get better. *Or...* I'm subconsciously relieved not to remember."

His voice sounded alien as he pushed an answer past the brutal temptation, the guilt, the rage, at her, at himself, at the whole damned universe. "Why wouldn't you want to remember?"

Her lips crooked. "If I knew, it wouldn't be a subconscious wish, would it? Am I still making sense only in my own ears?"

He tore his gaze away from her lips, focused on her eyes, cleared thorns from his throat. "No. I am not having an easy time processing the fact that you have total memory loss."

"And without memories, my imagination is having a field day thinking of outlandish explanations for why I'm not in a hurry to have my memories back. At least they seem outlandish. They might turn out to be the truth."

"And what are those theories?"

"That I was a notorious criminal or a spy, someone with a dark and dangerous past and who's in desperate need of a second chance, a clean slate. And now that it's been given to me, I'd rather not remember the past—my own identity most of all."

She struggled to sit up, groaning at the aches he knew her body had amassed. He tried to stop himself.

He failed. He lunged to help her, tried not to feel the supple heat of her flesh fill his hands as he pulled her up, adjusted her bed to a gentle slope. He struggled to ignore the gratitude filling her eyes, the softness of trust and willingness exhibited by every inch of her flesh. He roared inwardly at his senses as the feel and scent of her turned his insides to molten lava, his loins to rock. He gritted his teeth, made sure her intravenous line and the other leads monitoring her vital signs were secure.

Her hands joined his in checking her line and leads, an unconscious action born of engrained knowledge and ongoing application. He stepped away as if from a fiery pit.

She looked up at him, those royal blue eyes filling with a combo of confusion and hurt at his recoil. He took one more step back before he succumbed to the need to erase that crestfallen expression.

She lowered her eyes. "So—you're a doctor. A surgeon?"

He was, for once, grateful for her questions. "Neurosurgeon."

She raised her eyes again. "And from the medical terms filling my mind and the knowledge of what the machines here are and what the values they're displaying mean—I'm some kind of medical professional, too?"

"You were a senior trauma/reconstructive surgery resident."

"Hmm, that blows my criminal or spy theories out of the water. But maybe I was in another form of trouble before I ended up here? A ruinous malpractice suit? Some catastrophic mistake that killed someone? Was I about to have my medical license revoked?"

"I never suspected you had this fertile an imagination."

"Just trying to figure out why I'm almost relieved I don't remember a thing. Was I perhaps running away to start again where no one knows me? Came here and… hey, where *is* here?"

He almost kept expecting her to say *gotcha*. But the notion of Cybele playing a trick on him was more inconceivable than her total memory loss. "This is my private medical center. It's on the outskirts of Barcelona."

"We're in Spain?" Her eyes widened. His heart kicked. Even with her lids still swollen and her face bruised and pallid, she was the most beautiful thing he'd ever seen. "Okay, scratch that question. As far as my general knowledge can tell—and I feel it remains unaffected—there is no Barcelona anywhere else."

"Not that I know of, no."

"So—I sound American."

"You are American."

"And you're Spanish?"

"Maybe to the world, which considers all of Spain one community and everyone who hails from there as Spanish. But I am Catalan. And though in Catalonia we have the same king, and a constitution that declares 'the indissoluble unity of the Spanish nation,' we were the first to be recognized as a *Nacionalidad* and a *Comunidad Autónoma* or a distinct historical nationality and an autonomous community, along with the Basque Country and Galicia. There are now seventeen such communities that make up Spain, with our rights to self-government recognized by the constitution."

"Fascinating. Sort of a federation, like the United States."

"There are similarities, but it's a different system. The regional governments are responsible for education, health, social services, culture, urban and rural development and, in some places, policing. But contrary to the States, Spain is described as a decentralized country, with central government spending estimated at less than twenty percent." And he was damned if he knew why he was telling her all that, now of all times.

She chewed her lower lip that was once again the color of deep pink rose petals. His lips tingled with the memory of those lips, plucking at them, bathing them with intoxicating heat and moistness. "I knew some of that, but not as clearly as you've put it."

He exhaled his aggravation at the disintegration of his sense and self-control. "Pardon the lesson. My fascination with the differences between the two systems comes from having both citizenships."

"So you acquired the American citizenship?"

"Actually, I was born in the States, and acquired my Spanish citizenship after I earned my medical degree. Long story."

"But you have an accent."

He blinked his surprise at the implication of her words, something he'd never suspected. "I spent my first eight years in an exclusively Spanish-speaking community in the States and learned English only from then on. But I was under the impression I'd totally lost the accent."

"Oh, no, you haven't. And I hope you never lose it. It's *gorgeous*."

Everything inside him surged. This was something else he'd never considered. What she'd do to him if, instead of hostility, admiration and invitation spread on her face, invaded her body, if instead of bristling at the sight of him, she looked at him as if she'd like nothing more than to feast on him. As she was now.

What was going on here? How had memory loss changed her character and attitude so diametrically? Did that point to more neurological damage than he'd feared? Or was this what she was really like, what her reaction to him would have been if not for the events that had messed up their whole situation?

"So…what's your name? What's mine, too, apart from Cybele?"

"You're Cybele Wilkinson. I'm Rodrigo."

"Just… Rodrigo?"

She used to call him Dr. Valderrama, and in situations requiring informality she'd avoided calling him anything at all. But now she pressed back into her pillows, let his name melt on her tongue as if it were the darkest, richest chocolate. He felt her contented purr cascade down his body, caress his aching hardness….

This was unbelievable. That she could do this to him *now*. Or at all. It was worse than unbelievable. It was unacceptable.

He shredded his response. "Rodrigo Edmundo Arrellano i Bazán Valderrama i de Urquiza."

Her eyes widened a fraction more with each surname. Then a huff that bordered on a giggle escaped her. "I did ask."

His lips twisted. "That's an excerpt of my names, actually. I can rattle off over forty more surnames."

She giggled for real this time. "That's a family tree going back to the Spanish Inquisition."

"The Catalan, and the Spanish in general, take family trees very seriously. Because both maternal and paternal ancestors are mentioned, each name makes such a list. The Catalan also put *i* or *and* between surnames."

"And do I have more than the measly Wilkinson?"

"All I know is that your father's name was Cedric."

"Was? H-he's dead?"

"Since you were six or seven, I believe."

She seemed to have trouble swallowing again. He had to fist his hands against the need to rush to her side again.

His heart still hammered in protest against his restraint when she finally whispered, "Do I have a mother? A family?"

"Your mother remarried and you have four half siblings. Three brothers and one sister. They all live in New York City."

"D-do they know what happened to me?"

"I did inform them. Yesterday." He hadn't even thought of doing so until his head nurse had stressed the necessity of alerting her next of kin. For the seventh time. He hadn't even registered the six previous times she had mentioned it.

He waited for her next logical question. If they were on their way here to claim responsibility for her.

His gut tightened. Even with all he had against her, not the least of which was the reaction she wrenched from him, he hated to have to answer that question. To do so, he'd have to tell her that her family's response to her danger had been so offhand, he'd ended the phone call with her mother on a barked, "Don't bother explaining your situation to me, Mrs. Doherty. I'm sure you'd be of more use at your husband's business dinner than you would be at Cybele's bedside."

But her next question did not follow a logical progression. Just as this whole conversation, which she'd steered, hadn't. "So…what happened to me?"

And this was a question he wanted to avoid as fiercely.

No way to do that now that she'd asked so directly. He exhaled. "You were in a plane crash."

A gasp tore out of her. "I just knew I was in an accident, that I wasn't attacked or anything, but I thought it was an MVA or something. But…a plane crash?" She seemed to struggle with air that had gone thick, lodging in her lungs. He rocked on his heels with the effort not to rush to her with an oxygen mask and soothing hands. "Were there many injured o-or worse?"

Dios. She really remembered nothing. And he was the one who had to tell her. Everything. "It was a small plane. Seated four. There were only…two onboard this time."

"Me and the pilot? I might not remember anything, but I just know I can't fly a plane, small or otherwise."

This was getting worse and worse. He didn't want to answer her. He didn't want to relive the three days before she'd woken up, that had gouged their scars in his psyche and soul.

He could pretend he had a surgery, escape her interrogation.

He couldn't. Escape. Stop himself from answering her. "He was flying the plane, yes."

"Is—is he okay, too?"

Rodrigo gritted his teeth against the blast of pain that detonated behind his sternum. "He's dead."

"Oh, God…." Her tears brimmed again and he couldn't help himself anymore. He closed the distance he'd put between them, stilled the tremors of her hand with both of his. "D-did he die on impact?"

He debated telling her that he had. He could see survivor's guilt mushrooming in her eyes. What purpose did it serve to tell her the truth but make her more miserable?

But then he always told his patients the truth. Sooner or later that always proved the best course of action.

He inhaled. "He died on the table after a six-hour surgery."

During those hours, he'd wrestled with death, gaining an inch to lose two to its macabre pull, knowing that it would win the tug-of-war. But what had wrecked his sanity had been knowing that while he fought this losing battle, Cybele had been lying in his ER tended to by others.

Guilt had eaten through him. Triage had dictated he take care of her first, the one likely to survive. But he couldn't have let Mel go without a fight. It had been an impossible choice. Emotionally, professionally, morally. He'd gone mad thinking she'd die or suffer irreversible damage because he'd made the wrong one.

Then he'd lost the fight for Mel's life among colleagues' proclamations that it had been a miracle he'd even kept him alive for hours when everyone had given up on him at the accident scene.

He'd rushed to her, knowing that while he'd exercised the ultimate futility on Mel, her condition had worsened. Terror of losing her, too, had been the one thing giving him continued access to what everyone extolled as his vast medical knowledge and surgical expertise.

"Tell me, please. The details of his injuries."

He didn't want to tell her how terrible it had all been.

But he had to. He inhaled a stream of what felt like aerosolized acid, then told her.

Her tears flowed steadily over a face gone numb with horror throughout his chilling report.

She finally whispered, "How did the accident happen?"

He needed this conversation to be over. He gritted his teeth. "That is one thing only you can know for sure. And it'll probably be the last memory to return. The crash site and plane were analyzed for possible whys and hows. The plane shows no signs of malfunction and there were no distress transmissions prior to the crash."

"So the pilot just lost control of the plane?"

"It would appear so."

She digested this for a moment. "What about my injuries?"

"You should only concern yourself now with recuperating."

"But I need to know a history of my injuries, their progression and management, to chart my recuperation."

He grudgingly conceded her logic. "On site, you were unconscious. You had a severely bleeding scalp wound and bruising all over your body. But your severest injury was comminuted fractures of your left ulna and radius."

She winced as she looked down on her splinted arm. "What was my Glasgow Coma Scale scoring?"

"Eleven. Best eye response was three, with your eyes opening only in response to speech. Best verbal response was four, with your speech ranging from random words to confused responses. Best motor function was four with flexion withdrawal response to pain. By the time I operated on you, your GCS had plunged to five."

"Ouch. I was heading for decorticate coma. Did I have intracranial hemorrhage?"

He gave a difficult nod. "It must have been a slow leak. Your initial CTs and MRIs revealed nothing but slight brain edema, accounting for your depressed consciousness. But during the other surgery, I was informed of your deteriorating neurological status, and new tests showed a steadily accumulating subdural hematoma."

"You didn't shave my hair evacuating it."

"No need. I operated via a new minimally invasive technique I've developed."

She gaped at him. "You've developed a new surgical technique? Excuse me while my mind, tattered as it is, barrels in awe."

He grunted something dismissive. She eyed him with a wonder that seemed only to rise at his discomfort. Just as he almost growled *stop it*, she raised one beautifully dense and dark eyebrow at him. "I trust I wasn't the guinea pig for said technique?"

Cybele gazed up at Rodrigo, a smile hovering on her lips.

His own lips tightened. "You're fine, aren't you?"

"If you consider having to get my life story from you as *fine*."

The spectacular wings of his eyebrows snapped together. That wasn't annoyance or affront. That was mortification. Pain, even.

Words couldn't spill fast enough from her battered brain to her lips. "God, that was such a lame joke. Just shows I'm in no condition to know how or when to make one. I owe you my life."

"You owe me nothing. I was doing my job. And I didn't even do it well. I'm responsible for your current condition. It's my failure to manage you first that led to the deepening of the insult to your brai—"

"The pilot's worst injuries were neurological." She cut him short. It physically hurt to see the self-blame eating at him.

"Yes, but that had nothing to do with my decision—"

"And I bet you're the best neurosurgeon on the continent."

"I don't know about that, but being the most qualified one on hand didn't mea—"

"It *did* mean you had to take care of him yourself. And my initial condition misled you into believing my case wasn't urgent. You did the right thing. You fought for this man as he deserved to be fought for. And then you fought for me. And you saved me. And then, I'm certain my condition is temporary."

"We have no way of knowing that. Having total memory loss with the retention of all faculties of language and logic and knowledge and no problem in accumulating new memories is a very atypical form of amnesia. It might never resolve fully."

"Would that be a bad thing, in your opinion? If the idea of regaining my memories is almost...distressing, maybe my life was so bad, I'm better off not remembering it?"

He seemed at a loss for words. Then he finally found some. "I am not in a position to know the answer to that. But I am in a position to know that memory loss is a neurological deficit, and it's my calling to fix those. I can't under any circumstances wish that this wouldn't resolve. Now, if you'll excuse me, I need to tend to my other patients. I'll be back every three hours to check on you."

With a curt nod, he turned and left her, exiting the huge, opulent suite in strides loaded with tense grace.

She wanted to run after him, beg him to come back.

What could possibly explain all this turmoil and her severe attraction to him? Had they been lovers, married even, and they'd separated, or maybe divorced…?

She suddenly lurched as if from the blow of an ax as a memory lodged in her brain. No…a knowledge.

She *was* married.

And it was certainly not to Rodrigo.

Chapter 3

Rodrigo did come back in three hours. And stayed for three minutes. Long enough to check on her and adjust her medical management. Then he repeated that pattern for the next three days. She even felt him come in during her fitful sleep.

She hadn't had the chance to tell him what she'd remembered.

No. She hadn't *wanted* to tell him. Discovering she was married, even if she didn't know to whom, wasn't on her list of things to share with him of all people.

And he probably already knew.

She *could* have told him that she'd also remembered who she was. But then, she hadn't remembered much beyond the basics he'd told her.

This boded well for her memory deficit, if it was receding so early.

She didn't want it to recede, wanted to cling to the blankness with all her strength.

But it was no use. A few hours ago, a name had trickled into the parting darkness of her mind. Mel Braddock.

She was certain that was her husband's name. But she couldn't put a face to the name. The only memory she could attach to said name was a profession. General surgeon.

Beyond that, she remembered nothing of the marriage. She knew only that something dark pressed down on her every time the knowledge of it whispered in her mind.

She couldn't possibly feel this way if they'd been on good terms. And if he wasn't here, days after his wife had been involved in a serious accident, were they separated, getting divorced even? She was certain she was still married. Technically, at least. But the marriage was over. That would explain her overriding emotions for Rodrigo, that she innately knew it was okay to feel them.

On the strike of three hours, Rodrigo returned. And she'd progressed from not wanting to bring up any of it to wanting to scream it all at the top of her lungs.

He made no eye contact with her as he strode in flanked by two doctors and a nurse. He never came unescorted anymore. It was as if he didn't want to be alone with her again.

He checked her chart, informed his companions of his adjustment of her medications as if she wasn't in the room much less a medical professional who could understand everything they were saying. Frustration frothed inside her. Then it boiled over.

"I remembered a few things."

Rodrigo went still at her outburst. The other people in the room fidgeted, eyed her uncomfortably before turning uncertain gazes to their boss. Still without looking at her, he hung her chart back at the foot of the bed, murmured something clearly meant for the others' ears alone. They rushed out in a line.

The door had closed behind the last departing figure for over two minutes before he turned his eyes toward her.

She shuddered with the force of his elemental impact.

Oh, please. Let me have the right to feel this way about him.

The intensity of his being buzzed in her bones—of his focus, of his…wariness?

Was he anxious to know what she remembered? Worried about it? Because he suspected what it was—the husband she remembered only in name? He'd told her of her long-dead father, her existing family, but not about that husband. Would he have told her if she hadn't remembered?

But there was something more in his vibe. Something she'd felt before. After she'd kissed him. Disapproval? Antipathy?

Had they been on bad terms before the accident? How could they have been, if she felt this vast attraction to him, untainted by any negativity? Had the falling out been her fault? Was he bitter? Was he now taking care of her to honor his calling, his duty, giving her extra special care for old times' sake, yet unable to resume their intimacy? *Had* they been intimate? Was he her lover?

No. He wasn't.

She might not remember much about herself, but the thought of being in a relationship, no matter how unhealthy, and seeking involvement with another felt abhorrent to her, no matter how inexorable the temptation. And then, there was him. He radiated nobility. She just knew Rodrigo Valderrama would never poach on another man's grounds, never cross the lines of honor, no matter how much he wanted her or how dishonorable the other man was.

But there was one paramount proof that told her they'd never been intimate. Her body. It burned for him but knew it had never had him. It would have borne his mark on its every cell if it had.

So what did it all mean? He had to tell her, before something beside memories short-circuited inside her brain.

He finally spoke. "What did you remember?"

"Who I am. That I'm married." He showed no outward reaction. So he *had* known. "Why didn't you tell me?"

"You didn't ask."

"I asked about family."

"I thought you were asking about flesh-and-blood relatives."

"You're being evasive."

"Am I?" He held her gaze, making her feel he was giving her a psyche and soul scan. Maybe trying to steer her thoughts, too. "So you remember everything?"

She exhaled. "I said I remembered 'a few things.' Seems I'm a stickler for saying exactly what I mean."

"You said you remembered who you were, and your marriage. That's just about everything, isn't it?"

"Not when I remember only the basics about myself,

the name you told me, that I went to Harvard Medical School, that I worked at St. Giles Hospital and that I'm twenty-nine. I know far less than the basics about my marriage. I remembered only that I have a husband, and his name and profession."

"That's all?"

"The rest is speculation."

"What kind of speculation?"

"About the absence of both my family and husband more than a week after I've been involved in a major accident. I can only come up with very unfavorable explanations."

"What would those be?"

"That I'm a monster of such megaproportions that no one felt the need to rush to my bedside." Something flared in his eyes, that harshness. So she was right? He thought so, too? Her heart compressed as she waited for him to confirm or negate her suspicions. When he didn't, she dejectedly had to consider his silence as corroboration, condemnation. She still looked for a way out for herself, for her family. "Unless it is beyond them financially to make the trip here?"

"As far as I know, finances are no issue to your family."

"So you told them I was at death's door, and no one bothered to come."

"I told them no such thing. You weren't at death's door."

"It *could* have gone either way for a while."

Silence. Heavy. Oppressive. Then he simply said, "Yes."

"So I'm on the worst terms with them."

It seemed he'd let this go uncommented on, too. Then

he gave a noncommittal shrug. "I don't know about the worst terms. But it's my understanding you're not close."

"Not even with my mother?"

"Especially with your mother."

"Great. See? I was right when I thought I was better off not remembering. Not knowing."

"It isn't as bad as you're painting it. By the time I called your family, you were stable, and there really was nothing for any of them to do but wait like the rest of us. Your mother did call twice for updates, and I told her you were doing very well. Physically. Psychologically, I suggested it might not be a good thing in this early phase for you to be jogged by their presence or contact, any more than you already are."

He was making excuses for her family, her mother. If they'd cared, they wouldn't have been satisfied with long-distance assurances. Or maybe he had discouraged them from coming, so he wouldn't introduce an unpredictable emotional element into her neurological recovery?

The truth was, she didn't care right now how things really stood with her family. What she was barely able to breathe from needing to know was her status with her husband.

"And that's my not-so-bad situation with my family. But from my husband's pointed absence, I can only assume the worst. That maybe we're separated or getting divorced."

She wanted him to say, *Yes, you are.*

Please, say it.

His jaw muscles bunched, his gaze chilled. When he finally spoke it felt like an arctic wind blasting her, freezing her insides with this antipathy that kept spiking out of nowhere.

"Far from being separated, you and your husband have been planning a second honeymoon."

Cybele doubted the plane crashing into the ground had a harder impact than Rodrigo's revelation.

Her mind emptied. Her heart spilled all of its beats at once.

For a long, horrified moment she stared at him, speech skills and thought processes gone, only blind instincts left. They all screamed *run, hide, deny.*

She'd been so certain…so…certain…

"A second honeymoon?" She heard her voice croaking. "Does that mean we…we've been married long?"

He waited an eternity before answering. At least it felt that way. By the time he did, she felt she'd aged ten years. "You were married six months ago."

"Six *months?* And already planning a second honeymoon?"

"Maybe I should have said honeymoon, period. Circumstances stopped you from having one when you first got married."

"And yet my adoring husband isn't here. Our plans probably were an attempt to salvage a marriage that was malfunctioning beyond repair, and we shouldn't have bothered going through the motions…."

She stopped, drenched in mortification. She instinctively knew she wasn't one to spew vindictiveness like that. Her words had been acidic enough to eat through the gleaming marble floor.

Their corrosiveness had evidently splashed Rodrigo. From the way his face slammed shut, he clearly disapproved of her sentiments and the way she'd expressed them. Of her.

"I don't know much about your relationship. But his reason for not being at your bedside *is* uncontestable. He's dead."

She lurched as if he'd backhanded her.

"He was flying the plane," she choked.

"You remember?"

"No. Oh, God." A geyser of nausea shot from her depths. She pitched to the side of the bed. Somehow she found Rodrigo around her, holding her head and a pan. She retched emptily, shook like a bell that had been struck by a giant mallet.

And it wasn't from a blow of grief. It was from one of horror, at the anger and relief that were her instinctive reactions.

What kind of monster was she to feel like that about somebody's death, let alone that of her husband? Even if she'd fiercely wanted out of the relationship. Was it because of what she felt for Rodrigo? She'd wished her husband dead to be with him?

No. *No.* She just knew it hadn't been like that. It had to have been something else. Could her husband have been abusing her? Was she the kind of woman who would have suffered humiliation and damage, too terrified to block the blows or run away?

She consulted her nature, what transcended memory, what couldn't be lost or forgotten, what was inborn and unchangeable.

It said, no way. If that man had abused her, emotionally or physically, she would have carved his brains out with forceps and sued him into his next few reincarnations.

So what did this mess mean?

"Are you okay?"

She shuddered miserably. "If feeling mad when I should be sad is okay. There must be more wrong with me than I realized."

After the surprise her words induced, contemplation settled on his face. "Anger *is* a normal reaction in your situation."

"What?" He knew why it was okay to feel so mad at a dead man?

"It's a common reaction for bereaved people to feel anger at their loved ones who die and leave them behind. It's worse when someone dies in an accident that that someone had a hand in or caused. The first reaction after shock and disbelief is rage, and it's all initially directed toward the victim. That also explains your earlier attack of bitterness. Your subconscious must have known that he was the one flying the plane. It might have recorded all the reports that flew around you at the crash site."

"You're saying I speak Spanish?"

He frowned. "Not to my knowledge. But maybe you approximated enough medical terminology to realize the extent of his injuries…."

"Ya lo sé hablar español."

She didn't know which of them was more flabbergasted.

The Spanish words had flowed from a corner in her mind to her tongue without conscious volition. And she certainly knew what they meant. *I know how to speak Spanish.*

"I…had no idea you spoke Spanish."

"Neither did I, obviously. But I get the feeling that the knowledge is partial...fresh."

"Fresh? How so?"

"It's just a feeling, since I remember no facts. It's like I've only started learning it recently."

He fixed her with a gaze that seeped into her skin, mingled into the rapids of her blood. Her temperature inched higher.

Was he thinking what she was thinking? That she'd started learning Spanish because of him? To understand his mother tongue, understand *him* better, to get closer to him?

At last he said, "Whatever the case may be, you evidently know enough Spanish to validate my theory."

He was assigning her reactions a perfectly human and natural source. Wonder what he'd say if she set him straight?

She bet he'd think her a monster. And she wouldn't blame him. She was beginning to think it herself.

Next second she was no longer thinking it. She knew it.

The memory that perforated her brain like a bullet was a visual. An image that corkscrewed into her marrow. The image of Mel, the husband she remembered with nothing but anger, whose death aroused only a mixture of resentment and liberation.

In a wheelchair.

Other facts dominoed like collapsing pillars, crushing everything beneath their impact. Not memories, just knowledge.

Mel had been paralyzed from the waist down. In a car accident. *During* their relationship. She didn't know if it had been before or after they'd gotten married. She didn't think it mattered.

She'd been right when she'd hypothesized why no one had rushed to her bedside. She was heartless.

What else could explain harboring such harshness toward someone who'd been so afflicted? The man she'd promised to love in sickness and in health? The one she'd basically felt "good riddance" toward when death *did* them part?

In the next moment, the air was sucked out of her lungs from a bigger blow.

"Cybele? *¿Te duele?*"

Her ears reverberated with the concern in Rodrigo's voice, her vision rippled over the anxiety warping his face.

No. She wasn't okay.

She was a monster. She was amnesic.

And she was pregnant.

Chapter 4

Excruciating minutes of dry retching later, Cybele lay surrounded by Rodrigo, alternating between episodes of inertness and bone-rattling shudders.

He soothed her with the steady pressure of his containment, wiping her eyelids and lips in fragrant coolness, his stroking persistent, hypnotic. His stability finally earthed her misery.

He tilted the face she felt had swollen to twice its original size to his. "You remembered something else?"

"A few things," she hiccupped, struggled to sit up. The temptation to lie in his arms was overwhelming. The urge only submerged her under another breaker of guilt and confusion.

He helped her sit up, then severed all contact, no doubt not wanting to continue it a second beyond necessary.

Needing to put more distance between them, she swung her numb legs to the floor, slipped into the downy slippers that were among the dozens of things he'd supplied for her comfort, things that felt tailored to her size and needs and desires.

She wobbled with her IV drip pole to the panoramic window overlooking the most amazing verdant hills she'd ever seen. Yet she saw nothing but Rodrigo's face, seared into her retinas, along with the vague but nausea-inducing images of Mel in his wheelchair, his rugged good looks pinched and pale, his eyes accusing.

She swung around, almost keeled over. She gasped, saw Rodrigo's body bunch like a panther about to uncoil in a flying leap. He was across the room, but he'd catch her if she collapsed.

She wouldn't. Her skin was crackling where he'd touched her. She couldn't get enough of his touch but couldn't let him touch her again. She held out a detaining hand, steadied herself.

He still rose but kept his distance, his eyes catching the afternoon sun, which poured in ropes of warm gold through the wall-to-wall glass. Their amalgamated color glowed as he brooded across the space at her, his eyebrows lowered, his gaze immobilizing.

She hugged her tender left shoulder, her wretchedness thickening, hardening, settling into concrete deadness. "The things I just remembered… I wouldn't call them real memories. At least, not when I compare them to the memories I've been accumulating since I regained consciousness. I remember those in Technicolor, frame by frame, each accompanied by sounds and scents and sensations. But the things I just recalled came in colorless, soundless and shapeless, like skeletons of data and knowledge. Like headings without articles. If that makes any sense."

He lowered his eyes to his feet, before raising them again, the surgeon in him assessing. "It makes plenty of sense. I've dealt with a lot of post-traumatic amnesia cases, studied endless records, and no one described returning memories with more economy and efficiency than you just did. But it's still early. Those skeletal memories will be fleshed out eventually...."

"I don't want them fleshed out. I want them to stop coming, I want what came back to disappear." She squeezed her shoulder, inducing more pain, to counteract the skewer turning in her gut. "They'll keep exploding in my mind until they blow it apart."

"What did you remember this time?"

Her shoulders sagged. "That Mel was a paraplegic."

He didn't nod or blink or breathe. He just held her gaze. It was the most profound and austere acknowledgment.

And she moaned the rest, "And I'm pregnant."

He blinked, slowly, the motion steeped in significance. He knew. And it wasn't a happy knowledge. Why?

One explanation was that she'd been leaving Mel, but he'd become paralyzed and she'd discovered her pregnancy and it had shattered their plans. Was that the origin of the antipathy she had felt radiating from him from time to time? Was he angry at her for leading him on then telling him that she couldn't leave her husband now that he was disabled and she was expecting his child?

She wouldn't know unless he told her. It didn't seem he was volunteering any information.

She exhaled. "Judging from my concave abdomen, I'm in the first trimester."

"Yes." Then as if against his better judgment, he added, "You're three weeks pregnant."

"Three *weeks*...? How on earth do you know that? Even if you had a pregnancy test done among others before my surgery, you can't pinpoint the stage of my pregnancy that accurate—" Her words dissipated under another gust of realization. "I'm pregnant through IVF. That's how you know how far along I am."

"Actually, you had artificial insemination. Twenty days ago."

"Don't tell me. You know the exact hour I had it, too."

"It was performed at 1:00 p.m."

She gaped at him, finding nothing to explain that too-specific knowledge. And the whole scenario of her pregnancy.

If it had been unplanned and she'd discovered it after she'd decided to leave Mel, that would still make her a cold-blooded two-timer. But it hadn't been unplanned. Pregnancies didn't come more planned than *that*. Evidently, she'd *wanted* to have a baby with Mel. So much that she'd made one through a procedure, when he could no longer make one with her the normal way. The intimate way.

So their marriage *had* been healthy. Until then. Which gave credence to Rodrigo's claim that they'd been planning a honeymoon. Maybe to celebrate her pregnancy.

So how come her first reaction to his death was bitter relief, and to her pregnancy such searing dismay?

What kind of twisted psyche did she have?

There was only one way to know. Rodrigo. He kept filling in the nothingness that had consumed most of what seemed to have been a maze of a life. But he was doing so reluctantly, cautiously, probably being of the school that thought providing another person's memories would make reclaiming hers more difficult, or would taint or distort them as they returned.

She didn't care. Nothing could be more tainted or distorted than her own interpretations. Whatever he told her would provide context, put it all in a better light. Make her someone she could live with. She had to pressure him into telling her what he knew....

Her streaking thoughts shrieked to a halt.

She couldn't *believe* she hadn't wondered. About *how* he knew what he knew. She'd let his care sweep her up, found his knowledge of her an anchoring comfort she hadn't thought to question.

She blurted out the questions under pressure. "Just how do you know all this? How do you know me? And Mel?"

The answer detonated in her mind.

It was that look in his eyes. Barely curbed fierceness leashed behind the steel control of the surgeon and the suave refinement of the man. She remembered *that* look. *Really* remembered it. Not after she'd kissed him. Long before that. In that life she didn't remember.

In that life, Rodrigo had despised her.

And it hadn't been because she'd led him on, then wouldn't leave Mel. It was worse. Far worse.

He'd been Mel's best friend.

The implications of this knowledge were horrifying.

However things had been before, or worse, *after* Mel

had been disabled, if she'd exhibited her attraction to Rodrigo, then he had good reason to detest her. The best.

"You remembered."

She raised hesitant eyes at his rasp. "Sort of."

"Sort of? Now that's eloquent. More skeletal headlines?"

There was that barely contained fury again. She blinked back distress. "I remember that you were his closest friend, and that's how you know so much about us, down to the hour we had a procedure to conceive a baby. Sorry I can't do better." And she was damned if she'd ask him what the situation between *them* had been. She dreaded he'd verify her speculations. "I'm sure the rest will come back. In a flood or bit by bit. No need to hang around here waiting for either event. I want to be discharged."

He looked at her as if she'd sprouted two more sets of eyes. "Get back in bed, now, Cybele. Your lucidity is disintegrating with every moment on your feet, every word out of your mouth."

"Don't give me the patronizing medical tone, Dr. Valderrama. I'm a license-holding insider, if you remember."

"You mean if *you* remember, don't you?"

"I remember enough. I can recuperate outside this hospital."

"You can only under meticulous medical supervision."

"I can provide that for myself."

"You mean you don't 'remember' the age-proven adage that doctors make the worst patients?"

"It has nothing to do with remembering it, just not subscribing to it. I can take care of myself."

"No, you can't. But I will discharge you. Into my custody. I will take you to my estate to continue your recuperation."

His declaration took the remaining air from her lungs.

His custody. His estate. She almost swayed under the impact of the images that crowded her mind, of what both would be like, the temptation to jump into his arms and say *Yes, please.*

She had to say no. Get away from him. And fast. "Listen, I was in a terrible accident, but I got off pretty lightly. I would have died if you and your ultra-efficient medical machine hadn't intervened, but you did, and you fixed me. I'm fine."

"You're so far from fine, you could be in another galaxy."

It was just *wrong*. That he'd have a sense of humor, too. That it would surface now. And would pluck at her own humor strings.

She sighed at her untimely, inappropriate reaction. "Don't exaggerate. All I have wrong with me is a few missing memories."

"A few? Shall we make a list of what you do remember, those headlines with the vanished articles, and another of the volumes you've had erased and might never be able to retrieve, then revisit your definition of 'a few'?"

"Cute." And he was. In an unbearably virile and overruling way. "But at the rate I'm retrieving headlines, I'll soon have enough to fill said volumes."

"Even if you do, that isn't your only problem. You

had a severe concussion with brain edema and subdural hematoma. I operated on you for ten hours. Half of those were with orthopedic and vascular surgeons as we put your arm back together. Ramón said it was the most intricate open reduction and internal fixation of his career, while Bianca and I had a hell of a time repairing your blood vessels and nerves. Afterward, you were comatose for three days and woke up with a total memory deficit. Right now your neurological status is suspect, your arm is useless, you have bruises and contusions from head to toe and you're in your first trimester. Your body will need double the time and effort to heal during this most physiologically demanding time. It amazes me you're talking, and that much, moving at all and not lying in bed disoriented and sobbing for more painkillers."

"Thanks for the rundown of my condition, but seems I'm more amazing than you think. I'm pretty lucid and I can talk as endlessly as *you* evidently can. And the pain is nowhere as bad as before."

"You're pumped full of painkillers."

"No, I'm not. I stopped the drip."

"What?" He strode toward her in steps loaded with rising tension. He inspected her drip, scowled down on her. "When?"

"The moment you walked out after your last inspection."

"That means you have no more painkillers in your system."

"I don't need any. The pain in my arm is tolerable now. I think it was coming out of the anesthesia of unconsciousness that made it intolerable by comparison."

He shook his head. "I think we also need to examine your definition of 'pretty lucid.' You're not making sense to me. Why feel pain at all, when you can have it dealt with?"

"Some discomfort keeps me sharp, rebooting my system instead of lying in drug-induced comfort, which might mask some deterioration in progress. What about *that* doesn't make sense to you?"

He scowled. "I *was* wondering what kept you up and running."

"Now you know. *And* I vividly recall my medical training. I may be amnesic but I'm not reckless. I'll take every precaution, do things by the post-operative, post-trauma book…."

"I'm keeping you by my side until I'm satisfied that you're back to your old capable-of-taking-on-the-world self."

That silenced whatever argument she would have fired back.

She'd had the conviction that he didn't think much of her.

So he believed she was strong, but despised her because she'd come on stronger to him? Could she have done something so out-of-character? She abhorred infidelity, found no excuse for it. At least the woman who'd awakened from the coma did not.

Then he surprised her more. "I'm not talking about how you were when you were with Mel, but before that."

She didn't think to ask how he knew what she'd been like before Mel. She was busy dealing with the suspicion that he was right, that her relationship with Mel *had* derailed her.

More broad lines resurfaced. How she'd wanted to be nothing like her mother, who'd left a thriving career to serve the whims of Cybele's stepfather, how she'd thought she'd never marry, would have a child on her own when her career had become unshakable.

Though she didn't have a time line, she sensed that until months ago, she'd held the same convictions.

So how had she found herself married, at such a crucial time as her senior residency year, and pregnant, too? Had she loved Mel so much that she'd been so blinded? Had she had setbacks in her job in consequence, known things would keep going downhill and that was why she remembered him with all this resentment? Was that why she'd found an excuse to let her feelings for Rodrigo blossom?

Not that there could be an excuse for that.

But strangely, she wasn't sorry she was pregnant. In fact, that was what ameliorated this mess, the one thing she was looking forward to. That…and, to her mortification, being with Rodrigo.

Which was exactly why she couldn't accept his carte blanche proposal.

"Thank you for the kind offer, Rodrigo—"

He cut her off. "It's neither kind nor an offer. It's imperative and it's a decision."

Now *that* was a premium slice of unadulterated autocracy.

She sent up a fervent thank-you for the boost to her seconds-ago-nonexistent resistance. "Imperative or imperious? Decision or dictate?"

"Great language recall and usage. And take your pick."

"I think it's clear I already did. And whatever you choose to call your *offer*, I can't accept it."

"You mean you won't."

"Fine. If you insist on dissecting my refusal. I won't."

"It seems you *have* forgotten all about me, Cybele. If you remembered even the most basic things, you'd know that when I make a decision, saying no to me is not an option."

Cybele stared at him. Life was grossly, horribly unfair. How did one being end up endowed with all that?

And she'd thought he had it all before she'd seen him crook his lips in that I-click-my-fingers-and-all-sentient-beings-obey quasi smile.

Now there was one thought left in her mind. An urge. To get as far away from him as possible. Against all logic. And desire.

Her lips twisted, too. "I didn't get that memo. Or I 'forgot' I did. So *I* can say no to you. Consider it a one-off anomaly."

That tiger-like smirk deepened. "You can say what you want. I'm your surgeon and what *I* say goes."

The way he'd said *your surgeon*. Everything clamored inside her, wishing he was her anything-and-everything, for real.

She shook her head to disperse the idiotic yearnings. "I'll sign any waiver you need me to. I'm taking full responsibility."

"I'm the one taking full responsibility for you. If you do remember being a surgeon, you know that my being yours makes me second only to God in this situation. You have no say in God's will, do you?"

"You're taking the God complex too literally, aren't you?"

"My status in your case is an uncontestable fact. You're in my care and will remain there until I'm satisfied you no longer need it. The one choice I leave up to you is whether I follow you up in my home as my guest, or in my hospital as my patient."

Cybele looked away from his hypnotic gaze, his logic. But there was no escaping either. It *had* been desperation, wanting to get away from him. She *wasn't* in a condition to be without medical supervision. And who best to follow her up but her own surgeon? The surgeon who happened to be the best there was?

She knew he was. He was beyond the best. A genius. With billions and named-after-him revolutionary procedures and equipment to prove it.

But even had she been fit, she wouldn't have wanted to be discharged. For where could she go but home? A home she recalled with nothing but dreariness?

And she didn't want to be with anyone else. Certainly not with her mother and family. She remembered them as if they were someone else's unwanted acquaintances. Disappointing and distant. Their own actions reinforced that impression. The sum total of their concern over her accident and Mel's death had been a couple of phone calls. When told she was fine, didn't need anything, it seemed they'd considered it an excuse to stop worrying—if they *had* been worried—dismiss her and return to their real interests. She didn't remember specifics from her life with them, but this felt like the final straw in a string of lifelong letdowns.

She turned her face to him. He was watching her as if he'd been manipulating her thoughts, steering her toward the decision he wanted her to make. She wouldn't put mental powers beyond him. What was one more covert power among the glaringly obvious ones?

She nodded her capitulation.

He tilted his awesome head at her. "You concede

your need for my supervision?" He wanted a concession in words? Good luck with that. She nodded again. "And which will it be? Guest or patient?"

He wanted her to pick, now? She'd hoped to let things float for a couple of days, until she factored in the implications of being either, the best course of action….

Just great. A scrambled memory surely hadn't touched her self-deception ability. Seemed she had that in spades.

She knew what the best course of action was. She *should* say patient. Should stay in the hospital where the insanities he provoked in her would be curbed, where she wouldn't be able to act on them. She *would* say patient.

Then she opened her mouth. "As if you don't already know."

She barely held back a curse, almost took the sullen words back.

She didn't. She was mesmerized by his watchfulness, by seeing it evaporate in a flare of…something. Triumph?

She had no idea. It was exhausting enough trying to read her own thoughts and reactions. She wasn't up to fathoming his. She only hoped he'd say something superior and smirking. It might trip a fuse that would make her retreat from the abyss of stupidity and self-destructiveness, do what sense and survival were yelling for her to do. Remain here, remain a patient to him, nothing more.

"It'll be an honor to have you as my guest, Cybele." Distress brimmed as the intensity in his eyes drained, leaving them as gentle as his voice. It was almost spilling over when that arrogance she'd prayed for coated his face. "It's a good thing you didn't say 'patient,' though. I would have overruled you again."

She bristled. "Now look here—"

He smoothly cut across her offense. "I would have, because I built this center to be a teaching hospital, and if you stay, there is no way I can fairly stop the doctors and students from having constant access to you, to study your intriguing neurological condition."

Seemed not only did no one say no to him, no one ever won an argument with him, either. He'd given her the one reason that would send her rocketing out of this hospital like a cartoon character with a thick trail of white exhaust clouds in her wake.

No way would she be poked and prodded by med students and doctors-in-training. In the life that felt like a half-remembered documentary of someone else's, she'd been both, then the boss of a bunch of the latter. She knew how nothing—starting with patients' comfort, privacy, even basic human rights—stood in the way of acquiring their coveted-above-all experience.

She sighed. "You always get what you want, don't you?"

"No. Not always."

The tormented look that seized his face arrested her in midbreath. Was this about…her? Was *she* something he wanted and couldn't get?

No. She just knew what she felt for him had always been only on her side. On his, there'd been nothing inappropriate. He'd never given her reason to believe the feelings were mutual.

This…despondency was probably about failing to save Mel. That had to be the one thing he'd wanted most. And he hadn't gotten it.

She swallowed the ground glass that seemed to fill her throat. "I—I think I'll take a nap now."

He inhaled, nodded. "Yes, you do that."

He started to turn away, stopped, his eyes focusing far in the distance. He seemed to be thinking terrible things.

A heart-thudding moment later, without looking back again, he muttered, "Mel's funeral is this afternoon." She gasped. She'd somehow never thought of that part. He looked back at her then, face gripped with urgency, eyes storming with entreaty. "You should know."

She gave a difficult nod. "Thanks for telling me."

"Don't thank me. I'm not sure I should have."

"Why? You don't think I can handle it?"

"You seem to be handling everything so well, I'm wondering if this isn't the calm before the storm."

"You think I'll collapse into a jibbering mess somewhere down the road?"

"You've been through so much. I wouldn't be surprised."

"I can't predict the future. But I'm as stable as can be now. I—I want to go. I have to."

"You don't have to do anything, Cybele. Mel wouldn't have wanted you to go through the added trauma."

So Mel had cared for her? Wanted the best for her?

She inhaled, shook her head. "I'm coming. You're not going to play the not-neurologically-stable-enough card, are you?"

His eyes almost drilled a crater of conflicted emotions between her own. "You should be okay. If you do everything I say."

"And what is that?"

"Rest now. Attend the funeral in a wheelchair. And leave when I say. No arguments."

She hadn't the energy to do more than close her eyelids in consent. He hesitated, then walked back to her, took her elbow, guided her back to the bed. She sagged down on it.

He, too, dropped down, to his haunches. Heartbeats shook her frame as he took one numb foot after the other, slid off slippers that felt as if they were made of hot iron. He rose, touched her shoulder, didn't need to apply force. She collapsed like water in a fountain with its pressure lost. He scooped up her legs, swung them over the bed, swept the cotton cover over her, stood back and murmured, "Rest."

Without another look, he turned and crossed the room as if he'd been hit with a fast-forward button.

The moment the door clicked shut, shudders overtook her.

Rest? He really thought she could? After what he'd just done? Before she had to attend her dead husband's funeral?

She ached. For him, because of him, because she breathed, with guilt, with lack of guilt.

She could only hope that the funeral, the closure ritual, might open up the locked, pitch-black cells in her mind.

Maybe then she'd get answers. And absolution.

Chapter 5

She didn't rest.

Four hours of tossing in bed later, at the entry of a genial brunette bearing a black skirt suit and its accessories, Cybele staggered up feeling worse than when she'd woken from her coma.

She winced a smile of thanks at the woman and insisted she didn't need help dressing. Her fiberglass arm cast was quite light and she could move her shoulder and elbow joints well enough to get into the front-fastening jacket and blouse.

After the woman left, she stood staring at the clothes Rodrigo had provided for her. To attend the funeral of the husband she didn't remember. Didn't want to remember.

She didn't need help dressing. She needed help de-stressing.

No chance of that. Only thing to do was dress the part, walk in and out of this. Or rather, get wheeled in and out.

In minutes she was staring at her reflection in the full-wall mirror in the state-of-the-art, white and gray bathroom.

Black wool suit, white silk blouse, two-inch black leather shoes. All designer items. All made as if for her.

A knock on the door ripped her out of morbid musings over the origin of such accuracy in judging her size.

She wanted to dart to the door, snatch it open and yell, *Let's get it over with.*

She walked slowly instead, opened the door like an automaton. Rodrigo was there. With a wheelchair. She sat down without a word.

In silence, he wheeled her through his space-age center to a gigantic elevator that could accommodate ten gurneys and their attending personnel. This was obviously a place equipped and staffed to deal with mass casualty situations. She stared ahead as they reached the vast entrance, feeling every eye on her, the woman their collective boss was tending to personally.

Once outside the controlled climate of the center, she shivered as the late February coolness settled on her face and legs. He stopped before a gleaming black Mercedes 600, slipped the warmth of the cashmere coat she realized had been draped over his arm all along around her shoulders as he handed her into the back of the car.

In moments he'd slid in beside her on the cream leather couch, signaled the chauffeur and the sleek beast of a vehicle shot forward soundlessly, the racing-by vistas of the Spanish countryside the only proof that it was streaking through the nearly empty streets.

None of the beauty zooming by made it past the surface of her awareness. All deeper levels converged on him. On the turmoil in the rigidity of his profile, the coiled tension of his body.

And she couldn't bear it anymore. "I'm…so sorry."

He turned to her. "What are you talking about?"

The harshness that flickered in his eyes, around his lips made her hesitate. It didn't stop her. "I'm talking about Mel." His eyes seemed to lash out an emerald flare. She almost backed down, singed and silenced. She forged on. "About your loss." His jaw muscles convulsed then his face turned to rock, as if he'd sucked in all emotion, buried it where it would never resurface for anyone to see. "I don't remember him or our relationship, but you don't have that mercy. You've lost your best friend. He died on your table, as you struggled to save him…."

"As I *failed* to save him, you mean."

His hiss hit her like the swipe of a sword across the neck.

She nearly suffocated on his anguish. Only the need to drain it made her choke out, "You didn't fail. There was nothing you could have done." His eyes flared again, zapping her with the force of his frustration. "Don't bother contradicting me or looking for ways to shoulder a nonexistent blame. Everyone knew he was beyond help."

"And that's supposed to make me feel better? What if I don't want to feel better?"

"Unfounded guilt never did anyone any good. Certainly not the ones we feel guilty over."

"How logical you can be, when logic serves no purpose."

"I thought you advocated logic as what serves every purpose."

"Not in this instance. And what I feel certainly isn't hurting me any. I'm as fit as an ox."

"So you're dismissing emotional and psychological pain as irrelevant? I know that as surgeons we're mainly concerned with physical disorders, things we can fix with our scalpels, but—"

"But nothing. I'm whole and hearty. Mel is dead."

"Through no fault of yours!" She couldn't bear to see him bludgeoning himself with pain and guilt that way. "That's the only point I'm making, the only one to *be* made here. I know it doesn't make his loss any less traumatic or profound. And I am deeply sorry for—everyone. You, Mel, his parents, our baby."

"But not yourself?"

"No."

The brittle syllable hung between them, loaded with too much for mere words to express, and the better for it, she thought.

Twenty minutes of silence later her heart hiccupped in her chest. They were entering a private airport.

With every yard deeper into the lush, grassy expanses, tentacles of panic slid around her throat, slithered into her mind until the car came to a halt a few dozen feet from the stairs of a gleaming silver Boeing 737.

She blindly reached out to steady herself with the one thing that was unshakeable in her world. Rodrigo.

His arm came around her at the same moment she sought his support, memories billowing inside her head like the sooty smoke of an oil-spill fire. "This is where we boarded the plane."

He stared down at her for a suspended moment before closing his eyes. "*Dios, lo siento,* Cybele—I'm so sorry. I didn't factor in what it would do to you, being here, where your ordeal began."

She snatched air into her constricted lungs, shook her head. "It's probably the right thing to do, bringing me here. Maybe it'll get the rest of my memories to explode back at once. I'd welcome that over the periodic detonations."

"I can't take credit for attempting shock therapy. We're here for Mel's funeral." She gaped at him. He elaborated. "It's not a traditional funeral. I had Mel's parents flown over from the States so they can take his body home."

She struggled to take it all in. Mel's body. Here. In that hearse over there. His parents. She didn't remember them. At all. They must be in the Boeing. Which had to be Rodrigo's. They'd come down, and she'd see them. And instead of a stricken widow they could comfort and draw solace from, they'd find a numb stranger unable to share their grief.

"Rodrigo..." The plea to take her back now, that she'd been wrong, couldn't handle this, congealed in her throat.

He'd turned his head away. A man and a woman in their early sixties had appeared at the jet's open door.

He reached for his door handle, turned to her. "Stay here."

Mortification filled her. She was such a wimp. He'd felt her reluctance to face her in-laws, was sparing her.

She couldn't let him. She owed them better than that. She'd owe any grieving parents anything she could do to lessen their loss. "No, I'm coming with you. And no wheelchair, please. I don't want them to think I'm worse than I am." He pursed his lips, then nodded, exited the car. In seconds he was on her side, handing her out. She crushed his formal suit's lapel. "What are their names?"

His eyes widened, as if shocked all over again at the total gaps in her memory. "Agnes and Steven Braddock."

The names rang distant bells. She hadn't known them long, or well. She was sure of that.

The pair descended as she and Rodrigo headed on an intercept course. Their faces became clearer with every step, setting off more memories. Of how Mel had looked in detail. And in color.

Her father-in-law had the same rangy physique and wealth of hair, only it was gray where Mel's had been shades of bronze. Mel had had the startlingly turquoise eyes of her mother-in-law.

She stopped when they were a few steps way. Rodrigo didn't.

He kept going, opened his arms, and the man and woman rushed right into them. The three of them merged into an embrace that squeezed her heart dry of its last cell of blood.

Everything hurt. Burned. She felt like strips were being torn out of her flesh. Acid filled her eyes, burned her cheeks.

The way he held them, the way they sought his comfort and consolation as if it was their very next breath, the way they all clung together… The way he looked, wide open and giving everything inside him for the couple to take their fill of, to draw strength from…

Just when she would have cried out *Enough—please,*

the trio dissolved their merger of solace, turned, focused on her. Then Agnes closed the steps between them.

She tugged Cybele into a trembling hug, careful not to brush against her cast. "I can't tell you how worried we were for you. It's a prayer answered to see you so well." So well? She'd looked like a convincing post-mortem rehearsal last time she'd consulted a mirror. But then, compared to Mel, she was looking great. "It's why we were so late coming here. Rodrigo couldn't deal with this, with anything, until you were out of danger."

"He shouldn't have. I can't imagine how you felt, having to put th-this off."

Agnes shook her head, the sadness in her eyes deepening. "Mel was already beyond our reach, and coming sooner would have served no purpose. You were the one who needed Rodrigo's full attention so he could pull you through."

"He did. And while everyone says he's phenomenal with all his patients, I'm sure he's gone above and beyond even by his standards. I'm as sure it's because I was Mel's wife. It's clear what a close friend of the whole family he is."

The woman looked at her as if she'd said Rodrigo was in reality a reptile. "But Rodrigo isn't just a friend of the family. He's our son. He's Mel's brother."

Cybele felt she'd stared at Agnes for ages, feeling her words reverberating in her mind in shock waves.

Rodrigo. Wasn't Mel's best friend. Was his brother. *How?*

"You didn't know?" Agnes stopped, tutted to herself. "What am I asking. Rodrigo told us of your memory loss. You've forgotten."

She hadn't. She was positive. This was a brand-new revelation.

Questions heaved and pitched in her mind, splashed against the confines of her skull until she felt they'd shatter it.

Before she could relieve the pressure, launch the first few dozen, Rodrigo and Steven closed in on them. Rodrigo stood back as Steven mirrored his wife's actions and sentiments.

"We've kept Cybele on her feet long enough," Rodrigo addressed the couple who claimed to be his parents. "Why don't you go back to the car with her, Agnes, while Steven and I arrange everything."

Agnes? Steven? He didn't call them mother and father?

She would have asked to be involved if she wasn't burning for the chance to be alone with Agnes, to get to the bottom of this.

As soon as they settled into the car, Cybele turned to Agnes. And all the questions jammed in her mind.

What would she ask? How? This woman was here to claim her son's body. What would she think, feel, if said son's widow showed no interest in talking about him and was instead panting to know all about the man who'd turned out to be his brother?

She sat there, feeling at a deeper loss than she had since she'd woken up in this new life. Rodrigo's chauffeur offered them refreshments. She parroted what Agnes settled on, mechanically sipped her mint tea every time Agnes did hers.

Suddenly Agnes started to talk, the sorrow that coated her face mingling with other things. Love. Pride.

"Rodrigo was six, living in an exclusively Hispanic

community in Southern California, when his mother died in a factory accident and he was taken into the system. Two years later, when Mel was six, we decided that he needed a sibling, one we'd realized we'd never be able to give him."

So that was it. Rodrigo was adopted.

Agnes went on. "We took Mel with us while we searched, since our one criteria for the child we'd adopt was that he get along with Mel. But Mel antagonized every child we thought was suited to our situation, got them to turn nasty. Then Rodrigo was suggested to us. We were told he was everything Mel wasn't—responsible, resourceful, respectful, with a steady temperament and a brilliant mind. But we'd been told so many good things about other children and we'd given up hope that any child would pass the test of interaction with Mel. Then Rodrigo walked in.

"After he introduced himself in the little English he knew, enquired politely why we were looking for another child, he asked to be left alone with Mel. Unknown to both boys, we were taken to where children's meetings with prospective parents were monitored. Mel was at his nastiest, calling Rodrigo names, making fun of his accent, insulting his parentage and situation. We were mortified that he even knew those… words, and would use them so viciously. Steven thought he felt threatened by Rodrigo, as he had by any child we sought. I told him whatever the reason, I couldn't let Mel abuse the poor boy, that we'd been wrong and Mel didn't need a sibling but firmer treatment until he outgrew his sullenness and nastiness. He hushed me, asked me to watch. And I watched.

"Rodrigo had so far shown no reaction. By then,

other boys had lashed out, verbally and physically, at Mel's bullying. But Rodrigo sat there, watching him in what appeared to be deep contemplation. Then he stood up and calmly motioned him closer. Mel rained more abuse on him, but when he still didn't get the usual reaction, he seemed to be intrigued. I was certain Rodrigo would deck him and sneer *gotcha* or something. I bet Mel thought the same.

"We all held our breath as Rodrigo put a hand in his pocket. My mind streaked with worst-case scenarios. Steven surged up, too. But the director of the boys' home detained us. Then Rodrigo took out a butterfly. It was made of cardboard and elastic and metal springs and beautifully hand-painted. He wound it up and let it fly. And suddenly Mel was a child again, giggling and jumping after the butterfly as if it were real.

"We knew then that Rodrigo had won him over, that our search for a new son was over. I was shaking as we walked in to ask Rodrigo if he'd like to come live with us. He was stunned. He said no one wanted older children. We assured him that we did want him, but that he could try us out first. He insisted it was he who would prove himself to us. He turned and shook Mel's hand, told him he'd made other toys and promised to teach him how to make his own."

The images Agnes had weaved were overwhelming. The vision of Rodrigo as a child was painfully vivid. Self-possessed in the face of humiliation and adversity, stoic in a world where he had no one, determined as he proved himself worthy of respect.

"And did he teach him?" she asked.

Agnes sighed. "He tried. But Mel was short-fused, impatient, never staying with anything long enough for it to bear fruit. Rodrigo never stopped trying to involve him, get him to experience the pleasures of achievement. We loved him with all our hearts from the first day, but loved him more for how hard he tried."

"So your plan that a sibling would help Mel didn't work?"

"Oh, no, it did. Rodrigo did absorb a great deal of Mel's angst and instability. He became the older brother Mel emulated in everything. It was how Mel ended up in medicine."

"Then he must have grown out of his impatience. It takes a lot of perseverance to become a doctor."

"You really don't remember a thing about him, do you?" Now what did that mean? Before she pressed for an elaboration, Agnes sighed again. "Mel was brilliant, could do anything if only he set his mind to it. But only Rodrigo knew how to motivate him, to keep him in line. And when Rodrigo turned eighteen, he moved out."

"Why? Wasn't he happy with you?"

"He assured us that his need for independence had nothing to do with not loving us or not wanting to be with us. He confessed that he'd always felt the need to find his roots."

"And you feared he was only placating you?"

Agnes's soft features, which showed a once-great beauty lined by a life of emotional upheavals, spasmed with recalled anxiety. "We tried to help as he searched for his biological family, but his methods were far more effective, his instincts of where to look far sharper. He found his maternal relatives three years later and his grandparents were beside themselves with joy. Their whole extended family welcomed him with open arms."

Cybele couldn't think how anyone wouldn't. "Did he learn the identity of his father?"

"His grandparents didn't know. They had had a huge quarrel with his mother when she got pregnant and she wouldn't reveal the father's identity. She left home, saying she'd never return to their narrow-minded world. Once they had calmed down, they searched for her everywhere, kept hoping she'd come home. But they never heard from her again. They were devastated to learn their daughter was long dead, but ecstatic that Rodrigo had found them."

"And he changed his name from yours to theirs then?"

"He never took our name, just kept the name his mother had used. There were too many obstacles to our adopting him, and when he realized our struggles, he asked us to stop trying, said he knew we considered him our son and we didn't need to prove it to him. He was content to be our foster son to the world. He was eleven at the time. When he found his family, he still insisted *we* were his real family, since it was choice and love that bound us and not blood. He didn't legally take their names until he made sure we knew that it just suited his identity more to have his Catalan names."

"And you still thought he'd walk out of your life."

Agnes exhaled her agreement. "It was the worst day of my life when he told us that he was moving to Spain as soon as his medical training was over. I thought my worst fears of losing him had come true."

It struck Cybele as weird that Agnes didn't consider the day Mel had died the worst day of her life. But she was too intent on the story for the thought to take hold. "But you didn't lose him."

"I shouldn't have worried. Not with Rodrigo. I should have known he'd never abandon us, or even neglect us. He never stopped paying us the closest attention, was a constant presence in our lives—more so even than Mel, who lived under the same roof. Mel always had a problem expressing his emotions, and showed them with material, not moral, things. That's probably why he…he…" She stopped, looked away.

"He what?" Cybele tried not to sound rabid with curiosity. They were getting to some real explanation here. She knew it.

She almost shrieked with frustration when Agnes ignored her question, returned to her original topic. "Rodrigo continued to rise to greater successes but made sure we were there to share the joy of every step with him. Even when he moved here, he never let us or Mel feel that he was far away. He was constantly after us to move here, too, to start projects we've long dreamed of, offered us everything we'd need to establish them. But Mel said Spain was okay for vacations but he was a New Yorker and could never live anywhere else. Though it was a difficult decision, we decided to stay in the States with him. We thought he was the one who…needed our presence more. But we do spend chunks of every winter with Rodrigo, and he comes to the States as frequently as possible."

And she'd met him during those frequent trips. Over and over. She just knew it. But she was just as sure, no matter how spotty her memory was, that *this* story hadn't been volunteered by anyone before. She was certain she hadn't been told Rodrigo was Mel's foster brother. Not by Mel, not by Rodrigo.

Why had neither man owned up to this fact?

Agnes touched her good hand. "I'm so sorry, my dear. I shouldn't have gone on and on down memory lane."

And the weirdest thing was, Agnes's musings hadn't been about the son she'd lost, but the son she'd acquired thirty years ago. "I'm glad you did. I need to know anything that will help me remember."

"And did you? Remember anything?"

It wasn't a simple question to ascertain her neurological state. Agnes wanted to know something. Something to do with what she'd started to say about Mel then dropped, as if ashamed, as if too distressed to broach it.

"Sporadic things," Cybele said cautiously, wondering how to lead back to the thread of conversation she just knew would explain why she'd felt this way about Mel, and about Rodrigo.

Agnes turned away from her. "They're back."

Cybele jerked, followed Agnes's gaze, frustration backing up in her throat. Then she saw Rodrigo prowling in those powerful, control-laden strides and the sight of him drowned out everything else.

Suddenly a collage of images became superimposed over his. Of her and Mel going out with Rodrigo and a different sexpot each time, women who'd fawned over him and whom he'd treated with scathing disinterest, playing true to his reputation as a ruthless playboy.

Something else dislodged in her mind, felt as if an image had moved from the obscurity of her peripheral vision into the clarity of her focus. How Mel had become exasperating around Rodrigo.

If these were true memories, they contradicted everything Agnes had said, everything she'd sensed about Rodrigo. They showed him as the one who was erratic and inconstant, who'd had a disruptive, not a stabilizing, effect on Mel. Could she have overlooked all that, and her revulsion toward promiscuous men, under the spell of his charisma? Or could that have been his attraction? The challenge of his unavailability? The ambition of being the one to tame the big bad wolf? Could she have been that perverse and stupid…?

"Are you ready, Agnes?"

Cybele lurched at the sound of Rodrigo's fathomless baritone.

Stomach churning with the sickening conjectures, she dazedly watched him hand Agnes out of the car. Then he bent to her.

"Stay here." She opened her mouth. A gentle hand beneath her jaw closed it for her. "No arguments, remember?"

"I want to do what you're all going to do," she mumbled.

"You've had enough. I shouldn't have let you come at all."

"I'm fine. Please."

That fierceness welled in his eyes again. Then he gave a curt nod, helped her out of the car.

She didn't only want to be there for these people to whom she felt such a powerful connection. She also hoped she'd get more answers from Agnes before she and Steven flew back home.

Cybele watched Rodrigo stride with Steven to the hearse, where another four men waited. One was Ramón Velázquez, her orthopedic surgeon and Rodrigo's best friend—for real—and partner.

Rodrigo and Ramón shared a solemn nod then opened the hearse's back door and slid the coffin out.

Steven and the three other men joined in carrying it to the cargo bay of the Boeing.

Cybele stood transfixed beside Agnes, watching the grim procession, her eyes flitting between Rodrigo's face and Steven's. The same expression gripped both. It was the same one on Agnes's face. Something seemed… off about that expression.

Conjectures ping-ponged inside her head as everything seemed to fast-forward until the ritual was over, and Steven walked back with Rodrigo to join Agnes in hugging Cybele farewell. Then the Braddocks boarded the Boeing and Rodrigo led Cybele back to the Mercedes.

The car had just swung out of the airfield when she heard the roar of the jet's takeoff. She twisted around to watch it sail overhead before it hurtled away, its noise receding, its size diminishing.

And it came to her, why she knew that off expression. It was the exhausted resignation exhibited by families of patients who died after long, agonizing terminal illnesses. It didn't add up when Mel's death had been swift and shocking.

Something else became glaringly obvious. She turned to Rodrigo. He was looking outside his window.

She hated to intrude on the sanctity of his heartache. But she had to make sense of it all. "Rodrigo, I'm sorry, but—"

He rounded on her, his eyes simmering in the rays penetrating the mirrored window. "Don't say you're sorry again, Cybele."

"I'm sor—" She swallowed the apology he seemed unable to hear from her. "I was going to apologize for interrupting your thoughts. But I need to ask. *They* didn't ask. About my pregnancy."

He seemed taken aback. Then his face slammed shut. "Mel didn't tell them."

This was one answer she hadn't considered. Yet another twist. "Why? I can understand not telling them of our intention to have a baby this way, in case it didn't work. But after it did, why didn't he run to them with the news?"

His shrug was eloquent with his inability to guess Mel's motivations. With his intention to drop the subject.

She couldn't accommodate him. "Why didn't *you* tell them?"

"Because it's up to you whether or not to tell them."

"They're my baby's grandparents. Of course I want to tell them. If I'd realized they didn't know, I would have. It would have given them solace, knowing that a part of their son remains."

His jaw worked for a moment. Then he exhaled. "I'm glad you *didn't* bring it up. You're not in any shape to deal with the emotional fallout of a disclosure of this caliber. And instead of providing the solace you think it would have, at this stage, the news would have probably only aggravated their repressed grief."

But it *hadn't* been repressed grief she'd sensed from them.

Then again, what did she know? Her perceptions might be as scrambled as her memories. "You're probably right." *As usual,* she added inwardly. "I'll tell them when I'm back to normal and I'm certain the pregnancy is stable."

He lowered his eyes, his voice, and simply said, "Yes."

Feeling drained on all counts, she gazed up at him—the mystery that kept unraveling only to become more tangled. The anchor of this shifting, treacherous new existence of hers.

And she implored, "Can we go home now, please?"

Chapter 6

He took her home. His home.

They'd driven back from the airport to Barcelona city center. From there it had taken over an hour to reach his estate.

By the time they approached it at sunset, she felt saturated with the sheer beauty of the Catalan countryside.

Then they passed through the electronic, twenty-foot wrought iron gates, wound through the driveway, and with each yard deeper into his domain, she realized. There was no such thing as a limit to the capacity to appreciate beauty, to be stunned by it.

She turned her eyes to him. He'd been silent save for necessary words. She'd kept silent, too, struggling with the contradictions of what her heart told her and what her memories insisted on, with wanting to ask him to dispel her doubts.

But the more she remembered everything he'd said and done, everything everyone had said about him in the past days, the more only one conclusion made sense. Her memories had to be false.

He turned to her. After a long moment, he said, deep, quiet, "Welcome to Villa Candelaria, Cybele."

She swallowed past the emotions, yet her "Thank you" came out a tremulous gasp. She tried again. "When did you buy this place?"

"Actually, I built it. I named it after my mother."

The lump grew as images took shape and form. Of him as an orphan who'd never forgotten his mother until he one day was affluent enough to build such a place and name it after her, so her memory would continue somewhere outside of his mind and…

Okay, she'd start weeping any second now. Better steer this away from personal stuff. "This place looks… massive. Not just the building, but the land, too."

"It's thirty thousand square feet over twenty acres with a mile-long waterfront. Before you think I'm crazy to build all this for myself, I built it hoping it would become the home of many families, affording each privacy and land for whatever projects and pursuits they wished for. Not that it worked out that way."

The darkness that stained his face and voice seared her. He'd wished to surround himself with family. And he'd been thwarted at every turn, it seemed. Was he suffering from the loneliness and isolation she felt were such an integral part of her own psyche?

"I picked this land completely by chance. I was driving once, aimlessly, when I saw that crest of a hill overlooking this sea channel." She looked where he was pointing. "The vision slammed into my mind fully formed. A villa built into those rock formations as if it was a part of them."

She reversed the process, imagining those elements without the magnificent villa they now hugged as if it *were* an intrinsic part of their structure. "I always thought of the Mediterranean as all sandy beaches."

"Not this area of the northern Iberian coastline. Rugged rock is indigenous here."

The car drew to a smooth halt in front of thirty-foot wide stone steps among landscaped, terraced plateaus that surrounded the villa from all sides.

In seconds Rodrigo was handing her out and insisting she sit in the wheelchair she hadn't used much today. She acquiesced, wondered as he wheeled her up the gentle slope beside the steps if it had always been there, for older family members' convenience, or if it had been installed to accommodate Mel's condition.

Turning away from futile musings, she surrendered to the splendor all around her as they reached a gigantic patio that surrounded the villa. On one side it overlooked the magnificent property that was part vineyards and orchards and part landscaped gardens, with the valley and mountains in the distance, and on the other side, the breathtaking sea and shoreline.

The patio led to the highest area overlooking the sea, a massive terrace garden that was illuminated by golden lights planted everywhere like luminescent flowers.

He took her inside and she got rapid impressions of the interior as he swept her to the quarters he'd designated for her.

She felt everything had been chosen with an eye for uniqueness and comfort, simplicity and grandeur, blending sweeping lines and spaces with bold wall colors, honey-colored ceilings and furniture that complemented both. French doors and colonial pillars merged seamlessly with the natural beauty of hardwood floors accentuated by marble and granite. She knew she could spend weeks poring over every detail, but in its whole, she felt this was a place this formidable man had wanted his family to love, to feel at home in from the moment they set foot in it. She knew *she* did. And she hadn't technically set foot in it yet.

Then she did. He opened a door, wheeled her in then helped her out of the chair. She stood as he wheeled the chair to one side, walked out to haul in two huge suitcases that had evidently been transported right behind them.

He placed one on the floor and the other on a luggage stand at the far side of the room, which opened into a full-fledged dressing room.

She stood mesmerized as he walked back to her.

He was overwhelming. A few levels beyond that.

He stopped before her, took her hand. She felt as though it burst in flames. "I promise you a detailed tour of the place. Later. In stages. Now you have to rest. Doctor's orders."

With that he gave her hand a gentle press, turned and left.

The moment the door clicked closed behind him, she staggered to lean on it, exhaled a choppy breath.

Doctor's orders. *Her* doctor…

She bit her lip. Hours ago, she'd consigned her husband's body to his parents. And all she could think of was Rodrigo. There wasn't even a twinge of guilt toward Mel. There *was* sadness, but it was the sadness she knew she'd feel for any human being's disability and death. For his loved ones' mourning. Nothing more.

What was wrong with her? What had been wrong with her and Mel? Or was there more wrong with her mind than she believed?

Her lungs deflated on a dejected exhalation.

All she could do now was never let any of those who'd loved and lost Mel know how unaffected by his loss she was. What did it matter what she felt in the secrecy of her heart and mind if she never let the knowledge out to hurt others? She couldn't change the way she felt, should stop feeling bad about it. It served no purpose, did no one any good.

With that rationalization reached, she felt as if a ten-pound rock had been lifted off her heart. Air flowed into her lungs all of a sudden, just as the lovely surroundings registered in her appreciation centers.

The room—if a thirty-something- by forty-something-foot space with a twelve-foot ceiling could be called that—was a manifestation of the ultimate in personal space.

With walls painted sea-blue and green, furniture of dark mahogany and ivory ceilings and accents, it was soothingly lit by golden lamps of the side and standing variety. French doors were draped in gauzy powder-blue curtains that undulated in the twilight sea breeze, wafting scents of salt and freshness with each billow. She sighed away her draining tension and pushed from the wood-paneled door.

She crossed the gleaming hardwood floor to the suitcases. They were more evidence of Rodrigo's all-inclusive care. She was certain she'd never owned anything so exquisite. She wondered what he'd filled them with. If the outfit she had on was any indication, no doubt an array of haute couture and designer items, molding to her exact shape and appealing to her specific tastes.

She tried to move the one on the floor, just to set it on its wheels. Frantic pounding boomed in her head.

Man—what *had* he gotten her to wear? Steel armor in every shade? And he'd made the cases look weightless when he'd hauled them both in, simultaneously. She tugged again.

"*¡Parada!*"

She swung around at the booming order, the pounding in her head crashing down her spine to settle behind her ribs.

A robust, unmistakably Spanish woman in her late thirties was plowing her way across the room, alarm and displeasure furrowing the openness of her olive-skinned beauty.

"Rodrigo warned me that you'd give me a hard time."

Cybele blinked at the woman as she slapped her hand away from the suitcase's handle and hauled it onto the king-sized, draped-in-ivory-silk bed. She, too, made it look so light. Those Spaniards—uh, Catalans—must have something potent in their water.

The woman rounded on her, vitality and ire radiating from every line. Even her shoulder-length, glossy dark brown hair seemed pissed off. "He told me that you'd be a troublesome charge, and from the way you were trying to bust your surgery scar open, he was right. As he always is."

So it wasn't only she who thought he was always practically infallible. Her lips tugged as she tried to placate the force of nature before her. "I don't have a surgery scar to bust, thanks to Rodrigo's revolutionary minimally invasive approach."

"You have things in there—" the woman stabbed a finger in the air pointing at Cybele's head "—you can bust, no? What you busted before, necessitating such an approach."

From the throb of pain that was only now abating, she had to concede that. She'd probably raised her intracranial pressure tenfold trying to drag that behemoth of a bag. As she shrugged, she remembered Rodrigo telling her something.

She'd been too busy watching his lips wrap around each syllable to translate the words into an actual meaning. She now replayed them, made sense of them.

Rodrigo had said Consuelo, his cousin who lived here with her husband and three children and managed the place for him, would be with her shortly to see to her every need and to the correct and timely discharge of his instructions. She'd only nodded then, lost in his eyes. She now realized what he'd meant.

He didn't trust her to follow his instructions, was assigning a deputy to enforce their execution. And he certainly knew how to pick his wardens.

She stuck out her hand with a smile tugging at her lips. "You must be Consuelo. Rodrigo told me to expect you."

Consuelo took her hand, only to drag her forward and kiss her full on both cheeks.

Cybele didn't know what stunned her more, the affectionate salute, or Consuelo resuming her disapproval afterward.

Consuelo folded her arms over an ample bosom artfully contained and displayed by her floral dress with the lime background. "Seems Rodrigo didn't *really* tell you what to expect. So let *me* make it clear. I received you battered and bruised. I'm handing you back in tip-top shape. *I* won't put up with you not following Rodrigo's orders. I'm not soft and lenient like him."

"Soft and lenient?" Cybele squeaked her incredulity. Then she coughed it out on a laugh. "I wasn't aware there were two Rodrigos. I met the intractable and inexorable one."

Consuelo tutted. "If you think Rodrigo intractable and inexorable, wait till you've been around me twenty-four hours."

"Oh, the first twenty-four seconds were a sufficient demo."

Consuelo gave her an assessing look, shrewdness simmering in her dark chocolate eyes. "I know your type. A woman who wants to do everything for herself, says she can handle it when she can't, keeps going when she shouldn't, caring nothing about what it costs her, and it's all because she dreads being an imposition, because she hates accepting help even when she dearly needs it."

"Whoa. Spoken like an expert."

"*¡Maldita sea, es cierto!*—that's right. It takes one mule-headed, aggravatingly independent woman to know another."

Another laugh overpowered Cybele. "Busted."

"*Sí,* you are. And I'm reporting your reckless behavior to Rodrigo. He'll probably have you chained to my wrist by your good arm until he gives you a clean bill of health."

"Not that I wouldn't be honored to have you as my… keeper, but can I bribe you into keeping silent?"

"You can. And you know how."

"I don't try to lift rock-filled suitcases again?"

"And do everything I say. *When* I say it."

"Uh…on second thought, I'll take my chances with Rodrigo."

"Ha. Try another one. Now hop to it. Rodrigo told me what kind of day—what kind of *week* you've had. You're doing absolutely nothing but sleeping and resting for the next one. And eating. You look like you're about to vanish."

Cybele laughed as she whimsically peered down at her much lesser endowments. She could see how they were next to insubstantial by the super-lush Consuelo's standards.

This woman would be good for her. As she was sure Rodrigo had known she would be. Every word out of her mouth tickled funny bones Cybele hadn't known existed.

Consuelo hooked her arm through Cybele's good one, walked her to bed then headed alone to the en suite bathroom. She talked all the time while she ran a bubble bath, emptied the suitcases, sorted everything in the dressing room, and laid out what Cybele would wear to bed. Cybele loved listening to her husky, vibrant voice delivering perfect English dipped in the molasses of her all-out Catalan accent. By the time she led Cybele to the all-marble-and-gold-fixtures, salonlike bathroom, she'd told her her life story. At least, everything that had happened since she and her husband had become Rodrigo's house- and groundskeepers.

Cybele insisted she could take it from there. Consuelo insisted on leaving the door open. Cybele insisted she'd call out to prove she was still awake. Consuelo threatened to barge in after a minute's silence. Cybele countered she could sing to prove her wakefulness then everyone within hearing distance would suffer the consequences of Consuelo's overprotection.

Guffawing and belting out a string of amused Catalan, Consuelo finally exited the bathroom.

Grinning, Cybele undressed. The grin dissolved as she stared at herself in the mirror above the double sinks' marble platform.

She had a feeling there'd once been more of her. Had she lost weight? A lot of it? Recently? Because she'd been unhappy? If she had been, why had she planned a pregnancy and a second honeymoon with Mel? What did Rodrigo think of the way she looked? Not now, since she looked like crap, but before? Was she his type? Did he have a type? Did he have a woman now? More than one…?

Oh, God…she couldn't finish a thought without it settling back on him, could she?

She clamped down on the spasm that twisted through her at the idea, the images of him with a woman…any other woman.

How insane was it to be jealous, when up to eight days ago she'd been married to his brother?

She exhaled a shuddering breath and stepped into the warm, jasmine-and-lilac-scented water. She moaned as she submerged her whole body, felt as if every deep-seated ache surged to her surface, bled through her pores to mingle with the bubbles and fluid silk that enveloped her.

She raised her eyes, realized the widescreen window was right across from her, showcasing a masterpiece of heavenly proportions. Magnificent cloud formations in every gradation of silver morphing across a darkening royal blue sky and an incandescent half moon.

Rodrigo's face superimposed itself on the splendor, his voice over the lapping of water around her, the swishing of blood in her ears. She shut her eyes, tried to sever the spell.

"Enough."

Consuelo's yelled *"¿Qué?"* jerked Cybele's eyes open.

Mortification threatened to boil her bathwater.

God—she'd cried that out loud.

She called out the first thing that came to her, to explain away her outburst. "Uh… I said I'm coming out. I've had enough."

And she had. In so many ways. But there was one more thing that she prayed she would soon have enough of. Rodrigo.

Any bets she never would?

It was good to face her weakness. Without self-deception, she'd be careful to plan her actions and control her responses, accept and expect no more than the medical supervision she was here for during her stay. Until it came to an end.

As it inevitably would.

Rodrigo stood outside Cybele's quarters, all his senses converged on every sound, every movement transmitted from within.

He'd tried to walk away. He couldn't. He'd leaned on her door, feeling her through it, tried to contain the urge to walk back in, remain close, see and hear and feel for himself that she was alive and aware.

The days during which she'd lain inert had gouged a

fault line in his psyche. The past days since she'd come back, he hadn't been able to contemplate putting more than a few minutes' distance between them. It had been all he could do not to camp out in her room as he had during her coma. He had constantly curbed himself so he wouldn't suffocate her with worry, counted down every second of the three hours he'd imposed on himself between visits.

After he'd controlled the urge, he'd summoned Consuelo, had dragged himself away. Then he'd heard Consuelo's shout.

He hadn't barged into the room only because he'd frozen with horror for the seconds it took him to realize Consuelo had exclaimed *Stop,* and Consuelo's gregarious tones and Cybele's gentler, melodic ones had carried through the door, explaining the whole situation.

Now he heard Cybele's raised voice as she chattered with Consuelo from the bathroom. In a few minutes, Consuelo would make sure Cybele was tucked in bed and would walk out. He had to be gone before that. Just not yet.

He knew he was being obsessive, ridiculous, but he couldn't help it. The scare was too fresh, the trauma too deep.

He hadn't been there for Mel, and he'd died.

He had to be there for Cybele.

But to be there for her, he had to get ahold of himself. And to do that, he had to put today behind him.

It had felt like spiraling down through hell. Taking her to that airfield, realizing too late what he'd done, seeing his foster parents after months of barely speaking to them, only to give them the proof of his biggest failure. Mel's body.

The one thing mitigating this disaster was Cybele's memory loss. It *was* merciful. For her. For him, too. He didn't know if he could have handled her grief, too, had she remembered Mel.

But—was it better to have reprieve now, than to have it all come back with a vengeance later? Wouldn't it have been better if her grief coincided with his? Would he be able to bear it, to be of any help if she fell apart when he'd begun healing?

But then he had to factor in the changes in her.

The woman who'd woken up from the coma was not the Cybele Wilkinson he'd known the past year. Or the one Mel had said had become so volatile, she'd accused him of wanting her around only as the convenient help rolled into one with a medical supervisor—and who'd demanded a baby as proof that he valued her as his wife.

Rodrigo had at first found that impossible to believe. She'd never struck him as insecure or clingy. Just the opposite. But then her actions had proved Mel right.

So which persona was really her? The stable, guileless woman she'd been the past five days? The irritable introvert she'd been before Mel's accident? Or the neurotic wreck who'd made untenable emotional demands of him when he'd been wrecked himself?

And if this new persona was a by-product of the accident, of her injuries, once she healed, once she regained all her memories, would she revert? Would the woman who was bantering so naturally with Consuelo, who'd consoled him and wrestled verbally with him and made him forget everything but her, disappear?

He forced himself away from the door. Consuelo was asking what Cybele would like for breakfast. In a moment she'd walk out.

He strode away, speculations swarming inside his head.

He was staring at the haggard stranger in mourning clothes in his bathroom mirror when he realized something.

It made no difference. Whatever the answers were, no matter what she was, or what would happen from now on, it didn't matter.

She was in his life now. To stay.

Chapter 7

"You don't have post-traumatic amnesia."

Cybele's eyes rounded at Rodrigo's proclamation.

Her incredulity at his statement was only rivaled by the one she still couldn't get over; that he'd transferred a miniature hospital to his estate so he could test and chart her progress daily.

Apart from wards and ORs, he had about everything else on site. A whole imaging facility with X-ray, MRI, CT machines and even a PET scan machine, which seemed like overkill just to follow up her arm's and head's healing progress. A comprehensive lab for every known test to check up on her overall condition and that of her pregnancy. Then there were the dozen neurological tests he subjected her to daily, plus the physiotherapy sessions for her fingers.

They'd just ended such a session and were heading

out to the barbecue house at the seafront terrace garden to have lunch, after which he'd said they'd explore more of the estate.

He was walking beside her, his brows drawn together, his eyes plastered to the latest batch of results from another dozen tests. So what did he mean, she didn't have…?

Terrible suspicion mushroomed, clouding the perfection of the day.

Could he think she'd capitalized on a transient memory loss and had been stringing him along for the past four weeks? Or worse, that she'd never had memory loss, that she was cunning enough, with a convoluted enough agenda, to have faked it from the start?

And she blurted it out, "You think I'm pretending?"

"What?" He raised his eyes sluggishly, stared ahead into nothingness as if the meaning of her words was oozing through his mind, searching for comprehension. Then it hit him. Hard. His head jerked toward her, his frown spectacular. *"No."*

She waited for him to elaborate. He didn't, buried his head back into the tests.

So she prodded. "So what do you mean I don't have PTA? I woke up post-trauma with amnesia. Granted, it's not a classic case, but what else could it be?"

Instead of answering, he held the door of the terrace pergola open for her. She stepped out into the late March midday, barely stopped herself from moaning as the sweet saltiness of the sea breeze splashed her face, weaved insistent fingers through her hair.

He looked down at her as they walked, as if he hadn't heard her question. She shivered, not from the delicious coolness of the wind, but from the caress of his gaze, which followed the wind's every movement over her face and through her hair.

At least, that was how it felt to her. It was probably all in her mind, and he was lost in thought and not seeing her at all.

He suddenly turned his eyes again to the tests, validating her interpretation. "Let's review your condition, shall we? You started out having total retrograde amnesia, with all the memories formed before the accident lost. Then you started retrieving 'islands of memory,' when you recalled those 'skeletal' events. But you didn't suffer from any degree of anterograde amnesia, since you had no problems creating new memories after the injury. Taking all that into account, and that it has been over four weeks and the 'islands' have not coalesced into a uniform landmass…"

"As uniform as could be, you mean," she interrupted. "Even so-called healthy people don't remember everything in their lives—most things not in reliable detail and some things not at all."

"Granted. But PTA that lasts that long indicates severe brain injury, and it's clear from your clinical condition and all of your tests that you are not suffering from any cognitive, sensory, motor or coordination deficits. An isolated PTA of this magnitude is unheard of. That is why I'm leaning toward diagnosing you with a hybrid case of amnesia. The trauma might have triggered it, but the major part of your memory deficit is psychogenic, not organic."

She chewed her lip thoughtfully. "So we're back to what I said minutes after I regained consciousness. I *wanted* to forget."

"Yes. You diagnosed yourself fresh out of a coma."

"It wasn't really a diagnosis. I was trying to figure out why I had no other symptoms. When I didn't find an explanation, I thought either my medical knowledge had taken a hit, or that neurology was never my strong point in my parallel existence. I thought you would know that cases like mine exist. But they don't. Turns out I don't really have amnesia, I'm just hysterical."

His gaze whipped to hers, fierce, indignant. "Psychogenic amnesia is no less real than organic. It's a self-preservation mechanism. I also wouldn't label the psychogenic ingredient of your memory loss as hysterical, but rather functional or dissociative. In fact, I don't support the hysterical nomenclature and what it's come to be associated with—willful and weak-willed frenzy."

Hot sweetness unfurled inside her. He was defending her to herself. Pleasure surged to her lips, making them tingle. "So you think I have a repressed-memory type functional amnesia."

He nodded, ultraserious. "Yes. Here, take a look at this. This is your last MRI." She looked. "It's called functional imaging. After structural imaging revealed no physical changes in your brain, I looked at the function. You see this?" She did. "This abnormal brain activity in the limbic system led to your inability to recall stressful and traumatic events. The memories are stored in your long-term memory, but access to them has been impaired through a mixture of trauma and psychological defense mechanisms. The abnormal activity explains your partial memory recovery. But now that I'm certain there's nothing to worry about organically, I'm relaxed about when total recovery occurs."

"*If* it ever does." If he was right, and she couldn't think how he wasn't, she might be better off if it never did.

Psychogenic amnesia sufferers included soldiers and childhood abuse, rape, domestic violence, natural disaster and terrorist attack victims. Sufferers of severe enough psychological stress, internal conflict or intolerable life situations. And if her mind had latched on to the injury as a trigger to purge her memories of Mel and her life with him, she'd probably suffered all three.

But that still didn't explain her pregnancy or the honeymoon they were heading to when they'd had the accident.

Rodrigo stemmed the tide of confusion that always overcame her when she came up against those points.

"Anyway," he said. "While explanations have been proposed to explain psychogenic amnesia, none of them have been verified as the mechanism that fits all types. I prefer to set aside the Freudian, personal semantic belief systems and betrayal trauma theories to explain the condition. I lean toward the theory that explains the biochemical imbalance that triggers it."

"That's why you're a neurosurgeon and not a neurologist or psychiatrist. Where others are content to deal with insults to the psyche, you dig down to the building blocks of the nervous system, cell by cell, neurotransmitter by neurotransmitter."

"I admit, I like to track any sign or symptom, physical or psychological, back to its causative mechanism, to find the '*exactly* how' after others explain the 'why.'"

"And that's why you're a researcher and inventor."

He focused on her eyes for a second before he turned his own back to the tests, his skin's golden-bronze color deepening.

He was embarrassed!

She'd noticed on many occasions that, although he

was certain of his abilities, he wasn't full of himself and didn't expect or abide adulation, despite having every reason to feel superior and to demand and expect being treated as such.

But this—to actually blush at her admiration! Oh, Lord, but he was delicious, scrumptious. Edible. And adorable.

And he ignored her praise pointedly. "So—I favor the theory that postulates that normal autobiographical memory processing is blocked by altered release of stress hormones in the brain during chronic stress conditions. With the regions of expanded limbic system in the right hemisphere more vulnerable to stress and trauma, affecting the body's opioids, hormones and neurotransmitters, increased levels of glucocorticoid and mineralocorticoid receptor density affect the anterior temporal, orbitofrontal cortex, hippocampal and amygdalar regions."

She couldn't help it. Her lips spread so wide they hurt. "I bet you're having a ball talking to a doctor/patient. Imagine all the translation into layman's terms you'd have to do if you wanted to say *that* to someone who didn't get the lingo."

He blinked, surprise tingeing his incredible eyes. Then that incendiary smile of his flowed over his face, crooked his divine-work-of-art lips. "It has been a very freeing experience, spoiling even, not to keep looking for ways to explain what I'm doing or what's happening and fearing I won't be clear enough or that you'll misinterpret it no matter what I say and develop false expectations, positive or negative." He shook his head in self-deprecation, switching back to solemn in a blink. "But that was far too involved, anyway. My point is, you might have appeared or thought you were coping with your situation before the accident, but according to your current condition, you weren't."

She pursed her lips in an effort to stop herself from grinning uncontrollably and giving in to the urge to lunge at him, tickle him out of his seriousness. "So you're saying I was headed for psychogenic amnesia, anyway?"

"No, I'm saying the unimaginable stress of experiencing a plane crash, plus the temporary brain insult you suffered, disrupted the balance that would have kept your memory intact in the face of whatever psychological pressure you were suffering."

She raised an eyebrow, mock-indignant. "You're trying very hard to find neurologically feasible explanations backed by complex theories and medical expressions to dress up the fact that you've diagnosed me as a basket case, aren't you?"

"No! I certainly haven't. You're in no way..." He stopped abruptly when she couldn't hold back anymore, let the smile split her face. Incredulity spread over his face. "You're playing me!"

She burst out laughing. "Yep. For quite some time now. But you were so involved in your explanations, so careful not to give me any reason to feel silly or undeserving of concern or follow-up since my condition is 'only in my mind,' you didn't notice."

One formidable eyebrow rose, a calculating gleam entering his eyes, an unbearably sexy curl twisting his lips. "Hmm, seems I have underestimated the stage of your progress."

"Been telling you so for—"

"Quite some time now. Yes, I get it. But now that I'm

certain your brain is in fine working order, nuts-and-bolts-wise, being the guy who cares about nothing but the hardware, I think I can safely stop treating you like you're made of fresh paint."

A laugh cracked out of her at his metaphor. He kept surprising her. She'd be thinking he was this ultra-cerebral, all-work genius of a man, then out of the blue, he'd let this side of him show. The most witty and wickedly fun person she'd ever known. And she did know that for a fact. She remembered all of her life before Mel now.

She pretended to wipe imaginary sweat off her brow. "Phew, I thought I'd never get you to stop."

"Don't be so happy. Until minutes ago, I would have let you trampoline-jump all over me. Now I think you don't warrant the walking-on-eggshells preferential treatment anymore. You deserve some punishment for making fun of my efforts to appear all-knowing."

"Making fun of them, or debunking them?"

"Payback is getting steeper by the word."

She made a cartoonish face. "What can you do to a poor patient who has expanded limbic system issues and increased levels of glucocorticoid and mineralocorticoid receptor density messing with her anterior temporal, orbitofrontal cortex, hippocampal and amygdalar regions?"

"That's it. I'm exacting retribution."

"What will you do? Make me go to my room?"

"I'll make you eat what I cook. And that's for starters. I'll devise something heinous while phase one is underway."

"You mean *more* heinous than your cooking?"

He rumbled something from his gut, devilry igniting in his eyes. She giggled and rushed ahead, felt like she was flying there, borne on the giddy pleasure of his pursuing chuckles.

When she reached the steps, his voice boomed behind her, concern gripping its rich power. "Slow down."

She did, waited for him to catch up with her in those strides that ate up ten of her running steps in five.

She grinned up into his no-longer-carefree, admonishing eyes. "I thought I wasn't getting the fresh-paint treatment any longer."

"You've hereby moved to getting the uninsured, last-known-piece-of-Ming-dynasty-China treatment."

He slipped a steadying hand around her waist as they scaled the steps. She felt she'd be secure if the whole country fell into the sea. Or he'd clasp her to his body and take off into the sky.

She leashed her desire to press into him. "Aha! I should have known you'd default on your declaration of my independence."

He grinned down at her as they reached the barbecue house. "Tales of your independence *have* been wildly exaggerated."

She made a face, ducked under the shade of the canvas canopy.

He gave her a smug look as he seated her, then went to the kitchen area and began preparing her "punishment."

She watched his every graceful move as putting out cooking utensils and food items and chopping and slicing were turned into a precision performance like his surgeries. When he ducked inside to get more articles, she exhaled at the interruption of her viewing pleasure, swept her gaze to the sparkling azure-emerald waters of the magnificent, channellike part of the sea, the mile-long breathtaking sandy beach ensconced in a rocky hug.

The living, breathing tranquility imbued her. Most of the time she couldn't remember how she'd come to be here, or that she'd ever been anywhere else, that a world existed outside.

This place wasn't just a place. It was an...experience. A sense of completion, of arrival. A realm in time and space she'd never seen approximated, let alone replicated. An amalgam of nature's pristine grandeur and man's quest for the utmost in beauty and comfort. But all this would have been nothing without him.

It was being with him that made it embody heaven.

During the past weeks they'd made real fires, collected ripe fruits and vegetables, eaten their meals in the apartment-sized kitchen or in the cool barbecue house and held their after-dinner gatherings and entertainment in its lounge or in the huge pergola terrace.

She'd watched him play tennis on the floodlit court with the tireless Gustavo, swim endless laps in the half-Olympic-sized pool, drooled over his every move, longed to tear off her cast and shed her aches and throw herself into that pool after him....

"Ready for your punishment?"

She twinkled up at him. "Is it too heinous?"

He looked down at the salad bowls in his hands. "Atrocious."

"Gimme." She took her bowl, set it in front of her. And gaped. Then she crooked a challenging smile up at him. "It's colorful, I'll give you that. And...odorous." She tried not to wince as she picked up her fork. "*And* I didn't know these food items could go together."

He sat down across from her. "I didn't hear any objections as I tossed them into each other's company."

She chuckled. "I don't even know what said food items are."

His glance said her delaying tactics weren't working. "Eat."

She took a mouthful, trying not to inhale the stench, trying not to have what produced it hit her taste buds, to slide directly into her throat. Then it did hit, everywhere. And…wow.

She raised incredulous eyes to him. "You better get this patented. It's a-maaazing!"

He raised both eyebrows in disbelief. "You're just trying to prove nothing can gross you out, that I didn't and wouldn't succeed in punishing you, 'cause you can take anything."

"What am I, twelve?" She wolfed down another huge forkful.

He crooked his head to one side, considering. "So you like it."

"I love it," she exclaimed, mumbling around the food she'd stuffed into her mouth. "I *can* do without the smell, but it actually lessens as you eat, or your senses forgive it for being coupled with the delicious taste. At first I thought it was rotten fish."

"It *is* rotten fish."

She almost choked. "Now you're pulling my leg."

"Nope." The wattage of the wickedness in his eyes reached electrocuting levels. "But if you like it, does the label matter?"

She thought about that for a second, then said "Nah" and stuffed another forkful into her mouth.

He laughed as he began to eat his own serving. "It's

actually only *semi*-rotten. It's called *feseekh*—sun dried then salted gray mullet. It's considered an acquired taste—which you must be the quickest to ever acquire—and a delicacy around here. It came to Catalonia with the Berbers, and they brought it all the way from Egypt. But I bet I'm the first one to mix it with a dozen unnamed leafy greens and the wild berries Gustavo grows and collects and gives to me to consume, assuring me they're the secret to my never needing any of our esteemed colleagues' services."

"So you can give me rotten and unidentified food to consume, but you balk at my walking faster than a turtle."

"The rotten ingredient has proved through centuries of folk experience to have potent antibacterial and digestive-regulating properties. It and the rest of the unidentified food have been repeatedly tested on yours truly, and I'm living proof to their efficacy. I haven't been sick a day in the last twenty years."

Her eyes rounded in alarm. "Okay, jinx much?"

He threw his head back on a guffaw. "You're superstitious? You think I'll get deathly sick now that I've dared tempt fate?"

"Who knows? Maybe fate doesn't like braggarts."

"Actually, I think fate doesn't like gamblers." Something dark flitted across his face. Before she analyzed it, he lowered his gaze, hid it. "Since I'm anything but, I'm a good candidate for staying on its good side. For as long as possible. That brings us back to your hare tactics. Maybe you don't have loose components inside your brain to be shaken and stirred, but running like one, if you stumble, you have only one hand to ward off a fall, and you might injure it, too, or end up reinjuring your arm. And though your first trimester has been the smoothest I've ever heard about, probably as a compensation for what you're already dealing with, you *are* pregnant."

She *did* forget sometimes that she was. Not that she wanted to forget. When she did remember, it was with a burst of joy, imagining that she had a life growing inside her, that she'd have a baby to love and cherish, who'd be her flesh and blood, the family she'd never had. If there had been one thing to thank Mel for, it was that he'd somehow talked her into conceiving that baby. But because she had no symptoms whatsoever, sometimes it *did* slip her mind.

"Okay, no hare tactics." Her smile widened as she repeated his term for her jog. "But since I have no loose components, you must tell Consuelo to stop chasing me around as if I'll scatter them."

He turned his head to both sides, looked behind him. Then he turned back to her, palm over chest with an expression of mock horror. "You're talking to *me?*"

Her lips twitched. "You're the one who sicced her on me."

"A man can start a nuclear reaction, but he surely has no way of stopping it once it becomes self-perpetuating."

"You gotta call her off. She'll brush my teeth for me next!"

"You really expect me to come between her and her hurt chick? I may be lord of all I survey back at the center, but here I'm just another in the line that marches to Consuelo's tune."

"Yeah, I noticed." She chuckled, loving how he could be so alpha and capable and overriding and yet be totally comfortable letting another, and a woman, have the upper hand where she was best suited to take it. She cocked her head at him. "Families are very matriarchal here, aren't they?"

He tossed her a piece of breath-freshening gum then piled their bowls in one hand and raised the other, ring and middle fingers folded by his thumb, fore and little fingers pointing up. "Women rule."

She spluttered at the sight of him, so virile and formidable and poised, making that goofy expression and pop culture gesture.

He headed into the barbecue house and she melted back in her chair, replete and blissful. She'd never laughed like that before him. Before being here with him in his paradise of a home.

He'd only left her side to fly to work—literally, via helicopter—and had cut down on his working hours, to be there for her. She'd insisted he shouldn't, that she was perfectly all right on her own or with Consuelo, Gustavo and their children.

But she'd stopped objecting, certain he wasn't neglecting his work, had everything under control. And she couldn't get enough of being with him. Against all resolutions, she reveled in his pampering, wished with all she had in her that she could repay him in kind. But he had everything. Needed nothing. Nothing but to heal emotionally.

So she contented herself with being there for him, hoping to see him heal. And he was healing. His moroseness had dissipated and his distance had vanished, had become a closeness like she'd never known, as they discovered each other, shared so many things she'd never thought she'd share with another.

She kept waiting for him to do something to annoy her, to disappoint her, as all human beings inevitably did. But the impossible man just wouldn't. Then he went further into the realm of impossibility, kept doing things that shocked her by how much they appealed to her, delighted her.

He was everything his foster parents had said they'd picked him for and far more. Everything she admired in a human being and a man, and the most effective power for good she'd ever had the fortune to meet. And that was what he was to the world.

To her, he was all that resonated with her preferences and peculiarities. They agreed on most everything, and what they disagreed on, they discussed, came out conceding a respect for the other's viewpoint and thrilled to have gained a new awareness.

And when she added up everything he'd done for her, had been to her—her savior, protector and support—he was, yes, just incredible.

Which was why every now and then the question popped into her head—where had this man been before the accident?

From the tatters she remembered, besides his reported promiscuity, he'd treated Mel with fed-up annoyance and everyone else with abrasive impatience. His treatment of her had been the worst. He'd barely spoken to her, had watched her with something almost vicious in his eyes, as if he'd thought her beneath his friend—his brother.

And every time there was one answer. The conclusion she'd made the first day she'd come here. Her memories had to be faulty.

This, *he,* must be the truth. The magnificent truth.

"Ready to go back to your keeper?"

Everything became more beautiful with his return. She surrendered to his effortless strength, let him draw her to feet that barely touched the ground because he existed, was near.

She ended up ensconced in his protective embrace. His face clenched with the intensity she now adored, his freshness and potency filling her lungs. And it was as necessary as her next breath that she show him what he was to her.

She moved against his solid heat and power, raised her face to him, the invocation that filled her with life and hope and the will to heal, to be, trembling on her lips. "Rodrigo…"

Chapter 8

Cybele's whisper skewered through Rodrigo, wrenching at all the emotions and responses he'd been repressing.

From every point where her body touched his, torrents of what felt like molten metal zapped through his nerves, converging to roar through his spine, jamming into his iron-hard erection.

Nothing was left in his raging depths but the need to crush her to his aching flesh, claim her, assimilate her into his being.

And he couldn't.

But how could he not—and remain sane?

Not that he was sane anymore. He hadn't been since the first time he'd laid eyes on her. And with every moment in her company, he'd been surrendering any desire to cling to sanity.

He'd plunged into the wonder of experiencing her, discovering her, sharing with her everything from his daily routines and professional pressures to his deepest beliefs and slightest whims.

And she was far more than anything he'd ever dreamed of. She was the best thing that had ever happened to him.

But whenever he was away from her, he kept dredging up the past, the suspicions and antipathies that had at once poisoned his existence and fueled his resistance. He'd *wanted* to hate and despise her, to believe the worst of her then. Because she'd been the only woman he'd ever truly wanted—and she'd been forever off-limits.

She was no longer off-limits. Not on account of Mel, nor on that of his objections to her character.

He'd moved from condemning her for tormenting Mel with her volatility to suspecting that the instability had been created in Mel's twisted psyche. Now that he was no longer jumping on anything to paint her as black as possible, and had seen all the evidence to the contrary, it made sense that a man in Mel's condition could have interpreted her acts of love—which he couldn't reciprocate in any healthy fashion—as emotional pressure and blackmail.

Later on, after their relationship had deteriorated further under the harsh realities of Mel's disability, it stood to reason that the money Mel had asked Rodrigo for to buy her things hadn't been things she'd hinted that she'd wanted. Mel had said he'd understood her demands, that she deserved some compensation to cheer her up in their endlessly trying situation.

But it could have been Mel who'd tried to satisfy any material desire of hers to placate her, to express his love in the only way he'd ever known how, and then to keep her from walking out on him in a fit of despair. And when that, too, had failed, he'd been down to the last thing he could do to prove to her that he didn't consider her his live-in nurse—give her a baby.

Rodrigo now thought her memory loss was probably her mind's way of protecting itself from being pulverized by grief if she remembered Mel and the desperate, traumatic love she'd felt for him.

After he'd reached that conviction, he'd fluctuated between thinking she was being so wonderful to *him* because she subconsciously saw him as all she had left of Mel, to thinking she treated him as she did *because* she didn't remember loving Mel, and that when she did she'd become cold and distant again. He'd thought her coolness had been a reaction to his own barely leashed antipathy. But maybe she'd really disliked him, for reasons that were now gone with her memory. Or maybe the injury *had* caused some radical changes in her personality.

Too many maybes, too many questions the answers to which only she knew and no longer remembered. And it was driving him mad.

What if her dislike came back in full force, and this persona he adored vanished when her mind and psyche did heal completely?

The temptation to claim her now, bind her to him, negate the possibility, was too much.

He looked down in her eyes. They were fathomless with need. He could reach out and take her, and she'd be his. Ecstatically. She seemed to want him as much as he wanted her.

But did she? Or did she only think she did, because

of some need to reassert her own life after surviving the accident that had claimed Mel's? Was he merely convenient, close? Or was she responding to him out of gratitude?

Whatever the reason, he didn't believe she was responsible for her desires, or capable of making a decision with so much missing from her memory.

And then there was *his* side of the story.

He had no doubt he wouldn't be betraying Mel's memory. Mel was dead, and even while he'd lived, his relationship with Cybele had been anything but healthy or happy. If *he* could be the one to offer her that relationship, he would do anything for that chance.

But how could he live with himself if he betrayed *her* trust? And she did trust him. Implicitly. With her life. Was now showing him that she trusted him with her body, maybe her heart and future.

Yet how could he resist? Need was gnawing him hollow. And feeling her answering yearning was sending him out of his mind.

He had to plan a distraction, an intervention.

He stopped himself from cupping her face, running his fingers down her elegant nose, her sculpted cheekbones, teasing those dainty lips open, plunging his thumb inside their moistness and dampening their rose-petal softness, bending to taste her then absorbing her gasps, thrusting inside her….

He staggered away from temptation, rasped, "I have to get back to work."

She gasped at the loss of his support, bit her lip, nodded.

Coward. Work was a few hours' excuse to stay away.

He *had* to do whatever would keep him away from

her until she healed and came to him with her full, unclouded, unpressured choice.

He exerted what remained of his will. "And before I forget, I wanted to tell you that I'm inviting my family for a visit."

Cybele stared up at Rodrigo.

For a moment there, as he'd held her against him, she'd thought he felt what she did, wanted what she did. She'd thought he'd take her in his arms, and she'd never be homeless again.

But it had all been in her mind. He'd torn himself away, the fierceness and the bleakness that had evaporated during the past four weeks settling back over him. She'd read him all wrong.

But he'd read her all right. There was no way he hadn't seen her desire, understood her plea for him.

And he'd recoiled from her offer, from her need, as if they'd injured him, or worse, tainted him.

But though he was too kind to castigate her for testing the limits of their situation when he'd never encouraged her to, he'd still found a way to draw the line again and keep her behind it.

He was inviting his family over. Now that she'd been so stupid as to come on to him, to offer him what he hadn't asked for and didn't want, he was making sure she'd no longer have unsupervised access to him to repeat the mistake. He was inviting them as chaperones.

That had to be his reason for suddenly thinking of inviting them. Just yesterday, they'd been talking about their families and he hadn't brought up his intention. He'd even said it would be the first year that no one came to stay at his estate at all. And she'd gotten the distinct feeling he'd been...relieved about that fact. Probably because he'd had all the distractions he could afford in the form of Mel's death and her recuperation.

But her irresponsible behavior was forcing him to put up with even more distractions than she'd caused him, through his extensive family's presence, probably until he decreed she was well enough to be let back into the wild. Which could mean weeks, maybe months.

It felt like a wake-up slap. One she'd needed. Not only couldn't she let him swamp himself with family just to keep her at arm's length, she couldn't burden him with more responsibility toward her, this time over her emotions and desires—which in his terminal nobility he was probably taking full blame for inciting. She'd burdened him enough, when she had no right to burden him at all. She had to stop leaning on him, stop taking advantage of his kindness and support. And she had to do it now, before her emotions got any deeper.

Not that she thought they could. What she felt for him filled her, overflowed.

Only one bright side to this mess. Though she'd betrayed herself and imposed on him, she was now certain she hadn't done that when Mel had been in the picture. She'd repressed her feelings before, and they must have broken free after the accident.

All she could do now was fade from his life, let him continue it free from the liability of her. She had to pick up the pieces of her life, plan how to return to a demanding job with a baby on the way, without counting on the help of a mother she was now sure wouldn't come through for her as Cybele had remembered she'd promised.

Cybele didn't need her mother. She'd long ago

learned not to. And it wasn't Rodrigo's fault that she needed him emotionally. Any other kind of need had to end. Right now.

She had to leave immediately, so he wouldn't have to call his whole family to his rescue. She had to stop wasting his time, cutting into his focus and setting back his achievements.

The moment they reentered the house, she opened her mouth to say what she had to, but he talked over her.

"When I relocated here, it seemed to me that Catalans search for reasons to gather and celebrate. It was explained to me that because they've fought so fiercely to preserve their language and identity, they take extra pride in preparing and executing their celebrations. My family is thoroughly Catalan, and they're big on family unity and cultural traditions. And since I built this place over five years ago, it has replaced my grandparents' home as the place to gather. It would be a shame to interrupt the new tradition."

He was trying to make his sudden decision look as though it had nothing to do with her snuggling up against him like a cat in heat. She wanted to cry out for him to shut up and quit being so thoughtful. She had to say her piece and he was making it so much harder. Comparing those festivities and family gatherings with the barrenness of her own life was another knife that would twist in her heart once she was away from here.

She couldn't say anything. Her throat sealed over a molten pain that filled it as he escorted her like always to her quarters, continuing her education in Catalan traditions and his family's close-knit pursuits—all the things she'd never had and would never have. "Spring and summer are rife with *fiestas i carnaval*...that means—"

"Feasts and carnivals. I know," she mumbled. "But I—"

A smile invaded his eyes and lips again, cutting her off more effectively than if he'd shouted. "I sometimes forget how good your Spanish is, and I'm blown away by how colloquial your Catalan has become in this short period."

She nearly choked on the surge of emotion and pleasure his praise provoked, only for it to be followed by an even deeper dejection.

That deepened further when he swept his gaze ahead, animation draining from his voice, the newscaster-like delivery coming back. "The closest upcoming festival is *La Diada De Sant Jordi,* or St. George's Day, celebrating the patron saint of Catalonia, on the 23rd of April. There are many variations of the legend of St. George, but the Catalan version says there was a lake that was home to a dragon to which a maiden had to be sacrificed every day. One day, St. George killed the dragon and rescued that day's maiden. A red rose tree is supposed to have grown where the dragon's blood was spilled. Now on the day, the streets of Catalonia are filled with stands selling *rosas i libros*—roses and books. The rose is a symbol of love, while the book is a symbol of culture."

"I'm sure it would be a great time to be in Catalonia—"

He bulldozed over her attempt to interrupt him. "It certainly is. The celebrations are very lively and very participatory. Anyone walking down the streets anywhere in Catalonia is invited to join. Another similar celebration is Mother of God of Montserrat, on the 27th of April. In addition to these dates, each village and town has its own designated patron saint to pay homage to. Those celebrations are much like the larger celebrations, with parades of giants made of papier-mâché, fireworks, music from live bands and more. My family may stay until the 23rd of June, which is the shortest day of the year and coincides with the summer solstice celebration and the festival honoring St. John. Here in Catalonia, we light bonfires when the sun is at its most northern point. Catalans believe this wards off disease, bad luck and assorted other demons."

She tried again. "Sounds like a fun time ahead for you and your family—"

"And for you, too. You'll love the energy and sheer fun of this time of year."

"I'm sure I would. But I won't be here for all that, so maybe another time?"

She felt his eyes turn to her then, felt their gaze as if it were his powerful arms hauling her back to him.

"What are you talking about?"

She kept walking, struggled not to give in to the need to look at him and catch his uncensored reaction to her announcement before the barrier of his surgical composure descended, obscured it. Stupid. Still wishing she mattered beyond being a duty.

"Based on your latest tests and diagnosis of my condition, and since you obviously won't do it, I'm giving myself a clean bill of health. Time to return to my life and job."

"And how do you propose to do that?" He stopped her midway in the huge sunlit corridor leading to her quarters. "You're left-handed and can barely move your fingers. It's going to be weeks before you can do a lot of basic things for yourself, months before you can go back to work."

"Countless people with more severe and permanent disabilities are forced to fend for themselves, and they manage—"

"But you won't only be fending for yourself now. You're having a baby. And you're *not* forced to do anything—you don't have to manage on your own. I won't allow you to, and I sure as hell am not allowing you to leave. And this is the last time we have this conversation, Cybele Wilkinson."

Her heart flapped faster with each adamant word until it felt blurred like the wings of a hummingbird.

She tried to tell herself it was moronic to feel that way. That even if she had to concede that he was correct, she should listen to the voice telling her to be indignant at his overruling tactics, to rebel against his cornering her at every turn into doing what he thought was right for her. That voice also insisted there was nothing to be so giddy about, that he wasn't doing it out of concern for *her*, but for his patient.

She couldn't listen. And if another voice said she was criminally weak to be forgetting her minutes-ago resolution and clinging to whatever time she could get with him, she could only admit it. She wasn't strong enough to throw away one second she could have in his company, extensive family and all.

As for walking away for his peace of mind, she believed his acute feelings of duty wouldn't leave him any if he let her go before he judged she could handle being on her own. She also had to believe *he* could handle her being here, or he would have been relieved at her offer to leave. And since he wasn't, she shouldn't feel bad about staying. She'd offered to go, and he'd said no. Such an incredibly alpha, protective and overriding *no*.

Still, some imp inside her, which she was certain had come to life during this past month, wouldn't let her grab at his lifeline without contention. Or without trying to do what it could to erase the damage her blunder had caused to their newfound ease and rapport.

"Okay, it's clear you believe you're right—"

"I *am* right."

She went on as if he hadn't growled over her challenging opening "—but that doesn't automatically mean I agree. I came here as an alternative to staying in your center as a teaching pincushion. *But,* if I'd been there, you would have discharged me long ago. No one stays in hospital until their fractures heal."

His eyebrows descended a fraction more. "Do you enjoy futility, Cybele? We've established that when I make a decision—"

"—saying no to you isn't an option," she finished for him, a smile trembling on her lips, inviting him to smile back at her, light up the world again, tell her that he'd look past her foolish moment of weakness. "But that was a decision based on a clinical picture from a month ago. Now that I'm diagnosed as having no rattling components, I should be left to fend for myself."

She waited for him to smile back at her, decimate her argument, embroil her in another verbal tournament that neither of them wanted to win, just to prolong the match and the enjoyment.

He did neither. No smile. No decimation. He brooded down at her, seemed to be struggling with something. A decision.

Then he voiced it. "*Muy bien,* Cybele. You win. If you insist on leaving, go ahead. Leave."

Her heart plummeted down a never-ending spiral.

And he was turning around, walking away.

He'd taken no for an answer.

But he never did. He'd told her so. She'd believed him. That was why she'd said what she had.

He *couldn't* take no for an answer. That meant she'd lose him now, not later. And she couldn't lose him now. She wasn't ready to be without him for the rest of her life.

She wanted to scream that she took it all back. That she'd only been trying to do what she thought she should, assert an independence she still couldn't handle, to relieve him of the burden of her.

She didn't make a sound. She couldn't. Because her heart had splintered. Because she had no right to ask for more from him, of him. He'd given her far more than she'd thought anyone could ever give. He'd given her back her life. And it was time to give him back his, after she'd inadvertently hijacked it.

She turned away, feeling as though ice had skewered from her gut to her heart, only the freezing felt now, the pain and damage still unregistered.

Her numb hand was on her doorknob when she heard him say, "By the way, Cybele, good luck getting past Consuelo."

She staggered around. He was looking at her over his shoulder from the end of the corridor, the light from the just-below-the-ceiling windows pouring over him like a spotlight. He looked like that archangel she'd thought him before. His lips were crooked.

He was teasing her!

He didn't want her to leave, hadn't accepted that she could.

Before she could do something colossally stupid, like run and throw herself into his arms and sob her heart out, Consuelo, in a flaming red dress with a flaring skirt, swept by Rodrigo and down the corridor like a missile set on her coordinates.

She pounced on her. "You trying to undo all my work? *Seven* hours running around?" Consuelo turned and impaled Rodrigo with her displeasure. "And *you!* Letting your patient call the shots."

Rodrigo glared at her in mock-indignation before he gave Cybele a get-past-this wink. Then he turned and walked away, his bass chuckles resonating in the corridor, in her every cell.

Consuelo dragged her inside the room.

Feeling boneless with the reprieve, Cybele gave herself up to Consuelo's care, grinned as she lambasted her for her haggardness, ordered her on the scales and lamented her disappointing gains.

She'd missed out on having someone mother her. And for the time being, she'd enjoy Consuelo's mothering all she could. Along with Rodrigo's pampering and protection.

It would come to an end all too soon.

But not yet. *Not yet.*

Chapter 9

Rodrigo stood looking down at the approaching car procession.

His family was here.

He hadn't even thought of them since the accident. He hadn't for a while before that, either. He'd had nothing on his mind but Cybele and Mel and his turmoil over them both for over a year.

He'd remembered them only when he needed their presence to keep him away from Cybele. And he'd gotten what he deserved for neglecting them for so long. They'd all had other plans.

He'd ended up begging them to come. He'd evaded explaining the reason behind his desperation. They'd probably figure it out the moment they saw him with her.

In the end, he'd gotten them to come. And made them

promise to stay. Long. He'd always wished they'd stay as long as possible.

This time he wondered if he'd survive it.

And here began his torment.

His grandparents stepped out of the limo he'd sent them, followed by three of his aunts. Out of the vans poured the aunts' adult children and their families plus a few cousins and their offspring.

Cybele stepped out of the French doors. He gritted his teeth against the violence of his response. He'd been wrestling with it for the past three days since that confrontation. He'd still almost ended up storming her bedroom every night. Her efforts to offer him sexually neutral friendliness were inflaming him far worse than if she'd been coming on to him hot and heavy.

Now she walked toward him with those energetic steps of hers, rod-straight, no wiggle anywhere, dressed in dark blue jeans and a crisp azure blouse that covered her from throat to elbows.

The way his hormones thundered, she could have been undulating toward him in stilettos, a push-up bra and a thong.

Dios. The…containment he now lived in had better be obscuring his condition.

He needed help. He needed the invasion of his family to keep him away from her door, from carrying her off to his bed.

Before she could say anything, since anything she said blinded him with an urge to plunder those mind-destroying lips, he said, "Come, let me introduce you to my tribe."

Tribe is right, Cybele thought.

She fell in step with Rodrigo as she counted thirty-eight men, women and children. More still poured from the vans. Four generations of Valderramas.

It was amazing what one marriage could end up producing.

Rodrigo had told her that his mother had been Esteban and Imelda's first child, had been only nineteen when she had him, that his grandparents had been in their early twenties when they got married. With him at thirty-eight, his grandparents must be in their late seventies or early eighties. They looked like a very good sixty. Must be the clean living Rodrigo had told her about.

She focused on his grandfather. It was uncanny, his resemblance to Rodrigo. This was what Rodrigo would look like in forty-something years' time. And it was amazingly good.

Her heart clenched on the foolish but burning wish to be around Rodrigo through all that time, to know him at that age.

She now watched as he met his family three-quarters of the way, smile and arms wide. Another wish seared her—to be the one he received with such pleasure, the one he missed that much. She envied each of those who had the right to rush to fill his arms, to be blessed by the knowledge of his vast and unconditional love. Her heart broke against the hopelessness of it all as his family took turns being clasped to his heart.

Then he turned to her, covered in kids from age two to mid-teens, his smile blazing as he beckoned to her to come be included in the boisterous affection of his family reunion.

She rushed to answer his invitation and found herself being received by his family with the same enthusiasm.

For the next eight hours, she talked and laughed non-stop, ate and drank more than she had in the last three days put together, put a name and a detailed history to each of the unpretentious, vital beings who swept her along the wave of their rowdy interaction and infectious joie de vivre.

All along she felt Rodrigo watching her even as he paid attention to every member of his family, clearly on the best possible terms with them all. She managed not to miss one of his actions either, even as she kept up her side of the conversations. Her pleasure mounted at seeing him at such ease, surrounded by all these people who loved him as he deserved to be loved. She kept smiling at him, showing him how happy she was for him, yet trying her best not to let her longing show.

She was deep in conversation with Consuelo and two of Rodrigo's aunts, Felicidad and Benita, when he stood up, exited her field of vision. She barely stopped herself from swinging around to follow his movement. Then she felt him. At her back. His approach was like a wave of electromagnetism, sending every hair on her body standing on end, crackling along her nerves. She hoped she didn't look the way she felt, a woman in the grip of emotional and physical tumult.

His hands descended on her shoulders. Somehow she didn't lurch. "Who's letting her patient call the shots, now?"

She looked up, caught his eyebrow wiggle at Consuelo. The urge to drag him down and devour that teasing smile right off his luscious lips drilled a hole in her midsection.

The three vociferous women launched into a repartee match with him. He volleyed each of their taunts with a witticism that was more funny and inventive than the last, until they were all howling with laughter. She laughed, too, if not as heartily. She was busy having mini-heart attacks as one of his hands kept smoothing her hair and sweeping it off her shoulders absently.

By the time he bent and said, "Bed," she almost begged, *Yes, please.*

He pulled her to her feet as everyone bid her a cheerful good-night. She insisted he didn't need to escort her to her room, that he remain with his family. She didn't think she had the strength tonight not to make a fool of herself. Again.

On *La Diada De Sant Jordi*, St. George's Day, Rodrigo's family had been there for four weeks. After the first four weeks with him, they were the second-best days of her life.

For the first time, she realized what a family was like, what being an accepted member of such a largely harmonious one could mean.

And they had more than accepted her. They'd reached out and assimilated her into their passionate-for-life, close-knit collective. The older members treated her with the same indulgence as Rodrigo, the younger ones with excitement and curiosity, loving to have someone new and interesting enter their lives. She almost couldn't remember her life before she'd met these people, before they'd made her one of their own. She didn't want to remember any time when Rodrigo hadn't filled her heart.

And he, being the magnificent human being that he was, had felt the melancholy that blunted her joy, had once again asked if her problems with her own family couldn't be healed, if he could intervene, as a neutral mediator, to bring about a reconciliation.

After she'd controlled her impulse to drown him in tears and kisses, she'd told him there hadn't exactly been a rift, no single, overwhelming episode or grievance that could be resolved. It was a lifetime of estrangement.

But the good news was—and that might be a side effect of her injuries—she was at last past the hurt of growing up the unwanted child. She'd finally come to terms with it, could finally see her mother's side of things. Though Cybele had been only six when her father had died, she'd been the difficult child of a disappointment of a husband, a constant reminder of her mother's worst years and biggest mistake. A daddy's girl who'd cried for him for years and told her mother she'd wished she'd been the one who'd died.

She could also see her stepfather's side, a man who'd found himself saddled with a dead man's hostile child as a price for having the woman he wanted, but who couldn't extend his support to tolerance or interest. They were only human, she'd finally admitted to herself, not just the grown-ups who'd neglected her. And that made it possible for her to put the past behind her.

As more good news, her mother had contacted her again, and though what she'd offered Cybele was nowhere near the unreserved allegiance Rodrigo's family shared, she wanted to be on better terms.

The relationship would never be what she wished for, but she'd decided to do her share, meet her mother halfway, take what was on offer, what was possible with her family.

Rodrigo hadn't let the subject go until he'd pressed

and persisted and made sure she was really at peace with that.

She now stood looking down the beach where the children were flying kites and building sand castles. She pressed the sight between the pages of her mind, for when she was back to her monotone and animation-free life.

No. She'd never go back to that. Even when she exited Rodrigo's orbit, her baby would fill her life with—

"Do you have your book?"

She swung around to Imelda, her smile ready and wholehearted. She'd come to love the woman in that short time.

She admired Imelda's bottle-green outfit, which matched the eyes she'd passed on to Rodrigo, and was again struck by her beauty. She could barely imagine how Imelda might have looked in her prime.

Her eyes fell on the heavy volume in Imelda's hand. "What book?"

"*La Diada De Sant Jordi* is *rosas i libros* day."

"Oh, yes, Rodrigo told me."

"Men give women a red rose, and women give men a book."

Her heart skipped a beat. "Oh. I didn't know that."

"So now you know. Come on, *muchacha*, go pick a book. The men will be coming back any time now."

"Pick a book from where?"

"From Rodrigo's library, of course."

"I can't just take a book from his library."

"He'll be more than happy for you to. And then, it's what you choose that will have significance when you give it to him."

Okay. Why would Imelda suggest she give Rodrigo

a book? Had she realized how Cybele felt about him and was trying to matchmake? Rodrigo hadn't been the one to betray any special emotions. He'd been no more affectionate to her than he'd been to his cousins.

Better gloss over this. "So a woman picks any man she knows, and gives him a book?"

"She can. But usually she picks the most important man in her life."

Imelda knew what Rodrigo was to her. There was certainty in her shrewd eyes, along with a don't-bother-denying-it footnote.

Cybele couldn't corroborate her belief. It would be imposing on Rodrigo. He probably knew how she felt, but it was one thing to know, another to have it declared. And then, *he* wouldn't give her a rose. Even if he did, it would be because all the women had their husbands with them for the fiesta, or because she was alone, or any other reason. She wasn't the most important woman in his life.

But after she walked back into the house with Imelda and they parted ways, she found herself rushing to the library.

She came out with the book of her choice, feeling agonizingly exposed each time one of the women passed her and commented on her having a book like them.

Then the men came back from the next town, bearing copious amounts of prepared and mouthwatering food. And each man had a red rose for his woman. Rodrigo didn't have one.

Her heart thudded with a force that almost made her sick.

She had no right to be crushed by disappointment.

And no right to embarrass him. She'd give the book to Esteban.

Then she moved, and her feet took her to Rodrigo. Even if she had no claim on him, and there'd never be anything between them, he *was* the most important man in her life, and everyone knew it.

As she approached him, he watched her with that stillness and intensity that always made her almost howl with tension.

She stopped one step away, held out the book.

"Happy *La Diada De Sant Jordi*, Rodrigo."

He took the book, his eyes fixing on it, obscuring his reaction from her. She'd chosen a book about all the people who'd advanced modern medicine in the last century. He raised his eyes to her, clearly uncertain of the significance of her choice.

"Just a reminder," she whispered, "that in a collation of this century's medical giants, you'll be among them."

His eyes flared with such fierceness, it almost knocked her off her feet. Then he reached for her hand, pulled her to him. One hand clasped her back, the other traveled over her hair to cup her head. Then he enfolded her into him briefly, pressed a searing kiss on her forehead. "*Gracias mucho, querida.* It's enough for me to have your good opinion."

Next second, he let her go, turned to deliver a few festive words, starting the celebrations.

She didn't know how she functioned after that embrace. That kiss. Those words. That *querida.*

She evidently did function, even if she didn't remember anything she said or did during the next hours. Then Rodrigo was pulling her to her feet.

"Come. We're starting the Sardana, our national dance."

She flowed behind him, almost hovered as she smiled up at him, her heart jiggling at seeing him at his most carefree.

The band consisted of eleven players. They'd already taken their place at an improvised stage in the terrace garden that had been cleared for the dancers, evidently all of Rodrigo's family.

"I had the nearest town's *cobla*, our Catalan music ensemble, come over to play for us. The Sardana is never the same without live music. It's always made of four Catalan shawm players..." He pointed toward four men holding double-reed woodwinds. "Two trumpets, two horns, one trombone and a double bass."

"And what's with that guy with the flutelike instrument and the small drum attached to his left arm?"

"He plays the *flabiol*, that three-holed flute, with his left hand and plays that *tamborí* with the right. He keeps the rhythm."

"Why not just have twelve players, instead of saddling one with this convoluted setup?"

He grinned. "It's a tradition some say goes back two thousand years. But wait till you see him play. He'll make it look like the easiest thing in the world."

She grimaced down at her casted arm. "One thing's for sure, I'm not a candidate for a *flabiol/tamborí* player right now."

He put a finger below her chin, raised her face to him. "You soon will be." Before she gave in and dragged his head down to her to take that kiss she was disintegrating for, he turned his head away. "Now watch closely.

They're going to dance the first *tirada,* and we'll join in the second one. The steps are very simple."

Letting out a steaming exhalation, she forced her attention to the circle of dancers that was forming.

"It's usually one man, one woman and so on, but we have more women than men here, so excuse the nontraditional configuration."

She mimicked his earlier hand gesture, drawled, "Women rule."

He threw his head back on a peal of laughter at her reminder, kept chuckling as he watched his womenfolk herding and organizing their men and children. "They do indeed."

The dance began, heated, then Rodrigo tugged her to join the *rotllanes obertes,* the open circles. They danced the steps he'd rehearsed with her on the sidelines, laughed together until their sides hurt. Everything was like a dream. A dream where she felt more alert and alive than she ever had. A dream where she was one with Rodrigo, a part of him, and in tune with the music, his family and the whole world.

Then, like every dream, the festivities drew to an end.

After calling good-night to everyone, Rodrigo walked her as usual to her quarters, left her a few steps from her door.

Two steps into the room, she froze. Her mouth fell open. Her breath left her lungs under pressure, wouldn't be retrieved.

All around. On every surface. *Everywhere.*

Red roses.

Bunches and bunches and *bunches* of perfect, bloodred roses.

Oh. God. Oh… *God…*

She darted back outside, called out to him. But he'd gone.

She stood there vibrating with the need to rush after him, find him wherever he was and smother him in kisses.

But…since he hadn't waited around for her reaction, maybe he hadn't anticipated it would be this fierce. Maybe he'd only meant to give her a nice surprise. Maybe he'd had every other woman's room filled with flowers, too. Which she wouldn't put past him. She'd never known anyone with his capacity for giving.

She staggered back into her room. The explosion of beauty and color and fragrance yanked her into its embrace again.

The need expanded, compressing her heart, her lungs.

It was no use. She had to do it. She had to go to him.

She grabbed a jacket, streaked outside.

His scent, his vibe led her to the roof.

He was standing at the waist-high stone balustrade overlooking a turbulent, after-midnight sea, a lone knight silvered by the moon, carved from the night.

She stopped a dozen steps away. He didn't turn, stood like a statue of a Titan, the only animate things his satin mane rioting around his leonine head and his clothes rustling around his steel-fleshed frame. There was no way he could have heard the staccato of her feet or the labor of her breathing over the wind's buffeting whistles. But she knew he felt her there. He was waiting for her to initiate this.

"Rodrigo." Her gasp trembled against the wind's dissipation. He turned then. Cool rays deposited glimmers in the emerald of his eyes, luster on the golden bronze of his ruggedness. She stepped closer, mesmerized by his magnificence. A step away, she reached for his hand. She wanted to take it to her lips. That hand that had saved her life, that changed the lives of countless others daily, giving them back their limbs and mobility and freeing them from pain and disability. She settled for squeezing it between both of her trembling ones. "Besides everything you've done for me, your roses are the best gift I've ever been given."

His stare roiled with his discomfort at receiving gratitude. Then he simply said, "Your book beats my roses any day."

A smile ached on her lips. "You have issues with hearing thanks, don't you?"

"Thanks are overrated."

"Nothing sincere can be rated highly enough."

"I do what I want to do, what pleases me. And I certainly never do anything expecting…anything in return."

Was he telling her that his gift wasn't hinting at any special involvement? Warning her about getting ideas?

It wouldn't change anything. She loved him with everything in her, would give him everything that she was if he'd only take it. But if he didn't want it, she *would* give him her unending appreciation. "And I thank you because I want to, because it pleases me. And I certainly don't expect you to do anything in return but accept. I accepted your thanks for the book, didn't I?"

His lips spread in one of those slow, scorching smiles of his, as if against his will. "I don't remember if I gave you a choice to accept it or not. I sort of overrode you."

"Hmm, you've got a point." Then, without warning,

she tugged his hand. Surprise made him stumble the step that separated them, so that he ended up pressed against her from breast to calf. Her hand released his, went to his head, sifting through the silk of his mane, bringing it down to hers. How she wished she had the use of her other arm, so she could mimic his earlier embrace. She had to settle for pressing her longing against his forehead with lips that shook on his name.

They slid down his nose…and a cell phone rang.

He sundered their communion in a jerk, stared down at her, his eyes echoing the sea's tumult. It was shuddering, disoriented moments before her brain rebooted after the shock of interruption, of separation from him. That was her cell phone's tone.

It was in her jacket. Rodrigo had given it her, and only he had called her on it so far. Who could be calling her?

"Are you expecting a call?" His rasp scraped her nerves.

"I didn't even know anyone had this number."

"It's probably a wrong number."

"Yeah, probably. Just a sec." She fumbled the phone out, hit Answer. A woman's tear-choked voice filled her head.

"Agnes? What's wrong?" Instant anxiety gripped Rodrigo, spilled into urgency that had his hand at the phone, demanding to bear bad news himself. She blurted out the question that she hoped would defuse his agitation, "Are you and Steven okay?"

"Yes, yes…it's not that."

Cybele covered the mouthpiece, rapped her urgent assurance to Rodrigo. "They're both fine. This is something else."

His alarm drained, but tension didn't. He eased a fraction away, let her take the call, watching for any sign that necessitated his intervention, his taking over the situation.

Agnes went on. "I hate to ask you this, Cybele, but if you've remembered your life with Mel, you might know how this happened."

Foreboding closed in on her. "How *what* happened?"

"M-many people have contacted us claiming that Mel owes them extensive amounts of money. And the hospital where you used to work together says the funding he offered in return for being the head of the new general surgery department was withdrawn and the projects that were under way have incurred overdrafts in the millions. Everyone is suing us—and you—as his next of kin and inheritors."

Chapter 10

"So you don't have any memory of those debts."

Cybele shook her head, feeling crushed by doubts and fears.

It didn't sound as if Rodrigo believed her. She had a feeling Agnes hadn't, either. Did they think Mel had incurred all those debts because of her? Worse, had he? If he had, how? Why?

Was that what Agnes had almost brought up during Mel's funeral? She'd thought Mel, in his inability to express his emotions for her any other way, had showered her with extravagant stuff? Not that she could think what could be *that* extravagant.

If that hadn't been the case, she could think of only one other way. She'd made demands of him, extensive, unreasonable ones, and he'd gone to insane lengths to meet them. But what could have forced him to do so?

Threats to leave him? If that were true, then she hadn't been only a heartless monster, but a manipulative, mercenary one, too.

She had to know. She couldn't take another breath if she didn't. "Do *you* know anything about them?"

Rodrigo's frown deepened as he shook his head slowly. But his eyes were thoughtful. With suspicions? Deductions? Realizations?

"You know something. Please, tell me. I have to know."

He looked down at her for a bone-shaking moment, moonlight coasting over his beauty, throwing its dominant slashes and hollows into a conflict of light and darkness, of confusion and certainty.

Then he shook his head again, as if he'd made up his mind. To her dismay, he ignored her plea. "What I want to know is what has taken those creditors so long to come forward."

"They actually did as soon as Mel's death was confirmed."

"Then what has taken Agnes and Steven so long to relate this, and why have they come to *you* with this, and not me?"

She gave him his foster mother's explanations. "They wanted to make sure of the claims first, and then they didn't want to bother you. They thought they could take care of it themselves. They called me in case I knew something only a wife would know, that would help them resolve this mess. And because I'm involved in the lawsuits."

"Well, they were wrong, on all counts." She almost cried out at the incensed edge that entered his voice and expression. The words to beg him not to take it up with them, that they had enough to deal with, had almost shot from her lips when he exhaled forcibly. "Not that they need to know that. They've been through enough, and they were as usual misguidedly trying not to impose on me. I think those two still don't believe me when I say they *are* my parents. But anyway, none of you have anything to worry about. I'll take care of everything."

She gaped at him. *Was* he real? Could she love him more?

All she could say was, "Thank you."

He squeezed his eyes on a grimace. "Don't."

"I will thank you, so live with it." He glowered at her. She went on, "And since I'm on a roll, throwing my problems in your lap, I need your opinion on another one. My arm."

His eyes narrowed. "What about it?"

"My fractures have healed, but the nerve damage isn't clearing. Eight weeks ago, you said I wouldn't be able to operate for months. Were you being overly optimistic? Will I ever regain the precision I used to have and need as a surgeon?"

"It's still early, Cybele."

"Please, Rodrigo, just give it to me straight. And before you say anything conciliatory, remember that I'll see through it."

"I would never condescend to you like that."

"Even to protect me from bad news?"

"Even then."

She believed him. He would never lie to her. He would never lie, period. So she pressed on. Needing the truth. About this, if she couldn't have it about anything else.

"Then tell me. I'm a left-handed surgeon who knows

nothing else but to be one, and I need to know if in a few weeks I'll be looking to start a new career path. As you pointed out before, the arm attached to my hand had extensive nerve damage…."

"*And* I performed a meticulous peripheral nerve repair."

"Still, I have numbness and weakness, tremors—"

"It's *still* too early to predict a final prognosis. We'll start your active motion physiotherapy rehabilitation program the moment we have proof of perfect bone healing."

"We have that now."

"No, we don't. You're young and healthy and your bones *look* healed now, but I need them rock solid before I remove the cast. That won't be a day before twelve weeks after the surgery. Then we'll start your physiotherapy. We'll focus first on controlling the pain and swelling that accompanies splint removal and restoration of motion. Then we'll move to exercises to strengthen and stabilize the muscles around the wrist joint then to exercises to improve fine motor control and dexterity."

"What if none of it works? What if I regain enough motor control and dexterity to be self-sufficient but not a surgeon?"

"If that happens, you still have nothing to worry about. If worse comes to worst, I'll see to it that you change direction smoothly to whatever field of medicine will provide you with as much fulfillment. But I'm not giving up on your regaining full use of your arm and hand. I'm stopping at nothing until we get you back to normal. And don't even *think* about how long it will take, or what you'll do or where you'll be until it happens. You have all the time in the world to retrain your hand, to regain every last bit of power and control. You have a home here for as long as you wish and accept to stay. You have *me,* Cybele. *I'm* here for you, anytime, all the time, whatever happens."

And she couldn't hold back anymore.

She surged into him, tried to burrow inside him, her working arm shaking with the ferociousness of her hug. And she wept. She loved him so much, was so thankful he existed, it was agony.

He stilled, let her hug him and hold on to him and drench him in her tears. Then he wrapped her in his arms, caressed her from head to back, his lips by her ear, murmuring gentle and soothing words. Her heart expanded so quickly with a flood of love, it almost ruptured. Her tears gushed faster, her quakes nearly rattling flesh from bone.

He at last growled something as though agonized, snatched her from gravity's grasp into his, lifted her until she felt she'd float out to sea if he relinquished his hold.

He didn't, crushed her in his arms, squeezed her to his flesh until he forced every shudder and tear out of her.

Long after he'd dissipated her storm, he swayed with her, as if slow dancing the Sardana again, pressing her head into his shoulder, his other arm bearing her weight effortlessly as he raggedly swore to her in a loop of English and Catalan that he was there for her, that she'd never be without him. His movements morphed from soothing to inflaming to excruciating. But it was his promises that wrenched at the tethers of her heart.

For she knew he would honor every promise. He

would remain in her life and that of her baby's. As the protector, the benefactor, the dutiful, doting uncle. And every time she saw him or heard from him it would pour fresh desperation on the desolation of loving him and never being able to have him.

She had to get away. Today. Now. Her mind was disintegrating, and she couldn't risk causing herself a deeper injury. Her baby needed her healthy and whole.

"Cybele..." He shifted his grip on her, and his hardness dug into her thigh.

She groped for air, arousal thundering through her. Voices inside her yelled that this was just a male reaction to having a female writhing in his arms, that it meant nothing.

She couldn't listen. It didn't matter. He was aroused. This could be her only chance to be with him. And she had to take it. She needed the memory, the knowledge that she'd shared her body with him to see her through the barrenness of a life without him.

She rubbed her face into his neck, opened her lips on his pulse. It bounded against her tongue, as if trying to drive deeper into her mouth, mate with her. Every steel muscle she was wrapped around expanded, bunched, buzzed. She whimpered at the feel of his flesh beneath her lips, the texture, the taste, at the sheer delight of breathing him in, absorbing his potency.

"Cybele, *querida...*" He began to put her down and she clung, captured his lips before he said any more, before he could tell her no.

She couldn't take no for an answer. Not this time. She had to have this time.

She caught his groans on her tongue, licked his lips of every breath, suckled his depths dry of every sound.

She arched into his arousal, confessing hers without words. Then with them.

"Rodrigo—I *want* you." That came out a torn sob. "If you want me, *please*—just take me. Don't hold back. Don't think. Don't worry. No consequences or considerations. No tomorrows."

Rodrigo surrendered to Cybele, let her take of him what she would, his response so vast it was like a hurricane building momentum before it unleashed its destruction.

But her tremulous words replayed in his mind as she rained petal softness and fragrant warmth all over his face, crooning and whimpering her pleas for his response, her offer of herself. He felt things burning inside him as he held back, the significance of her words expanding in his mind.

Carte blanche. That was what she was giving him. With her body, with herself. No strings. No promises. No expectations.

Because she didn't want any? Because her need was only sexual? Or because she couldn't handle more than that? But what if she couldn't handle *even* that? If he gave her what she thought she wanted and ended up damaging her more?

And though he was nearly mindless now, powerless against the force of her desire, he'd conditioned himself to protect her from his own. "Cybele, you're distraught—"

She sealed his lips again, stopping his objection, her tongue begging entry, her kisses growing fevered, singeing the last of his control. "With need for you. I sometimes feel it will shatter me. I know what I'm asking. Please, Rodrigo, please…just give me this time."

This time. She thought he could stop at once, that he could possess her then walk away? It wasn't carte blanche, just a one-time offer? Would all that need she talked about then be quenched? Did she not feel more for him because her emotions had been buried with Mel, even if she didn't remember?

That thought gave him the strength to put her down, step out of reach when she stumbled to embrace him again.

Her arms fell to her sides, her shoulders hunching as she suddenly looked fragile and lost.

Then her tears flowed again, so thick it seemed they shriveled up her face. "Oh, no—y-you already showed me that you don't want me, and I—I came on to you again…."

She choked up, stumbled around and disappeared from the roof.

He should let her go. Talk to her again when his body wasn't pummeling him in demand for hers. But even if he could survive his own disappointment, he couldn't survive hers. He couldn't let her think he didn't want her. He had to show her the truth, even if the price was having her only once. He would take anything he could have of her, give her anything she needed.

He tore after her, burst into her room, found her crumpled facedown on her bed, good arm thrown over one of the bouquets he'd flooded her room with. She lurched at his entry, half-twisted to watch his approach, her wet gaze wounded and wary.

He came down on his knees at the foot of the bed. Her smooth legs, which had tanned honey-colored under his agonized eyes these past weeks, were exposed as the long, traditionally Catalan red skirt he'd picked for her to wear today rode up above her knees.

He wanted to drag her to him, slam her into his flesh, overpower and invade her, brand her, devour her whole.

He wanted to cherish her, savor and pleasure her more.

She gasped as he slipped off her shoes, tried to turn to him fully. He stopped her with a gentle hand at the small of her back. She subsided with a whimpering exhalation, watched him with her lip caught in her teeth as he prowled on all fours, advancing over her, kissing and suckling his way from the soles of her feet, up her legs, her thighs, her buttocks and back, her nape. She lay beneath him, quaking and moaning at each touch until he traced the lines of her shuddering profile. The moment he reached her lips, she cried out, twisted onto her back, surged up to cling to his lips in a desperate, soul-wrenching kiss.

Without severing their meld, he scooped her up and stepped off the bed. She relinquished his lips on a gasp of surprise.

"I want you in my bed, *querida*."

She moaned, shook her head. "No, please." He jerked in alarm. She didn't want to be in his bed? He started to put her down when she buried her face and lips in his neck. "Here. Among the roses."

"Dios, si..."

He'd fantasized about having her in his bed from the day he'd first laid eyes on her. Even when she'd become a forbidden fantasy, her image, and the visualization of all the things he'd burned to do to her, with her, even when he'd hated her and himself and the whole world for it, had been what had fueled his self-pleasuring, providing the only relief he'd had.

He'd covered his bed with the royal blue of her eyes. The rest of the room echoed the mahogany of her hair and the honey of her skin. He'd needed to sleep surrounded by her.

But this was far better than his fantasies. To have her here, among the blazing-red beauty of his blatant confession that she was his most important woman. His most important person.

He hadn't meant to confess it, but couldn't stop himself. He also hadn't dreamed it would lead to this. To beyond his dreams.

He laid her back on the bed, stood back taking her in. Unique, a ravishing human rose, her beauty eclipsing that of the flowers he'd filled her room with. She must have realized their significance, encouraging her to divulge her own need.

He felt his clothes dissolve off his body under the pressure of his own, under her wide-eyed awe, her breathless encouragement.

Then he was all over her again, caressing her elastic-waist skirt from her silky legs, kneading her jacket off, then the ensemble blouse over her head. Her bra and panties followed as he traced the tide of peach flooding her from toes to cheeks, tasting each tremor strumming her every fiber.

Then he was looking down on what no fantasy had conjured. Thankfully. Or he would have lost his mind for real long ago.

He remained above her, arms surrounding her head, thighs imprisoning hers, vibrating as the sight, the scent and sounds of her surrender pulverized his intentions to be infinitely slow and gentle. Blood thundered in his head, in his loins, tearing the last tatters of control from his grasp in a riptide.

Then she took it all out of his hands, her hand trembling over his back in entreaty, its power absolute.

He surrendered, moved between her shaking thighs, pressed her shuddering breasts beneath his aching chest. Then she conquered him, irrevocably.

Her lips trembled on his forehead, his name a litany of tremulous passion and longing as she enveloped him, clasped him to her body as if her life depended on his existence, his closeness, on knowing he was there, as if she couldn't believe he was.

Tenderness swamped him, choked him. He had to show her, prove to her, that he was there, was hers. He'd already given her all he had. All he had left to give her was his passion, his body.

He rose on his knees, cupped her head in one hand, her buttocks in the other, tilted one for his kiss, the other for his penetration. He bathed the head of his erection in her welcoming wetness, absorbed her cries of pleasure at the first contact of their intimate flesh, drank her pleas to take her, fill her.

He succumbed to the mercilessness of her need and his, drew back to watch her eyes as he started to drive into her, to join them. Her flesh fluttered around his advance, hot and tight almost beyond endurance, seeming to drag him inside and trying to push him out at once, begging for his invasion while resisting it.

He tried again and again, until she was writhing beneath him, eyes streaming, her whole body shaking and stained in the flush of uncontrollable arousal and unbearable frustration.

His mind filled with confusion and colliding diagnoses.

"Please, just do it, Rodrigo, hard, just take me."

The agony in her sobs was the last straw. He had to give her what she needed, couldn't draw his next breath if he didn't.

He thrust past her resistance, buried half of his shaft inside her rigid tightness.

It was only when her shriek tore through him that he understood what was that ripping sensation he'd felt as he'd driven into her. And he no longer understood anything.

It was impossible. Incomprehensible.

She was a *virgin?*

Chapter 11

Rodrigo froze on top of Cybele, half-buried in her depths, paralyzed. A virgin? *How?*

He raised himself on shaking arms. Her face contorted and a hot cry burst from her lips. He froze in midmotion, his gaze pinned on hers as he watched her eyes flood with the same confusion, the same shock along with tears.

"It shouldn't hurt that much, should it?" she quavered. "I couldn't have forgotten *that*."

Dios. He'd wanted to give her nothing but pleasure and more pleasure. And all he'd done was *hurt* her.

"No" was all he could choke out.

She digested that, reaching the same seemingly impossible explanation he had. "Then you have to be… my first."

Her first. The way she said that, with such shy wonder, made him want to thrust inside her and growl, *And your only.*

Something far outside his wrecked restraint—probably the debilitating cocktail of shock and shame at causing her pain—held him back from that mindless display of caveman possessiveness.

"I remember I wanted to wait until, y'know, I met… the one. I assumed that when I met Mel… But it—it seems I wanted to wait until we were married. But…"

He'd been trying to get himself to deflate, enough to slip out of her without causing her further pain. He expanded beyond anything he'd ever known instead. His mind's eye crowded with images of him devouring those lips that quivered out her earnest words, those breasts that swelled with her erratic breathing.

"But since there are ways for paraplegics to have sex, I still assumed we did one way or…" She choked with embarrassment. It was painfully endearing, when their bodies were joined in ultimate intimacy. "But it's clear we didn't, at least nothing invasive, and artificial insemination is essentially noninvasive…."

He shouldn't find her efforts at a logical, medically sound analysis that arousing as she lay beneath him, shaking, her impossible tightness throbbing around his shaft, her torn flesh singeing his own. But—curse him—it was arousing him to madness. He wanted to *give* her invasive.

He couldn't. He had to give her time, for the pain that gripped her body to subside. He started to withdraw. Her sob tore through him.

He froze, his own moan mingling with hers until she subsided. Then he tried to move again. But she clamped quaking legs around his hips, stopping him from exiting her body, pumping her own hips, impaling herself further on his erection.

"I'm hurting you." He barely recognized the butchered protest that cracked the panting-filled silence as his.

"Yes, oh, *yes*..." He heaved up in horror. She clung harder, her core clamping him like a fist of molten metal. "It's...*exquisite*. *You* are. I dreamed—but could have never dreamed how you'd feel inside me. You're burning me, filling me, making me feel—feel so—so—oh, Rodrigo, take me, do everything to me."

He roared with the spike of arousal her words lashed through him. Then, helpless to do anything but her bidding, he thrust back into her, shaking with the effort to be gentle, go slow. She thrashed her head against the sheets, splashing her satin tresses, bucking her hips beneath his, engulfing more of his near-bursting erection into her heat. "*Don't*. Give me...all of you, do it...hard."

He growled his capitulation as he rose, cupped her hips in his palms, tilted her and thrust himself to the hilt inside her.

At her feverish cry, he withdrew all the way, looked down at the awesome sight of his shaft sinking slowly inside her again.

He raised his eyes to hers, found her propped up on her elbows, watching too, lips crimson, swollen, open on frantic pants, eyes stunned, wet, stormy. He drew out, plunged again, and she collapsed back, crying out a gust of passion, opening wider for each thrust, a fusion of pain and pleasure slashing across her face, rippling through her body.

He kept his pace gentle, massaging her all over with

his hands, his body, his mouth, bending to suckle her breasts, drain her lips, rain wonder all over her.

"Do you know what you are? *Usted es divina, mi belleza, divina.* Do you see what you do to me? What I'm doing to you?"

She writhed beneath him with every word, her hair rippling waves of copper-streaked gloss over the crisp white sheet, her breathing fevered, her whole body straining at him, around him, forcing him to pick up speed—though he managed not to give in to his body's uproar for more force.

"I *love* what you're doing to me—your flesh in mine—give it to me—give it all to me...."

He again obeyed, strengthened his thrusts until her depths started to ripple around him and she keened, bucked up, froze, then convulsion after convulsion squeezed soft shrieks out of her, squeezed her around his erection in wrenching spasms.

The force, the sight and sound and knowledge of her release smashed the last of his restraint. He roared, let go, his body all but detonating in ecstasy. His hips convulsed into hers and he felt his essence flow into her as he fed her pleasure to the last tremor, until her arm and legs fell off him in satiation.

He collapsed beside her, shaking with the aftershocks of his life's most violent and first profound orgasm, moved her over him with extreme care, careful to remain inside her.

She spread over him, limp, trembling and cooling. He'd never known physical intimacy could be like this, channeling into his spirit, his reason. It had been merciful he hadn't imagined how sublime making love to her would be. He *would* have long ago gone mad.

He encompassed her velvet firmness in caresses, letting the sensations replay in his mind and body, letting awe overtake him.

He was her first. And she'd needed him so much that even through her pain, she'd felt so much pleasure at their joining.

Not that it had mattered to him in any way when he'd thought she'd belonged to Mel, had probably been experienced before him.

But now he knew she'd been with no one else, he almost burst with pride and elation. She *was* meant to be his alone.

And he had to tell her that he was hers, too. He had to offer her. Everything. *Now.*

"Cybele, *mi corazón,*" he murmured into her hair as he pressed her into his body, satiation, gratitude and love swamping him. *"Cásate conmigo, querida."*

Cybele lay draped over Rodrigo, shell-shocked by the transfiguring experience.

Every nerve crackled with Rodrigo-induced soreness and satiation and a profundity of bliss, amazement and disbelief.

She'd been a virgin. Wow.

And what he'd done to her. A few million wows.

The wows in fact rivaled the number of his billions since he'd given her all that pleasure when she'd simultaneously been writhing with the pain of his possession. But the very concept of having him inside her body, of being joined to him in such intimacy, at last, had swamped the pain, turned it into pleasure so excruciating she thought she *had* died in his arms for moments there.

Love welled inside her as she recalled him looking down at her in such adorable contrition and stupefaction. The latter must have been because she'd babbled justifications for her virginal state with him buried inside her. Another breaker of heat crashed over her as she relived her mortification. Then the heat changed texture when she recalled every second of his domination.

What would he do to her when pain was no longer part of the equation? When he no longer feared hurting her? When he lost the last shred of inhibition and just plundered her?

She wondered if she'd survive such pleasure. And she couldn't wait to risk her life at the altar of his unbridled possession.

She was about to attempt to beg for more, needing to cram all she could into her one time in his arms. But she lost coherence as he caressed and crooned to her. Then his words registered.

Cásate conmigo, querida.

Marry me, darling.

Instinctive responses and emotions mushroomed, paralyzed her, muted her. Heart and mind ceased, time and existence froze.

Then everything rushed, streaked. Elation, disbelief, joy, shock, delight, doubt. The madly spinning roulette of emotions slowed down, and one flopped into the pocket. Distress.

She pushed away from the meld of their bodies, moaning at the burn of separation, rediscovering coordination from scratch. "I meant it when I said no tomorrows, Rodrigo. I don't expect anything."

He rose slowly to a sitting position, his masculinity taking on a harsher, more overwhelming edge among the dreamy softness of a background drenched in red roses. He looked like that wrathful god she'd seen in the beginning, decadent in beauty, uncaring of the effect his nakedness and the sight of his intact arousal had on flimsy mortals like her. "And you don't want it, either?"

"What I want isn't important."

He stopped her as she turned away, his grip on her arm gentleness itself, belying his intensity as he gritted, "It's *all*-important. And we've just established how much you want me."

"It still makes no difference. I—I can't marry you."

He went still. "Because of Mel? You feel guilty over him?"

She huffed a bitter laugh. "And you don't?"

"No, I don't," he shot back, adamant, final. "Mel is no longer here and this has nothing to do with him."

"Says the man whose every action for the last ten weeks had everything to do with Mel."

He rose to his knees, blocked her unsteady attempt to get off the bed. "Care to explain that?"

Air disappeared as his size dwarfed her, his heat bore down on her, as his erection burned into her waist. She wanted to throw herself down, beg him to forget about his honor-bound offer and just ride her to oblivion again.

She swallowed fire past her hoarse-with-shrieks-of-pleasure vocal cords. "I'm Mel's widow, and I'm carrying his unborn child. Need more clues?"

"You think all I did for you was out of duty for him?"

She shrugged dejectedly. "Duty, responsibility, dependability, heroism, nobility, honor. You're full of 'em."

And he did the last thing she'd expected in this tension.

He belted out one of those laughs that turned her to boiling goo. "You make it sound like I'm full of…it."

Words squeezed past the heart bobbing in her throat. "I wish. You make it impossible to think the least negative thing of you."

He encroached on her as he again exposed her to that last thing she'd thought she'd ever see from him. Pure seduction, lazy and indulgent and annihilating. "And that's bad…why?"

Oh, *no*. She'd been in deep…it, when he'd been only lovely and friendly. Now, after he'd kick-started her sexuality software with such an explosive demonstration, had imprinted his code and password all over her cells, to all of a sudden see fit to turn on his sex appeal intentionally was cruel and unusual overkill.

She tried to put a breath between them. He wouldn't let her, backed her across the bed, a panther crowding his prey into a corner. She came up against the brass bars, grabbed them, tried to pull up from her swooning position.

"It's bad because it makes it impossible to say no to you."

His lips twitched as he prowled over her, imprisoning her in a cage of muscle and maleness. But instead of his previous solemn and tender intensity, that mind-messing predatory sexiness spiked to a whole new level. "That has always been my nefarious plan."

"Okay, Rodrigo, I'm confused here," she panted. "What's brought all…*this* about?"

His eyebrows shot up in mock-surprise and affront. "You mean you don't remember? Seems I have to try much…harder—and longer—to make a more lasting impression."

She coughed in disbelief. "You're telling me you suddenly want to marry me because of the mind-blowing pleasure?"

He tightened his knees around her thighs, winding the pounding between them into a tighter rhythm, licking his lips as his gaze melted over her captive nakedness, making her feel as if he'd licked her all over again. "So it was mind-blowing for you?"

"Are you kidding? I'm surprised my head is still screwed on. But I can't believe it was for *you*. I'm not by any stretch hot stuff, not to mention I must have cramped your style, being your first pregnant virgin and all."

"I admit, I was and am still agonizingly cramped, as you can see. And feel." He pressed his erection into her belly. Feeling the marble smooth and hard column of hot flesh against hers, the awe that she'd accommodated all that inside her, the carnality of the sharply recalled sensations as he'd occupied her, stretched her into mindlessness made her gasp, arch up involuntarily into his hardness. He ground harder into her as he drove a knee between her thighs, coaxing their rigidity to melt apart for him. "And in case you want to know my style…" His other knee joined in splaying her thighs apart as he leaned over her, teasing her aching nipples with the silk-sprinkled power of his chest. "…it's a woman who has no idea she's inferno-level stuff who happens to be a pregnant virgin. Or who was one, until I put an end to that condition."

She couldn't wrap her head around this. "So if it isn't out of duty to Mel, it isn't something more moronically honorable as doing the 'right thing' since you took my 'innocence,' is it?"

He chuckled. "*Dios,* you say the funniest things. First, I don't equate virginity with innocence. Second, *your* innocence seems to be almost intact. But don't worry. I didn't even scratch the surface of all the ways I plan to rectify that." He nipped her nipple, had her coming off the bed with a sharp slam of pleasure. He withdrew on a sigh of satisfaction. "Any more far-fetched reasons you can come up with to explain why I'm proposing to you?"

"Why don't you tell me your not-so-far-fetched ones?" she gasped. "And don't say because I'm your one and only aphrodisiac. That wasn't the case up until a few hours ago."

"Up until a few hours ago, I didn't know you wanted me."

"That's as straight-faced a lie as I've ever heard," she scoffed. "I'm as transparent as the windows Consuelo keeps spotless. I showed you I wanted you weeks ago. Hell, I showed you I wanted you two minutes after I regained consciousness."

He tasted her nipples in soft pulls as if compelled. "That you did so soon, coupled with your loss of memory, made me wonder if your mind wasn't scrambled and you didn't know what you wanted, or why. I thought I might be what you clung to, to reaffirm your life after surviving such a catastrophe, or because I was the one closest to you, or the one you seemed to perceive as your savior."

She pushed his head away before her breasts—her whole body—exploded. "You *are* my savior, but that has nothing to do with my wanting you." She devoured his beauty as he loomed over her, felt her core clench with the memory, the knowledge of what he could do to it. “I remember you had hordes of women you didn’t save panting for you. I think *not* wanting you is a feminine impossibility.”

The intimacy and seduction on his face turned off like a light, plunging her world into darkness. “So it’s only sexual for you? That’s why you wanted it to be only once?”

“Which part of me lauding your responsibility, dependability, heroism, nobility and honor didn’t you get?”

The mesmerizing heat flared back on like floodlights, making her squirm. “So you like me for my character not just my body?”

“I *love* you for your character.” That made that smug, male assurance falter, crack. He stared at her, stunned, almost vulnerable. She groaned. “I didn’t intend to say that, so don’t go all noble pain-in-the-derriere on me and find it more reason to—”

He crashed his lips onto hers, silencing her, wrenching keens from her depths on scorching, devouring kisses. He came fully over her body, grinding into her belly, lifting her off the bed, one hand supporting her head for his ravaging, the other at her back holding her for his chest to torment her breasts into a frenzy.

She tore her lips away before she combusted and it was too late to vent her reservations. “Please, Rodrigo, don’t feel you owe me anything. And I can’t owe you any more than I already do.”

He plastered her back to the bed, seemingly by the force of his conviction alone. “You owe me nothing, do you hear? It’s been my privilege to see to your health, my joy to have you in my home, and yes, my mind-blowing pleasure to have you in my bed.”

She started shaking again. It was too much. Loving him, needing to grab at him, to take him at his every magnificent word, blocking her mind to the fear that she'd be taking advantage of him, end up causing them both misery and heartache.

She trembled caresses over his beloved face. "I know you're always right, but you're totally wrong here. I owe you far more than medical care and shelter. And mind-blowing pleasure. I owe you for restoring my faith in humanity, for showing me what a family could be like, and letting me be a part of yours for a while, for stabilizing my outlook so much that I feel I will at last have a relationship with my own family, not just cynical and bitter avoidance. I owe you memories and experiences that have made me a stronger, healthier person, that will be a part of me forever. And that was before what you offered me today."

He grabbed her hand, singed it in kisses, all lightness burned away as he, too, vibrated with emotion. "Mel's debts..."

She rushed to make one thing clear. "I don't know what hand I had in them, but if I had any, I'll pay my part, I swear."

"No, you won't. I said I'd take care of them."

"You'd do anything to protect your foster parents, and me, too, won't you? And *this* is what I'm indebted to you for. The—the...carte blanche support. And you're offering it forever now. And I can't accept. I can't burden you anymore with my problems. Any more support from you would burden *me.* Whatever your reasons are for offering to marry me, I have nothing to offer you in return."

His hands convulsed in her hair, pinned her for the

full impact of his vehemence. "You have everything to offer me, *querida.* You've *already* offered me everything and I want it all for the rest of my life. I want your passion, your friendship, and now that I know I have it, I want your love. I *need* your love. And I want your baby as mine. I want us to be lovers, to be a family. And the only reason I want all this is because I love you."

She lurched so hard she nearly threw him off her. He pressed down harder, holding her head tighter to imprint her with every nuance of his confession. "I love you, *mi amor,* for your character and your body, for being such a responsible, dependable, heroic, noble and honorable pregnant has-been-virgin who had no idea you started a fire in me that can never be put out."

She broke into sobs. "How can you say that? I was going to leave, and if I hadn't almost attacked you, you would have never—"

"I would have *never* let you leave. Don't you get that yet? I was going to keep shooting down your reasons and demands to leave for months to come, and when I was out of arguments, I was going to make you offers you can't refuse so you'd have to stay. I would have confessed my feelings to you when I felt secure you could make such a life-changing decision and lifelong commitment, could handle my feelings and my passion. You only freed me from the agonizing wait. Thankfully. I was suffering serious damage holding back."

Her tears slowed down with each incredible word out of that mouth that sent her to heaven no matter what it did or said. Scary joy and certainty started to banish the agony of grief and doubt.

"You hid that perfectly," she hiccupped, her face

trembling, with a smile of burgeoning belief in his reciprocated emotions.

His sincerity and intensity switched to bedevilment in a flash as his hands and lips started to roam her again. "I'm a neurosurgeon. Covert turmoil is one of my middle names."

"Another one?" She spluttered on mirth and emotion, finally felt she had the right to reciprocate his caresses, delighting in the silk of his polished, muscled back and swimmer's shoulders.

But she had to voice her concerns one last time. "This is a major step. Are you sure you considered all the ramifications?"

"The only thing that stopped me from snatching you up the first time you offered yourself was that I thought *you* were nowhere near aware of the ramifications, had no idea what you'd be letting yourself in for, weren't ready for a relationship so soon after such a loss and trauma. I, on the other hand, am positive of what I want. What I *have* to have. You, the baby. *Us*."

She cried out and dragged him down to her, surging up to meet his lips, devouring with her own. She was begging when he suddenly rose, swept her up in his arms and strode into her bathroom.

He put her down on the massage table and ran a bubble bath, came back to slide her off it, locking her thighs around his hips, gliding his erection along her core's molten lips before he leaned forward, pressed it to her belly, undulated against her, filled her gasping mouth with his tongue.

She arched, tried to bring him inside her. He held her down, wouldn't let her have what she felt she was imploding for.

"You haven't said yes."

"I've been saying 'yes…but' for a while now," she moaned.

"Didn't sound like that to me."

"Is that why you're punishing me now?"

"I would be punishing you if I gave you what you think you want again tonight. But don't worry, there are so many other ways I'll go about erasing that innocence of yours."

"No, please… I want you again."

"Let me hear that *yes* without the *but* and you can have me. For the rest of our lives."

"Yes."

And for the rest of the night, she lost count of how many *yeses* she said.

Chapter 12

Three months and a half to the day that Cybele opened her eyes in Rodrigo's world, she was trying not to run down the aisle to him.

She rushed down the path between their guests, his family and friends and colleagues, in one of the plateau gardens overlooking his vineyards on one side and the sea on the other, feeling like she was treading air, forging deeper into heaven.

He'd insisted on scheduling the wedding two weeks after he'd removed her cast, to give time for the physiotherapy to control any lingering discomforts. But he hadn't insisted on holding the wedding in Barcelona's biggest cathedral as he'd first planned, succumbing to her desire to hold it on his estate. The land that was now theirs. Their home. And their baby's home.

That was what completed her happiness. That it

wasn't only she who was being blessed by the best gift the world had to offer, but her baby, too. Only Rodrigo would love as his own the baby of the man he'd loved like a brother.

He stood there looking godlike in his tuxedo, his smile growing more intimate and delighted as she neared him. She only noticed Ramón standing beside him when she stumbled the last steps to grab Rodrigo's outstretched hand. She absently thought that they could be brothers. Not that Ramón, who was arguably as esthetically blessed as Rodrigo, was anywhere near as hard-hitting. Or perhaps it was she who had terminal one-man-one-woman syndrome.

Ramón winked at her as he kissed her and left them to the minister's ministrations. He'd come to her quarters an hour ago, where Rodrigo had insisted she remain until their wedding night, and performed the Catalan best man's duty of giving the bride her bouquet, which he'd picked for her, while reciting a poem he'd written. She'd almost had a heart attack laughing as he turned the poem that was supposed to extol her virtues and that of her groom into a hilariously wicked medical report.

Apart from that, and standing by Rodrigo's side until she reached him, Ramón's role had ended. In Catalonia there were no wedding rings for the best man to bear. Rodrigo would transfer the engagement ring from her right hand to her left one.

He was doing that now. She barely remembered the preceding ritual beyond repeating the vows, crying a river as Rodrigo made his own vows to her, lost in his eyes, singed by his love.

She watched their hands entwine as he slipped the ring onto her trembling finger, the ten-carat blue diamond part of the set she was wearing that totaled a breath-depleting fifty carats. He'd said he'd picked them for being a lighter version of her eyes.

Then he kissed her. As if they were now one. Forever.

From then on, everything blurred even more as their guests carried them away to another extensive session of Sardana dances and many other wedding customs and festivities.

At one point she thought she'd had a brief exchange with Mel's parents. She had the impression that they were doing much better and seemed genuinely happy for her and Rodrigo. Her family was here, too, flown in by Rodrigo. His magic had encompassed them, as well, had infused them with a warmth they'd never exhibited before.

Then the dreamlike wedding was over and he carried her to his quarters. Theirs now. At last.

She'd almost lost her mind with craving these past weeks, as she hadn't slept curved into his body, or taken him inside of hers.

She was in a serious state by now. She'd die if he took her slowly and gently like he'd done that first night.

She was about to beg him not to when he set her down, pressed her against the door and crashed his lips onto hers.

She cried out her welcome and relief at his fierceness, surrendered to his surging tongue. His hands were all over her as he plundered her mouth, removing the *peineta* and pins that held her cutwork lace veil in place, shaking her hair out of the imprisonment of her Spanish chignon, undoing the string lacing of her traditional wedding gown's front.

He pushed it off her shoulders, spilling her breasts

into his palms, weighing and kneading them until she felt they would burst if he didn't devour them. He was looking down at them as if he really would. Then he crushed them beneath his chest, her lips beneath his, rubbing, thrusting, maddening.

"Do you have any idea how much I've hungered for you?" he groaned against her lips. "What these past weeks were like?"

"If it's half as much as I hungered for you, and they were half as excruciating as mine, then…serves you right."

He grunted a sound so carnal and predatory yet amused, sowed a chain of nips from her lips to her nipples in chastisement as he dragged her dress down. It snagged on her hips.

He reversed his efforts, tried to get it over her head, and she hissed, "Rip it."

His eyes widened. Then with a growl, he ripped the white satin in two. She lurched and moaned, relishing his ferocity, fueling it.

He swept her underwear down her legs, then stood to fling away his jacket, cummerbund and tie then gave her a violent strip-show shredding of his shirt. Candlelight cast a hypnotic glow to accompany his performance. Passion rose from her depths at the savage poetry of his every straining muscle. To her disappointment, he kept his pants on.

Before she could beg him to complete his show, he came down before her, buried his face in her flesh, in her core, muttered love and lust. When she was begging for him, he rose with her wrapped around him, took her to bed, laid her on her back on its edge, kneeled between her thighs, probed her with deft fingers.

He growled his satisfaction as her slick flesh gripped them. "Do you know what it does to me—to feel you like this, to have this privilege, this freedom? Do you know what it means to me, that you let me, that you want me, that you're mine?"

Sensation rocketed, more at the emotion and passion fueling his words than at his expert pleasuring. She keened, opened herself fully to him, now willing to accept pleasure any way he gave it, knowing he craved her surrender, her pleasure. She'd always give him all he wanted.

He came over her, thrust his tongue inside her mouth to the rhythm of his invading fingers, his thumb grinding her bud in escalating circles. He swallowed every whimper, every tremulous word, every tear, until she shuddered apart in his arms.

She collapsed, nerveless and sated. For about two minutes.

Then she was all over him, kissing, licking, nipping and kneading him through his pants. He rasped, "Release me."

She lowered the zipper with shaking hands. Her mouth watered as he sprang heavy and hard into her palms. He groaned in a bass voice that spilled magma from her core, "Play with me, *mi amor*. Own me. I'm yours."

"And do you know what hearing you say this means to me?" she groaned back.

He growled as her hands traveled up and down his shaft, pumping his potency in delight. She slithered down his body, tasted him down to his hot, smooth crown. His scent, taste and texture made her shudder with need for all of him. She spread her lips over him, took all she could of him inside. He grunted his ecstasy, thrust his mighty hips to her suckling rhythm.

His hand in her hair stopped her. "I need to be inside you."

She clambered over him, kissing her way to his lips, "And I need you inside me. Don't you dare go slow or gentle…*please*…"

With that last plea, she found herself on her back beneath him, impaled, filled beyond capacity, complete, the pleasure of his occupation insupportable.

"Cybele, *mi amor, mi vida,*" he breathed into her mouth, as he gave her what she'd been disintegrating for, with the exact force and pace that had her thrashing in pleasure, driving deeper and deeper into her, until he nudged her womb.

Her world imploded into a pinpoint of shearing sensation, then exploded in one detonation after another of bone-rattling pleasure. He fed her convulsions, slamming into her, pumping her to the last abrading twitches of fulfillment.

Then he surrendered to his own climax, and the sight and sound of him reaching completion inside her, the feel of his body shuddering over hers with the force of the pleasure he'd found inside her, his seed jetting into her core, filling her to overflowing, had her in the throes of another orgasm until she was weeping, the world receding as pleasure overloaded her.

She came to, to Rodrigo kissing her, worry roughening his voice. "Cybele, *mi alma, por favor,* open your eyes."

Her lids weighed tons, but she opened them to allay his anxiety. "I thought you knocked me senseless the first time because it *was* the first time. Seems it's going to be the norm. Not that you'll hear anything but cries for an encore from this end."

She felt the tension drain from his body, pour into the erection still buried inside her. His gaze probed her tear-drenched face, proprietary satisfaction replacing the agitation in eyes that gleamed with that Catalan imperiousness. "In that case, prepare to spend half of our married life knocked senseless."

She giggled as he wrapped her nerveless body around him and prowled to the bathroom. He took her into the tub, already filled, laid her between his thighs, her back to his front, supporting her as she half floated. He moved water over her satiated body, massaging her with it as he did with his legs and lips. She hummed with the bliss reverberating in her bones.

She would have taken once with him, would have lived on the memory forever. But this *was* forever. It was so unbelievable that sometimes she woke up feeling as if she were suffocating, believing that it had all been a delusion.

She had serious security issues. This perfection was making her more scared something would happen to shatter it all.

He sighed in contentment. *"Mi amor milagrosa."*

She turned her face into his chest, was about to whisper back that it was he who was the miracle lover when a ring sounded from the bedroom. The center calling.

He exhaled a rough breath. "They've *got* to be kidding."

She turned in his arms. "It has to be something major, if they're calling you on your wedding night. You have to answer."

He harrumphed as he rose, dried himself haphazardly and went to answer. He came back frowning. "Pile up, serious injuries. Son and wife of an old friend among them." He drove his fingers in his hair. "*¡Maldita sea!* I only started making love to you."

"Hey. Surgeon here, too, remember? Nature of the beast." She left the tub, dried quickly, hugged him with both arms—an incredible sensation. "And you don't have to leave me behind. Let me come. I hear from my previous employers that I was a damn good surgeon. I can be of use to you and the casualties."

His frown dissolved, until his smile blinded her with his delight. "This isn't how I visualized spending our wedding night, *mi corazon*. But having you across a table in my OR is second on my list only to having you wrapped all around me in my bed."

After the emergency, during which their intervention was thankfully lifesaving, they had two weeks of total seclusion on his estate.

The three weeks after that, Cybele ticked off the two top items on Rodrigo's list, over and over. Daily, in fact.

They worked together during the days, discovering yet another area in which they were attuned. It became a constant joy and stimulation, to keep realizing how fully they could share their lives and careers.

Then came the nights. And if their first time and their semi-aborted wedding night had been world-shaking, she'd had no idea how true intimacy would escalate the pleasure and creativity of their encounters. Even those momentous occasions paled by comparison.

It was their five-week anniversary today.

She was in her twenty-second week of pregnancy and she'd never felt healthier or happier. Not that that convinced Rodrigo to change her prenatal checkups from weekly to biweekly.

"Ready, *mi amor?*"

She sprang to her feet, dissolved into his embrace. He kissed her until she was wrapped around him, begging him to postpone her checkup. She had an emergency only he could handle.

He bit her lip gently, put her away. "It'll take all of fifteen minutes. Then I'm all yours. As always."

She hooked her arm through his, inhaled his hormone-stimulating scent. "Do you want to find out the gender of the baby?"

He looked at her intently, as if wanting to make sure of her wish before he voiced his opinion. Seemed he didn't want to risk volunteering one that opposed hers. "Do you?"

She decided to let the delicious man off the hook. "I do."

His smile dawned. He *did* want to know, but considered it up to her to decide. Surely she couldn't love him more, could she?

"Then we find out."

"So what do you hope it is?"

He didn't hesitate, nuzzled her neck, whispered, "A girl. A tiny replica of her unique mother."

She surrendered to his cosseting, delight swirling inside her. "Would you be disappointed if it's a boy?"

His smile answered unequivocally. "I'm just being greedy. And then, you know how seriously cool it is to be female around here."

She made the goofy gesture and expression that had become their catchphrase. "Women rule."

* * *

Four hours later, they were back in their bedroom.

They'd made love for two of those, only stopped because they had a dinner date with Ramón and other colleagues in Barcelona.

She was leaning into him, gazing in wonder at his reflection in the mirror as he towered behind her, kissing her neck, caressing her zipper up her humming body, taking extra care of her rounding belly. She sighed her bliss. "Think Steven and Agnes will be happy it's a boy?"

His indulgent smile didn't waver. But she was so attuned to his every nuance of expression now, she could tell the question disturbed him. Since it indirectly brought up Mel.

And the mention of Mel had been the only thing to make him tense since they'd gotten married, to make him even testy and irritated. He'd once even snapped at her. She'd been shocked that day. And for a moment, black thoughts had swamped her.

She'd wondered if this fierceness was different from his early moroseness concerning Mel, if now that he was her husband, Mel was no longer simply his dead foster brother, but her dead first husband and he hated her mentioning Mel, out of jealousy.

The implications of that were so insupportable, she'd nearly choked on them. But only for a moment. Then he'd apologized so incredibly and she'd remembered what he was, what Mel had been to him.

She'd come to the conclusion that the memory of Mel was still a gaping wound inside him. One that hurt more as time passed, as the loss solidified. With him busy being the tower of strength everyone clung to, he hadn't dealt with his own grief. He hadn't attained the closure he'd made possible for everyone else to have. She hoped their baby would heal the wound, provide that closure.

His hands resumed caressing her belly. "I think they'll be happy as long as the baby is healthy."

And she had to get something else out of the way. "I called Agnes this morning and she sounded happier than I've ever heard her. She said those who filed the lawsuits weren't creditors but investors who gave Mel money to invest in the hospital, and that the money was found in an account they didn't know about."

His hands stopped their caresses. "That's right."

"But why didn't they ask for their money instead of resorting to legal action, adding insult to injury to bereaved parents? A simple request would have sent Agnes and Steven looking through Mel's documents and talking to his lawyer and accountant."

"Maybe they feared Agnes and Steven wouldn't give back the money without a strong incentive."

"Apart from finding this an incredibly irrational fear since Mel and his parents are upstanding people, there must have been legal provisos in place to assure everyone's rights."

"I don't know why they acted as they did. What's important is that the situation's over, and no harm's done to anyone."

And she saw it in his eyes. The lie.

She grabbed his hands. "You're not telling me the truth." He tried to pull his hand away. She clung. "Please, tell me."

That bleak look, which she'd almost forgotten had ever marred his beauty, was back like a swirl of ink muddying clear water.

But it was worse. He pushed away from her, glared at her in the mirror like a tiger enraged at someone pulling on a half ripped-out claw.

"You want the truth? Or do you just want me to confirm that those people acted irrationally, that Mel was an upstanding man? If so, you should do like Agnes and Steven, grab at my explanation for this mess, turn a blind eye and cling to your illusions."

She swung around to face him. "You made up this story to comfort them. The debts were real. And you must have done more than settle them to make Mel's creditors change their story."

"What do you care about the sordid details?"

Sordid? Oh, God. "Did…did I have something to do with this? Are you still protecting me, too?"

"*No.* You had nothing to do with any of it. It was just more lies Mel fed me, poisoned me with. I lived my life cleaning up after him, covering up for him. And now he's reaching back from the grave and forcing me to keep on doing it. And you know what? I'm *sick* of it. I've been getting sicker by the day, of embellishing his image and memory to you, to Agnes and Steven, of gritting my teeth on the need to tell you what I figured out he'd done to me. To *us*."

She staggered backward under the impact of his exasperated aggression. "What did he do? And what do you mean, to 'us'?"

"How can I tell you? It would be my word against a man who can't defend himself. It would make me a monster in your eyes."

"No." She threw herself in his path. "Nothing would make you anything but the man I love with every fiber of my being."

He held her at arm's length. "Just forget it, Cybele. I shouldn't have said anything… *Dios,* I wish I could take it back."

But the damage had been done. Rodrigo's feelings about Mel seemed to be worse than she'd ever feared. And she had to know. The rest. Everything. Now. "Please, Rodrigo, I have to know."

"How can I begin to explain, when you don't even remember how *we* first met?"

She stared at him, the ferocity of his frustration pummeling her, bloodying her. She gasped, the wish to remember so violent, it smashed at the insides of her skull like giant hammers.

Suddenly, the last barricade shattered. Memories burst out of the last dark chasm in her mind, snowballing into an avalanche.

She remembered.

Chapter 13

She swung away, a frantic beast needing a way out.

The world tilted, the ground rushed at her at a crazy angle.

"Cybele."

Her name thundered over her, then lightning hit her, intercepted her fall, live wires snaring her in cabled strength before she reinjured her arm beneath her plummeting weight.

Memories flooded through her like water through a drowning woman's lungs. In brutal sequence.

She'd first seen Rodrigo at a fundraiser for her hospital. Across the ballroom, towering above everyone, canceling out their existence. She'd felt hit by lightning then, too.

She'd stood there, unable to tear her eyes off him as people kept swamping him in relentless waves, moths to his irresistible fire. All through, he'd somehow never taken his eyes off her. She'd been sure she'd seen the same response in his eyes, the same inability to believe its power, to resist it.

Then Ramón had joined him, turned to look at her, too, and she knew Rodrigo was telling him about her. He left Ramón's side, charted a course for her. She stood there, shaking, knowing her life would change the moment he reached her.

Then a man next to her had collapsed. Even disoriented by Rodrigo's hypnotic effect, her doctor autofunction took over, and she'd rushed to the man's rescue.

She'd kept up her resuscitation efforts until paramedics came, and then she'd swayed up to look frantically for Rodrigo. But he'd vanished.

Disappointment crushed her even when she kept telling herself she'd imagined it all, her own response, too, that if she'd talked to him she would have found out he was nothing like the man she'd created in her mind.

Within days, she'd met Mel. He came with a huge donation to her hospital and became the head of the new surgery department. He offered her a position and started pursuing her almost at once. Flattered by his attention, she'd accepted a couple of dates. Then he proposed. By then, she had suspected he was a risk-taking jerk, and turned him down. But he'd said he used that persona at work to keep everyone on their toes, and showed himself to be diametrically different, everything she'd hoped for in a man, until she accepted.

Then Mel had introduced Rodrigo as his best friend.

She was shocked—and distraught that she hadn't imagined his effect on her. But she'd certainly imagined her effect on him. He seemed to find her abhorrent. Mel, unaware of the tension between the two people he said meant the most to him, insisted on having Rodrigo with them all the time. And though Mel's bragging accounts of his friend's mile-high bedpost notches had her despising Rodrigo right back, she'd realized she couldn't marry Mel while she felt that unstoppable attraction to his best friend. So she broke off the engagement. And it was then that Mel drove off in a violent huff and had the accident that had crippled him.

Feeling devastated by guilt when Mel accused her of being the reason he'd been crippled, Cybele took back her ring. They got married in a ceremony attended by only his parents a month after he was discharged from hospital. Rodrigo had left for Spain after he'd made sure there was nothing more he could do for his friend at that time, and to Cybele's relief, he didn't attend.

But the best of intentions didn't help her cope with the reality of living with a bitter, volatile man. They'd discussed with a specialist the ways to have a sex life, but his difficulties had agonized him even though Cybele assured him it didn't matter. She didn't feel the loss of what she'd never had, was relieved when Mel gave up trying, and poured her energy into helping him return to the OR while struggling to catch up with her job.

Then Rodrigo came back, and Mel's erratic behavior spiked. She'd confronted him, and he said he felt insecure around any able-bodied man, especially Rodrigo, but needed him more than ever. He was the world's leading miracle worker in spinal injuries, and he was working on putting Mel back on his feet.

But there was one thing Mel needed even more now. He was making progress with the sex therapy specialists, but until he could be a full husband to her, he wanted something to bind them, beyond her sense of duty and honor and a shared house. A baby.

Cybele had known he was testing her commitment. But was feeling guiltier now that she'd lived with his affliction reason enough to take such a major step at such an inappropriate time? Would a baby make him feel more of a man? Was it wise to introduce a baby into the instability of their relationship?

Guilt won, and with her mother promising she'd help out with the baby, she had the artificial insemination.

Within a week, her conception was confirmed. The news only made Mel unbearably volatile, until she'd said she was done tiptoeing around him since it only made him worse. He apologized, said he couldn't take the pressure, needed time off. And again Cybele succumbed, suspended her residency even knowing she'd lose her position, to help him and to work out their problems. Then he dropped another bombshell on her. He wanted them to spend that time off on Rodrigo's estate.

When she'd resisted, he said it would be a double benefit, as Rodrigo wanted Mel there for tests for the surgeries that would give Mel back the use of his legs. And she'd had to agree.

When they'd arrived in Barcelona, Rodrigo had sent them a limo. Mel had it drive them to the airfield where his plane was kept. When she objected, he said he didn't need legs to fly, that flying would make him feel like he was whole again.

But during the flight, in answer to some innocuous comments, he got nasty then abusive. She held her tongue and temper, knowing it wasn't the place to escalate their arguments, but she decided that once they landed, she'd face him, as she'd faced herself, and say that their relationship wasn't working, and it wasn't because of his turmoil, but because of who he was. A man of a dual nature, one side she'd loved but could no longer find, and the other she couldn't bear and seemed was all that remained.

But they hadn't landed.

Now she heaved as the collage of the crash detonated in image after shearing image, accompanied by a hurricane of deafening cacophony and suffocating terror.

Then the maelstrom exchanged its churning motion for a linear trajectory as all trivial memories of every day of the year before the accident burst like flashes of sickening light, obliterating the blessed darkness of the past months.

Everything decelerated, came to a lurching stop.

Her face was being wiped in coolness, her whole self bathed in Rodrigo's concern. She raised sore eyes to his reddened ones.

His lips feathered over them with trembling kisses. "You remember."

"My end of things," she rasped. "Tell me yours."

The heart beneath her ear felt as if it would ram out of his chest.

Then he spoke. "When I saw you at that fundraiser, it was like seeing my destiny. I told Ramón that, and he said that if anyone else had said that, he would have laughed. But coming from me, I, who always know what's right for me, he believed it, and to go get you. But as I moved to do that, all hell broke loose. You rushed to that man's aid and I was called to deal with multiple neuro-trauma cases back here. I asked Ramón to find out all he could about you, so I could seek you out the moment I came back.

"I tried for the last almost eighteen months not to reconstruct what I instinctively knew and didn't want to—*couldn't* face. But the more I knew you, the more inconsistencies I discovered since the accident, the more I couldn't pretend not to know how it all happened anymore. Mel was there, too, that initial day. He was right behind me as I turned away from Ramón. He must have overheard my intentions. And he decided to beat me to you."

She couldn't even gasp. Shock fizzled inside her like a spark in a depleted battery.

"And he did. Using money I gave him to gain his new position, he put himself where he'd have access to you. For the six weeks I stayed away performing one surgery after another, all the time burning for the moment I could come back and search you out, he was pursuing you. The moment you accepted his proposal, he called me to tell me that he was engaged. He left your name out.

"The day I rushed back to the States to find you, he insisted I go see him first, meet his fiancée. I can never describe my horror when I found out it was you.

"I kept telling myself it couldn't have been intentional, that he wouldn't be so cruel, that he couldn't be shoving down my throat the fact that he was the one who'd gotten you. But I remember his glee as he recounted how it had been love at first sight, that you couldn't get enough of him, and realized he was having a huge laugh at my expense, wallowing in his triumph over me, all the while dangling you in front of me until I was crazed with pain."

"Was that why…?" She choked off. It was too much.

"Why I behaved as if I hated you? *Sí*. I hated everything at the time. Mel, myself, you, the world, the very life I woke up to every morning in which you could never be mine."

"B-but you had so many other lovers."

"I had *nobody.* Since I laid eyes on you. Those women were smoke screens so that I wouldn't sit through our outings like a third-wheel fool, something to distract me so I wouldn't lose my mind wanting you more with each passing day. But nothing worked. Not my efforts to despise you, not your answering antipathy. So I left, and would have never come back. But he forced me back. He crippled himself, as I and his parents always warned him he one day would."

A shudder rattled her at the memory. "He said I made him lose his mind, drove him to it…."

He looked beyond horrified. "*No. Dios,* Cybele… it had *nothing* to do with you, do you hear? Mel never took responsibility for any problem he created for himself. He always found someone else to accuse, usually me or his parents. *Dios*—that he turned on you, too, accused you of this!" His face turned a burnt bronze, his lips worked, thinning with the effort to contain his aggression. She had the feeling that if Mel were alive and here, Rodrigo would have dragged him out of his wheelchair and taken him apart.

At last he rasped, "It had to do with his own gambler's behavior. He always took insane risks, in driving, in sports, in surgeries. One of those insane risks was the gambling that landed him in so much debt. I gave him the money to gamble, too. He told me it was to buy you the things you wanted. But I investigated. He never bought you anything."

So this was it. The explanation he'd withheld.

"As for the stunt that cost him his life and could have cost yours, it wasn't his first plane crash but his third. He walked away from so many disasters he caused without a scratch that even the one that cut him in half didn't convince him that his luck had run out and the next time would probably be fatal. As it was."

For a long moment, all she heard was her choppy breath, the blood swooshing in her ears, his harsh breathing.

Then he added, "Or maybe he wanted to die."

"Why would he?" she rasped. "He believed you'd put him back on his feet. He said you were very optimistic."

He looked as if he'd explode. "Then he lied to you. Again. There was nothing I could do for him. I made it absolutely clear."

She squeezed her eyes shut. "So he was really desperate."

"I think he was worse than that." His hiss felt as if it would scrape her flesh from her bone. "I think he'd gone over the edge, wanted to take you with him. So I would never have you."

She lurched as if under a flesh-gouging lash.

Rodrigo went on, bitterness pouring out of him. "Mel always had a sickness. Me. Since the first day I set foot in the Braddocks' house, he idolized me and seethed with jealousy of me, alternated between emulating me to the point of impersonation, to doing everything to be my opposite, between loving and hating me."

It all made so much sense it was horrifying. How she'd found Mel so different at first, how he'd switched to the seamless act of emulating Rodrigo. So it *had* been Rodrigo she'd fallen in love with all along. It was unbelievable. Yet it was the truth.

And it dictated her next action. The only thing she could do.

She pushed out of his arms, rose to unsteady feet, looked down at him, the man she loved beyond life itself.

And she cut her heart out. "I want a divorce."

Cybele's demand fell on Rodrigo like a scythe.

Rage, at himself, hacked him much more viciously.

He'd been so *stupid.* He'd railed at a dead man, not just the man he'd considered his younger brother, but the man Cybele still loved, evidently more than she could ever love him.

He shot to his feet, desperation the one thing powering him. "Cybele, *no. Lo siento, mi amor.* I didn't mean…"

She shut her eyes in rejection, stopping his apology and explanation. "You meant every word. And you had every right. Because you *are* right. You at last explained my disappointment in Mel, my resentment toward him. You rid me of any guilt I ever felt toward him."

Rodrigo reeled. "You—you didn't love Mel?"

She shook her head. Then in a dead monotone, she told him her side of the story.

"Seems I always sensed his manipulations, even if I would have never guessed their reason or extent. My subconscious must have considered it a violation, so it wiped out the traumatic time until I was strong enough. I still woke up with overpowering gut feelings. But without context, they weren't enough to stop me from tormenting myself when I felt nothing but relief at his death and anger toward him, when I wanted you from the moment I woke up. Now I know. I always wanted you."

Elation and confusion tore him in two. "You did? *Dios*—then why are you asking for a divorce?"

"Because I don't matter. Only my baby does. I would never have married you if I'd realized you would be the worst father for him. Instead of loving his father, you hate Mel with a lifelong passion. And though you have every right to feel that way, I can never subject my child to the life I had. Worse than the life I had. My stepfather didn't know my father, and he also didn't consider me the bane of his life. He just cared nothing for me. But it was my mother's love for him, her love for the children she had with him, that alienated her from me. And she doesn't love him a fraction of how much I love you."

He should have realized all that. He knew her scars in detail, knew she was barely coping now, as an adult, with her alienated childhood and current bland family situation. But he got it now. The sheer magnitude of his blunder. It could cost him his life. *Her.*

"I never hated Mel," he pleaded. "It was Mel who considered me the usurper of his parents' respect and affection. I loved him, like brothers love their imperfect siblings. Mel did have a lot to him that I appreciated, and I always hoped he'd believe that, be happy playing on his own strengths and stop competing with me in mine. But I could never convince him, and it ate at him until he lashed out, injured you while trying to get to me, the source of his discontent. It was foolish, tragic, and I *do* hate his taking you away from me, but I don't hate *him*. You have to believe that."

She clearly didn't. And she had every reason to distrust his words after that moronic display of bitterness and anger.

She confirmed his worst fears, her voice as inanimate as her face. "I can't take the chance with my baby's life."

Agony bled out of him. "Do you think so little of me, Cybele? You claim to love me, and you still think I'd be so petty, so cruel, as to take whatever I felt for Mel out on an innocent child?"

She stumbled two steps back to escape his pleading hands. "You might not be able to help it. He did injure you, repeatedly, throughout his life. That he's now dead doesn't mean that you can forget. Or forgive. I wouldn't blame you if you could do neither."

"But that baby is *yours,* Cybele. He could be yours from the very devil and I'd still love and cherish him because he's yours. Because I love you. I would die for you."

The stone that seemed to be encasing her cracked, and she came apart, a mass of tremors and tears. "And I would d-die for you. I feel I *will* die without you. And that only makes me more scared, of what I'd do to please you, to keep your love, if I weaken now, and it turns out, with your best intentions, you'd never be able to love my baby as he deserves to be loved. And I—I can't risk that. Please, I beg you, don't make it impossible to leave you. *Please*…let me go."

He lunged for her, as if to grab her before she vanished. "I *can't*, Cybele."

She wrenched away, tears splashing over his hands. His arms fell to his sides, empty, pain impaling his heart, despair wrecking his sanity.

Suddenly, realization hit him like a vicious uppercut.

He couldn't *believe* it. *Dios*, he was far worse than a moron.

He *did* have the solution to everything.

He blocked her path. "*Querida*, forgive me, I'm such an idiot. I conditioned myself so hard to never let the truth slip, that even after you told me your real feelings for Mel, it took seeing you almost walking out on me to make me realize I don't have to hide it anymore. It is true I would have loved any baby of yours as mine, no matter what. But I love *this* baby, I want him and I would die for him, too. Because he *is* mine. Literally."

Chapter 14

"I *am* the baby's father."

Cybele stared at Rodrigo, comprehension suspended.

"If you don't believe me, a DNA test will prove it."

And it ripped through her like a knife in her gut.

One thing was left in her mind, in the world. A question.

She croaked it. "How?"

He looked as if he'd rather she asked him to step in front of a raging bull. Then he exhaled. "A few years back, Mel had a paternity suit. During the tests to prove that he didn't father the child, he found out that he was infertile. Then he told me that you were demanding proof of his commitment to your marriage, the emotional security of a baby. He said he couldn't bear to reveal another shortcoming to you, that he couldn't lose you, that you were what kept him alive. He asked me to donate the sperm. Just imagining you blossoming with my baby, nurturing it, while I could never claim it or you, almost killed *me*.

"But I believed him when he said he'd die if you left him. And even suspecting how he'd stolen you from me, I would have done anything to save him. And I knew if I said no, he would have gotten any sperm donor sample and passed it as his. I couldn't have you bear some stranger's baby. So I agreed.

"But believing you were suffering from psychogenic amnesia so that your mind wouldn't buckle under the trauma of losing him, I couldn't let you know you'd lost what you thought remained of him. I wouldn't cause you further psychological damage. I would have settled for being my baby's father by adoption when he was mine for real."

So that was why. His change toward her after the accident, treating her like she was the most precious thing in the world, binding himself to her forever. This explained everything much more convincingly than his claim that he'd loved her all along.

It had all been for his baby.

"Te quiero tanto, Cybele, *más que la vida. Usted es mi corazón, mi alma."*

Hearing him say he loved her, more than life, that she was his heart, his soul now that she knew the truth was…unbearable.

Feeling her life had come to an end, she pushed out of his arms and ran.

Rodrigo restrained himself from charging after her and hauling her back and never letting her go ever again with an exertion of will that left him panting.

He had to let her go. She had to have time alone to come to terms with the shocks, to realize that although they'd taken a rough course to reach this point, both Mel and fate had ended up giving them their future and perfect happiness together.

He lasted an hour. Then he went after her. He found her gone.

Consuelo told him Cybele had asked Gustavo to drive her to the city, where he'd dropped her off at a hotel near the center.

He felt as if the world had vanished from around him.

She'd left him. But…why? She'd said she loved him, too.

When his head was almost bursting with confusion and dread, he found a note on their bed.

The lines swam as if under a lens of trembling liquid.

Rodrigo,

You should have told me that my baby was yours from the start. I would have accepted your care for its real reason—a man safeguarding the woman who is carrying his baby. Knowing you and your devotion to family, your need to have your flesh and blood surrounding you, I know you want this baby fiercely, want to give him the most stable family you can, the one neither of us had. Had you told me, I would have done anything to cooperate with you so the baby would have parents who dote on him and who treat each other with utmost affection and respect. I don't have to be your wife to do that. You can divorce me if you wish, and I'll still remain your friend and

colleague, will live in Spain as long as you do, so you'll have constant access to your son.
Cybele.

Rodrigo read the note until he felt the words begin to burn a brand into his retinas, his brain.

After all the lies and manipulations she'd been victim to, she had every right to distrust his emotions and motives toward her. From her standpoint, he could be saying and doing whatever it took to get his son.

But he'd prove his sincerity if it was the last thing he did.

If he lost her, it just might be.

Twenty-four hours later, he stood outside her hotel room door, feeling he'd aged twenty-four years.

She opened the door, looking as miserable as he felt.

All he wanted was to take her in his arms, kiss her until she was incoherent with desire, but he knew that might only prove to her that he was manipulating her even worse than Mel had.

He never gambled. But he'd never known true desperation, either. Now a gamble, with potentially catastrophic results, was the last resort he had left.

Without a word, he handed her the divorce papers.

Cybele's heart stopped, felt it would never beat again.

She'd made a desperate gamble. And lost. She'd owed him the choice, the freedom to have his baby without remaining her husband. She'd prayed he'd choose to be with her anyway.

He hadn't. He was giving her proof, now that she'd assured him he'd always have his son, that he'd rather be free of her.

Then her eyes fell on the heading of one of the papers.

Before the dread fully formed inside her mind, it spilled from her lips. “You won’t take the baby away, will you? Any court in the world would give you custody, I know, but please don’t—”

He grimaced as if she’d stabbed him. “Cybele, *querida, por favor, le pido.* I beg you…stop. Do you distrust me that much?”

Mortification swallowed her whole. “No…no—oh, God. But I—I don’t *know.* Anything. It’s like you’re three people in my mind. The one who seemed to hate me, the one who saved me, took such infinite care of me, who seemed to want me as much as I want you, and the one who always had an agenda, who’s handing me divorce papers. I don’t know who you are, or what to believe anymore.”

“Let me explain.” His hands descended on her shoulders.

“No.” She staggered around before his grip could tighten. She couldn’t hear that he cared, but not enough to remain married to her. She fumbled for a pen by the hotel’s writing pad. The papers slid from her hands, scattered across the desk. Fat tears splashed over the blurring lines that mimicked the chaos inside her. “After I sign these papers, I want a couple of days. I’ll call you when I’m thinking straight again and we can discuss how we handle things from now on.”

His hands clamped the top of her arms, hauled her back against the living rock of his body. She struggled to escape, couldn’t bear the agony his feel, his touch, had coursing in hers.

He pressed her harder to his length. She felt his hardness digging into her buttocks, couldn't understand.

He still wanted her? But if he was divorcing her, then all the hunger she'd thought only she could arouse in him had just been the insatiable sexual appetite of the hot-blooded male that he was. And now…what? Her struggles were arousing him?

All thought evaporated as his lips latched on to her neck, drew on her flesh, wrenching her desire, her very life force with openmouthed kisses and suckles. She tried to twist away, but he lifted her off the ground, carried her to the wall, spread her against it and pinned her there with his bulk, his knee driven between her thighs, his erection grinding against her belly.

He caught her lower lip in a growling bite, sucked and pulled on it until she cried out, opened wide for him. Then he plunged, took, gave, tongue and teeth and voracity. Wave after wave of readiness flooded her core. She squirmed against him, everything disintegrating with her need to crawl under his skin, take him into hers. His fingers found her under her panties, probed her to a screeching climax. Then she begged for him.

In a few moments and moves, he gave her more than she could take, all of him, driving inside her drenched, clenching tightness. Pleasure detonated from every inch of flesh that yielded to the invasion of the red-hot satin of his thickness and length. He powered into her, poured driven words in an inextricable mix of English and Catalan, of love and lust and unbearable pleasure into her gasping mouth as his thrusting tongue ravaged her with possession and mindlessness.

Pleasure reverberated inside her with each thrust, each word, each melding kiss, like the rushing and receding of a tide gone mad. It all gathered, towered, held at its zenith like a tidal wave before the devastating crash. Then the blows of release hit like those of a giant hammer, striking her core again and again, expanding shock waves that razed her, wrung her around his girth in contractions so violent they fractured breath and heartbeats. She clung to him in the frenzy, inside and out as if she'd assimilate him, dissolve around him. Then she felt him roar his release as he jammed his erection to her womb, jetting his pleasure to fill it, causing another wave to crash over her, shattering her with the power of the sensations, of wishing that they'd make a baby this way in the future. When they didn't have one…

She came back to awareness to find him beneath her on the bed, still hard and pulsating inside her, setting off mini quakes that kept her in a state of continuous orgasm.

A question wavered from her in a scratchy rasp. "So was that goodbye sex?"

He jerked beneath her. "You go out of your way to pick the exact words that will cut me deepest, don't you?"

And she wailed, "What else could it be?"

"It was you-turn-me-into-a-raging-beast-in-perpetual-mating-frenzy sex. It was I-can't-have-enough-of-your-pleasure-and-your-intimacy lovemaking." Every word flowed over her like a balm on a wound, drowning the doubt demons who whispered he was just over-endowed and would enjoy any sexually voracious female. "Not that that excuses what I did. I didn't come here intending to take you like that. I was resolved not to confuse issues. But I saw you about to sign those papers and almost burst an artery."

Her lips twitched in spite of her confusion. "Glad the pressure found another outlet." She relived the moments when it had, splashing against her inner walls, filling her with his scalding essence, mixing with her pleasure… But…wait a sec! "But you *want* me to sign the papers."

He rose onto his elbow, looked at her with the last trace of heavy-lidded male possession vanishing, that bleakness taking over his eyes. "I want a bullet between the eyes more." She gasped, the thought of anything happening to him paralyzing her with terror. "But since I can't prove that to you by words or lovemaking, and you have every right not to accept either as proof, after all the lies that almost cost you your mind and your very life, I'm down to action. And the proof of time."

He extricated himself from her, rose off the bed, walked to gather the papers and came back to lay them beside her.

Before she could say she didn't want any proof, just wanted to be his, if he really wanted her, he turned and gathered his clothes.

She sat up shakily as he started dressing, his movements stiff, his face clenched with that intensity she now believed betrayed his turmoil. And finally, she understood. Just as she'd given him the freedom to divorce her, the divorce papers were his proof that she was equally free. Even if he'd rather end his life than lose her, he was letting her go, if it meant her peace of mind. Oh, God…

She'd caused him so much pain, even if inadvertently. Then, when he'd told her how long and how much he'd been hurting, she'd added indelible insult to injury when she'd imposed her distrust of those who'd blighted her life with letdowns, who'd made her doubt that she was deserving of love, as pretext to condemn his motivations.

But a man who wanted only his child wouldn't have done one thousandth of the things he'd done for her. He would never have said he loved her, would rather die than lose her. And even if any other man might have lied to that extent to achieve what he considered a highest cause, the stability of his child's family life, Rodrigo wouldn't. He was too honorable.

Even when he'd kept the truth about their baby's paternity from her, he'd done it only to protect her, had been willing to never proclaim his baby as his own flesh and blood, to preserve the illusion he'd thought essential to her well-being.

She made a grab for the papers, sprang off the bed and ran to him, grabbed one of his hands as he started buttoning up his shirt, tears of humility and contrition and heart-piercing adoration pouring from her very soul to scorch down her cheeks. "Those papers are your I'm-free-to-come-back-to-you-of-my-own-free-will gesture, right?"

He seemed to struggle to stop himself. He lost the fight, reached out with his other hand, wiped away her tears, cupped her cheek, his face the embodiment of tenderness. "They're not a gesture. You *are* free. And you must not consider me in your decision. You're not responsible for how I feel." Exactly the opposite of what Mel and her family had done to her. They'd made her feel responsible for their feelings toward her, guilty of inciting Mel's pathological possessiveness or their equally unnatural negligence. "In time, if you become satisfied that I am what you need, what will make you happy, come back to me. If you don't, then sign those papers and send them back to me instead. The other documents should prove you are in no way pressured to make the best of it for anybody else's sake but yours."

And she revealed her last and biggest fear. "W-what if in time *you* decide I'm not what you need?"

He huffed a harsh laugh, as if she were asking if he might one day fly under his own power. Certainty solidified in her every cell as she grinned up at him with sudden unbridled ecstasy. Then the rest of his words registered. "The other documents..."

She looked through the papers, found those with the heading that had triggered her crazy doubt that he'd take the baby.

Custody papers. Giving away his parental rights. To her. Unconditionally. She'd choose if he was part of his baby's life.

She stared at the words, their meaning too huge to take in.

Her eyes flew dazedly up to his solemn ones. "Why?"

"Because without you, nothing is worth having, not even my child. Because I trust you not to deprive him of my love even if you decide to end our marriage. Because I want you to be totally free to make that decision if you need to, without fearing you'll lose your baby, or become embroiled in a custody case. Because I need to know that if you come back to me, you do it not out of need or gratitude or for our baby's best interests, but because it's in *your* best interests. Because you want me."

Then he turned away, looking like a man who had

nothing to look forward to but waiting for an uncertain verdict.

She flew after him, joy and distress tearing at her. She wrenched him around, jumped on him, climbed him, wrapped herself around him and squeezed him as if she'd merge them. His shuddering groan quaked through her as he hugged her back, crushed her to him, his arms trembling his relief.

She covered his face and neck and anything she could reach of him in tear-drenched kisses and wept. "I don't just *want* you! I worship you, I crave and adore and love you far more than life. And it's not out of need or gratitude. Not the way you fear. I don't need you to survive, but I need you to be alive. I'm grateful you exist, and a few light years beyond that that you love me, too. I don't deserve you or that you should feel the same for me. I—I hurt you and mistrusted you and it doesn't matter that I was reeling from the shock of the regained memories and the revelations—"

His lips crushed the rest of her outburst in savage kisses. Then she was on the bed again, on her back, filled with him as he drove into her, growled to her again and again that he believed her and in her, and she screamed and sobbed her relief and gratitude and love and pleasure.

It was hours before that storm abated and she lay over him, free of doubt or worry, of gravity and physical limitations.

She told him, "You make me feel—limitless, just like what I feel for you. But you are too much, give too much. It would have been criminal to have all this without paying in advance with some serious misery and heartache. I love the fates that tossed me around only to land me in your lap, and by some miracle make you love me, too. I just adore every bit of misfortune and unhappiness I had that now make me savor every second of what we share all the more."

Rodrigo swept Cybele with caresses, agreed to every word she said. They were the exact ones that filled his being. He did believe they wouldn't have come to share this purity and intensity without surviving so many tests and…

He shot up, his nerves going haywire.

Under his palm. He'd felt it.

"The baby…" he choked. "He moved." And for the first time since he'd shed tears over his mother's death, his tears flowed. With too much love, pride and gratitude.

She pushed him onto his back, rained frantic kisses all over his face. "No, please—I can't bear seeing your tears, even ones of joy." That only made the tears flow thicker. After moments of panting consternation, wickedness replaced the stricken look on her face and she attacked him with tickling.

He guffawed and flopped her onto her back, imprisoning what he swore were electricity- and magic-wielding hands over her head with one of his, his other returning the sensual torment.

She squirmed under his hand, nuzzled his chest. "I can't wait to have our baby. And I can't wait to have another one. One we'll make as we lose ourselves in love and pleasure, flesh in flesh."

"This one *was* made of our love…well, my love, at least."

She nipped him. "Yeah, I have to make up for my

initial lack of participation in the love department. But from now on, I'm sharing everything with you. And not only about our baby. I want to be involved in everything you do, your research, your surgeries…." The radiant animation on her face faltered. "Uh—that came out as if I'll hound your every step…."

He squeezed her, cutting short her mortification, laughter booming out of his depths. "Oh, please, do. Gives me an excuse to hound yours." Then he grew serious. "But I know exactly how you meant it. I want you involved in everything I do, too. I've never felt more stimulated, more empowered, more satisfied with my work than when you were there with me. And then there's every other instance when I see or feel or think anything, and it isn't right, isn't complete until I share it with you, knowing you're the only one who'll understand, appreciate."

She attacked him with another giggling, weeping kiss that almost extracted his soul. Then she raised a radiant face, gestured for him to stay where he was.

He watched her bounce out of bed to rummage in her suitcase. He hardened to steel again, licking at the lingering taste of her on his lips as she walked back, ripe and tousled and a little awkward, all the effects of his love and loving, short- and long-term ones. She was holding something behind her back, impishness turning her beauty from breathtaking to heartbreaking.

"Close your eyes." He chuckled, obeyed at once. He couldn't wait to "see" what she had in store for him.

Her weight dipped the mattress. Then he almost came off it.

She was licking him. All over his chest and abdomen.

He growled, tried to hold her head closer, thrusting at her, offering all of him for her delicate devouring.

"Keep those lethal weapons of yours closed."

He did, his heart almost rattling the whole bed in anticipation. Then he felt a sting on his chest.

The tail end of the sensation was a lance of pleasure that corkscrewed to his erection. It slammed against his abdomen. Air left his lungs on a bellow of stimulation.

Another sting followed. Then another and another, on a path of fiery pain and pleasure down his body. He'd never felt anything like this sourceless manipulation of his sensations. He could swear she wasn't touching him, was pricking each individual nerve cluster mentally.

He thrust at her, incoherent with arousal, his growls becoming those of a beast in a frenzy. He at last thrust his hands into her hair, tugged until she moaned with enjoyment.

"Tell me to open my eyes," he panted the order, the plea.

Another skewer of delight. "Uh-uh."

"I don't need them open to take you until you weep with pleasure," he threatened, almost weeping himself again with the sharpness of the sensations she'd buried him under.

"Which you routinely do." Another sting. He roared. She purred, "Okay, just because you threatened so nicely. Open 'em."

He did. And couldn't credit their evidence for moments.

Then he rasped between gasps as she continued her meticulous sensual torture, "This is—hands down—the most innovative use of a micro-grasping forceps I've ever seen."

She was tugging at his hairs using the most delicate forceps used in micro-neurosurgery. And sending him stark raving mad.

"It's also the most hands-on method I could think of to say thanks." Her eyes glittered up at him, flooding him with love.

"Not that I'm not deliriously thankful for whatever made you invent this new…procedure, but thanks for what, *mi vida?*"

"Thanks for all the patience and perseverance you put into getting my hand back to this level of fine coordination."

He dropped his gaze to her hand. It was true. There was no sign of clumsiness, weakness or pain as her precious hand performed her pioneering form of carnal torment.

He groaned, glided her over his aching body, grasped her hand gently and took it to his lips, thanked the fates for her, for letting him be the instrument of her happiness and well-being.

"Thank *you*, for existing, for letting me be forever yours."

Cybele cupped his face as he continued his homage, wondering how one being could contain all the love she felt for him.

She caressed his hewn cheek, traced the planes of his chiseled lips. "If you're satisfied with my precision, can I apprentice at your hands in neurosurgery?"

He enfolded her and she felt as if his heart gave her the answer. To everything. "Just wish for it and it's done, *mi alma*. Anything you want, the whole world is yours for the asking."

She took his lips with a whimper, then she whispered into his mouth, "I already have the whole world. You, our baby and our love."

* * * * *

Isa disappeared six years ago, taking Marc's trust with her. Now that he's found her again, he won't let go...

Read on for a sneak peek at CLAIMED,
the first of the **DIAMOND TYCOONS** *duet*
by New York Times *bestselling author*
Tracy Wolff

Isabella was somehow even more beautiful than he'd remembered. And probably more treacherous, Marc reminded himself as he fought for control.

It had been six years since he'd seen her.

Six years since he'd held her, kissed her, made love to her.

Six years since he'd kicked her out of his apartment and his life.

And still, he wanted her.

It came as something of a shock, considering he'd done his best not to think about her in the ensuing years. All it had taken was a glimpse of her gorgeous red hair, her warm brown eyes, from the small window embedded in the classroom door to throw him right back into the seething, tumultuous heat that had characterized so much of their relationship. He hadn't cared about anything but getting into that room to see if his mind was playing tricks on him.

Six years ago he had kicked Isa Varin—now, apparently, Isabella Moreno—out of his life in the cruelest manner possible. He didn't regret making her leave—how could he when she'd betrayed him so completely?—but in the time since, he had regretted how he'd done it. When he'd come to his senses and sent his driver to find her and deliver her things, including her purse and cell phone and some money, she had vanished into thin air. He'd looked for her, but he'd never found her.

Now he knew why. The very passionate, very beautiful, very bewitching Isa Varin had ceased to exist. In her place was this buttoned-down professor, her voice and face as cool and sharp as any diamond his mines had ever produced. Only the hair—that glorious red hair—was the same. Isabella Moreno wore it in a tight braid down her back instead of in the wild curls favored by his Isa, but he would know the color anywhere.

Black cherries at midnight.

Wet garnets shining in the filtered light of a full moon.

And when her eyes had met his over the heads of her students, he'd felt a punch in his gut—in his groin—that couldn't be denied. Only Isa had ever made his body react so powerfully.

One look into her eyes used to bring him to his knees. But those days were long gone. Her betrayal had destroyed any faith he might have had in her. He'd been weak once, had fallen for the innocence she could project with a look, a touch, a whisper.

He wouldn't make that mistake again.

Will Marc have Isa back in his bed, trust be damned?

Find out in CLAIMED, the first of the DIAMOND TYCOONS duet by New York Times *bestselling author Tracy Wolff, available wherever Harlequin® Desire books and ebooks are sold.*

www.Harlequin.com

HDEXP0815